Book One of the Rich...
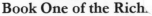

Three magnificent mansions share a cul-de-sac on a beautiful Florida bay. But for three unforgettable couples, the exclusive neighborhood opens their hearts to the humble richness of hope, love and faith.

When Ann Thomas is summoned to Florida for the reading of the will of the father she never knew, her life is forever changed. She learns she has a half-sister, she has the chance to inherit millions, and her name is really Angelina. Brett Hamilton, CPA, is assigned to help Ann spend a lot of money in a short period of time. As soon as his 'assignment' with her is over, he's headed to Peru to be a missionary, something he's felt called to do his whole life. Ann still lives with the pain of having a mother who chose world missions over her. Can Ann risk giving her love to someone who might give it back, or should she ignore her growing feelings towards Brett to keep her heart safe?

"*Rich in Love* . . . makes my Top Ten for 2013 list. I loved her characters and felt like they were friends. I cheered for them, I laughed with them, and I wept in places. The one thing I didn't want was for it to end. Novel Rocket and I give Rich in Love our highest recommendation. It's a dynamite read."
—Ane Mulligan, Sr. editor, *Novel Rocket*

"I love Lindi Peterson's writing style . . . Sweet, funny, and great exploration of relationships with moms all wrapped up in a lovely, satisfying romance. But also a fresh look (and that's hard to do) at the question: what if I could spend all the money I wanted? What would I do versus what do I think I would do? . . . Ms. Peterson has some very surprising twists in store . . ."
—Angela Breidenbach, author of *A Healing Heart*, Abingdon Press Quilts of Love Books

"*Rich in Love* is a heartwarming and powerful tale of one girl's search to find God and herself. The hero is sigh-worthy, and the heroine is full of inner-strength, compassion, and emotional turmoil. This is a compassionate tale grounded by faith but full of romance, secrets, heartbreak and love. A story that will warm your heart and soothe your soul."
—Ciara Knight author of *The Neumarian Chronicles*

Other Novels by Lindi Peterson

Her Best Catch

Summer's Song

Rich in Love

by

Lindi Peterson

Bell Bridge Books

Bell Bridge Books
PO BOX 300921
Memphis, TN 38130
Print ISBN: 978-1-61194-295-8

Bell Bridge Books is an Imprint of BelleBooks, Inc.

We at BelleBooks enjoy hearing from readers.
Visit our websites – www.BelleBooks.com and www.BellBridgeBooks.com.

10 9 8 7 6 5 4 3 2 1

Cover design: Debra Dixon
Interior design: Hank Smith
Photo credits:
Woman (manipulated) © Lja | Dreamstime.com
Texture (manipulated) © Ka Ho Leung | Dreamstime.com
Dove graphic (manipulated) © Ka Ho Leung | Dreamstime.com

:Lihl:01:

Dedication

To the Quest Church. Every day you show the world the true meaning of love. I am blessed to have you in my life as we refuse to give up on God's dream for the world.

"For God so loved the world that He gave His only begotten Son, that whoever believes in Him should not perish but have everlasting life."

John 3:16

Invitation

HAVE YOU EVER wished for an April fool's joke?

Right now I'm sitting in the Atlanta airport atrium waiting for my mom to bring us coffee. My mom, the queen of arriving at the airport hours early. My mom, the queen of world missions.

My mom, the reason I was fired today.

I was recently overlooked for a promotion, but managed to work through my feelings of disappointment. Imagine my surprise when the related-by-marriage-to-the-owner-of-the-business recipient of the promotion gave me a pink slip today. I waived it in the air and asked her if it was a joke. You know, I said, because it *is* the first day of April.

She assured me it wasn't a joke and reiterated how sorry she was before leaving my office.

And, okay, I guess I can't really blame it on mom. And they didn't use the word fired, per say. They said I was laid off. But if I hadn't asked off half a day to take my mom to the airport they would have had to wait until five o'clock to let me go and I would still be sitting at my desk preparing excel spreadsheets for clients.

"Here you are, Ann. Extra sugar and a dollop of cream. Just like you like it."

"Thanks, Mom," I say as she slides the brown paper cup towards me. She settles into the chair while I don't mention that I don't like any sugar let alone extra, and I load my coffee with creamer. Any kind. And dollop? Really, who uses that word?

But that's okay. Trixie, my mom, has other things she remembers to perfection. Like making sure her passport is current. Like mailing my birthday cards from wherever she is in the world. Even if they do arrive a few days late.

I spent the first fifteen years of my life traipsing around the world with her, then the next fifteen years saying good-bye when she left. By herself. I was through.

Honestly, if you were fifteen and had a choice between embracing poverty to show people who Jesus is or watching cute Leonardo

DiCaprio on the big screen (even though he did go down with the ship) which would you have chosen?

So while mom played traveling missionary I lived with my Aunt Venus, Mom's twin sister. Twins, but they couldn't be more different.

Mom reaches across the small, round table like she's going to brush my hair out of my eyes. Startled at the unfamiliar gesture, I lean back. "What?"

Her lips are pursed as she rubs her thumb and index finger together. Then she retreats to her side of the table. "Nothing. I was just going to pluck out that gray hair I saw."

I straighten my shoulders. "I don't think so. I don't have gray hair."

"My eyes see differently." She kind of rolls her eyes.

I sigh. "Impossible. You're almost fifty and don't have any gray."

Mom pats her pixie cut. "Good genes."

Rubbing strands of my hair between my fingers, I broach the forbidden subject. "Of course, I could have genes from the other side of my family. But you won't talk about them."

She takes a long swig of her coffee then starts fiddling with her backpack before setting the little zippered wallet that houses her passport and tickets and whatever else it is she needs to travel the world, on the table. "I should get to my gate if I don't want to miss the flight."

I pull her wallet toward me. "You have plenty of time. That's why we're here now. Early." I sigh, taming down the frustration which surfaces whenever I bring up the subject of my father. "I won't bring up the 'other' side anymore."

Once again I glean no information from my mom regarding my dad. I'll be thirty next week and to this day mom refuses to talk about him.

She drags her wallet back to her. "I'm sure you'll have no trouble finding a job."

Change of subject done quickly. Trixie-style. "I hope you're right."

"You have savings, right? You'll be okay for a while if nothing comes through, won't you?"

"I guess. I did just buy the condo six months ago. Between the down payment and the incidentals my nest egg needs more eggs."

Immediately I regret my words. It wasn't my intent to burden her before she leaves for another month.

"I told you purchasing the condo might not have been the best move. I mean, you seem like you know what you want in life, but you never know when Jesus might take hold of that heart of yours again and send you with me. You know, like before. When we did this together."

Her big smile and dreamy gaze quit making me feel guilty years ago. "I don't think that's going to happen."

"Those were such fun days, Ann. Remember the Psalms? How we used to sing them all the time? Lord our Lord, how excellent is thy name . . ."

Psalm 8:1. Some habits never die. "Stop singing, Mom. It's not working." She doesn't understand. I'm not like her. It's her dream, her calling, to live in airports and impoverished villages with people who don't speak the same language and whose eyes are filled with hope.

A hope I don't understand at times. How can they keep hoping when nothing ever changes?

And I love Jesus. I just choose to love him in the Atlanta area.

Locally. "Mom, you know the condo was a great purchase. I bought it for half its original price. I'll figure it all out. Like you said, I'm sure I'll have no trouble finding something else."

I speak the words with a confidence I don't feel. Jobs are scarce. And I need a high-paying one, like the one I left. Or rather the one that left me.

My mom's fingers brush the top of mine. "You know, Ann, I do enjoy and appreciate this time we have together. I know I'm never home for long, but it does my heart good to see my girl when I'm here."

A lot of moms would have tears in their eyes at a moment like this, but not mine. I believe she firmly means what she says, but I learned long ago that Trixie either has no emotions or she keeps them hidden. I guess if she didn't it would be too hard to live through her days in the mission field.

The only topic that seems to unnerve her is any discussion of my father. And that has been frustrating. I've seen my birth certificate. I know my father's name. Antonio Thomas. I also know I was born in Hampton Cove, Florida and my father's occupation was listed as unemployed.

Maybe that's why mom left.

A strange sense of loyalty to my mom keeps me from digging deeper right now. Maybe later. But the older I get, the harder it is to squelch the urge that will probably be her undoing.

BACK IN MY condo I'm supposed to be looking for a job, but instead I'm scouring the internet for shoes. Not just any shoes, mind you. No,

I'm looking for very special shoes.

Shoes I can't afford.

Crazy, isn't it? But it's my obsession I guess you can say.

Looking is my obsession, not buying.

I tried one time. Tried to spend hundreds of dollars on a pair of shoes with a surprise bonus from work. I planned to walk into the shoe store and purchase the beautiful shoes I passed by every day, wishing they were mine. I did make it through the door.

I actually sat in the luxurious chair and gave the sales girl my shoe size.

But while she went to the back to find the amazingly beautiful shoe I panicked.

Okay, maybe using the word panic is infusing a little too much drama. But visions of my mom, visions of the people she ministered to day after day, year after year, walked that Jimmy Choo shoe right out of my mind.

Slipping my own worn-out sandal on my foot, I high-tailed it out of the store. Once at home, I mailed a check to HOW, Hearts of the World, the organization my mom missions through.

That's how I became a monthly donor to HOW.

But the longing for nice shoes is still there. The Jimmy Choo page looms in front of me. I can't look too long before reality sets in. No job and a one-room condo. A condo with a mortgage.

And I love my condo.

The Atlanta skyline is visible from my window. Tall buildings of different heights jut toward the sky. Today low hanging clouds and rain put a damper on the normally beautiful view. Thunder rumbles a short distance away.

I hope this weather isn't a forecast for the rest of spring.

But even though the weather is dreary my condo is cozy. My daybed with its chocolate, sky blue and white striped comforter sits along the same wall as my desk. Two wall screens, arranged perfectly, give the illusion I have an actual bedroom. My fluffy white cat, Princess Sari, otherwise known as PS, sits in the middle of my bed bathing herself. PS is terribly spoiled, but I can't help it. *I take care of what I love.*

And I love my little abode. So I realize the need to minimize the Jimmy Choo page and start submitting my resume.

The need?

The mortgage company.

Running my tongue over my lips reminds me how thirsty I am. I grab a Coke from my apartment-sized refrigerator. A real Coke. Not a fake, diet one. Making my way back to my desk I wonder how long I will stay a size six without trying. Thirty will be here next week and I hear things go downhill from there.

I hope not.

They are already pretty much at the bottom.

Digging a hole might be an option, I guess. Burrow down just a little deeper.

With a sigh I minimize the JC page. With a bigger sigh I stare at my resume.

Ann Thomas. Accountant.

Really, can I sound any more boring?

I wish I could send a picture when I send my resume. Not because I'm beauty personified or anything. I just don't think I look like an Ann Thomas, numbers cruncher. That girl sounds like she'd have drab brown hair, maybe some out-of-style glasses and a collared shirt with a big bow.

I was blessed with my mom's red hair. (Earlier, I searched for that stray gray my mom pointed out, but I didn't find it.) A couple of friends have commented how my hair has just the right amount of blonde in it. It hangs below my shoulders and has a lot of body. Okay, I'll be totally honest. All my friends want my hair.

And my eyes? I once had a guy tell me they were green like the emerald lakes in Ireland. There are no emerald lakes and he was never in Ireland. So much for flattery. In this case it got him nowhere.

Frankly, right now I'd trade the hair and the eyes for a more interesting name.

Back to the resume.

I'm compiling a list of firms to send it to. I really need to make a few calls, see if anyone has any leads.

A knock sounds on my door causing me to jump. It's now late afternoon on this Friday, my mom is safely on her way to South America and I'm not expecting anyone, which is why peepholes rock.

As I put my eye up to the little window a delivery man of some sort is distorted on the other end. Only after securing the chain do I open the door slightly. "Can I help you?"

"I have a delivery for a Miss Ann Thomas. It needs to be signed for."

"Delivery? What kind of delivery?"

"This kind."

He holds up a standard overnight letter package then shoves an electronic device at me. I'm thankful this can all be done without taking the chain off. A woman can't be too careful in these times.

In moments he's gone and I'm holding a white express envelope marked urgent. The return name and street address I don't recognize.

The city, I do.

Hampton Cove, Florida.

As I sit down, my swivel desk chair rattles slightly, kind of like my nerves. Hampton Cove, the city listed on my birth certificate. My fingers shake as I pull the tab to open the package. Inside I find a single sheet of paper addressed to Ann Thomas.

That would be me.

As I start reading my breathing becomes somewhat erratic. I squint, an unnecessary action, as if it will change the words. But the words don't change.

My presence is required at the reading of a will of one Antonio Thomas. And the only Antonio Thomas I know of is the one who was listed on my birth certificate.

The name listed as my father.

And now this man is dead?

I read the letter three times, each time understanding less than I did the previous time because the letter becomes more real.

An ache of sorts fills me. How can I be numb at the passing of someone I'd never met?

Grabbing my cell phone I speed-dial my Aunt Venus. Other than Mom, Aunt Venus is the only family I have.

Or rather, the only family I know.

"Aunt Venus. Thank goodness you're home." A bit of relief flows through my tense body.

"Ann, what's wrong?" Her calm tone does nothing to calm me.

I jump up and shove my feet into my two for five dollars flip-flops. You know, the ones I can afford. "I'm fine, but I need to talk to you. In person. I'm on my way."

I click off my cell phone and shove it in my purse before grabbing PS. Yes, my cat goes with me.

The rain and the Friday afternoon traffic in Atlanta make the drive to Aunt Venus's a slow, tedious one. My nerves aren't helping either. The traffic light turns red, causing me to slam on the brakes. The letter slides off the passenger seat and floats to the floorboard, where it lands on PS, who is curled up on her zebra-striped bed.

I reach down, then set the letter back on the seat.

My palms are sweaty as they grip the steering wheel. They probably wouldn't be sweating if I was driving my dream car. A picture of a Jaguar XK rests next to my odometer. At approximately one hundred thousand dollars the car will always remain a dream. But I'm thinking the luxurious interior would be of some comfort in times of chaos.

Right now Aunt Venus is my only hope for comfort.

And answers.

I'M TAPPING MY foot, trying not to burst out of my skin. Aunt Venus has read the letter, but wants to make some coffee before we discuss.

Are you serious? My mind screams the words, but I don't. I stay seated in her cheery yellow kitchen wishing I could be just as cheery.

PS purrs gently on my lap. At least she's content. She has no idea that her world might be turned upside down by a letter from Florida.

"I still don't understand why you have to take your cat everywhere you go. It's not normal, you know. And I told you I might be allergic."

Aunt Venus is standing in front of the coffee maker, waiting for the brown liquid to fill the pot. She has the creamer and the sugar at the ready. Two mugs decorated with peace signs sit on the counter.

"The Princess is special, Aunt Venus. She loves to travel. And you're not allergic."

"Well, the last time you brought her over I had to go to the doctor the next day because my throat was scratchy and I kept sneezing. If it happens again I'm sending you the bill."

I'm not sure if she's trying to take my mind off of the letter, or if she's simply being Aunt Venus. I wouldn't know what to do if she ever changed. She's the only constant I have in my life. As short as my mom's hair is, Venus's reddish-brown hair is long. She always wears it in a bun or ponytail. I think she does that to show off her big earrings. Her face has a few wrinkles, a few laugh lines, but her bluish-green eyes still have a sparkle to them. Her long-time boyfriend Trevor plays a big part in that sparkle. They've been dating over twenty years and Aunt Venus still sticks to her mantra that she will never marry.

Trevor seems okay with it, but for some reason it bothers me.

Blue jeans and loose, colorful shirts are her normal attire. What she switches up are her shoes. My love of footwear came from her. She has the coolest shoes, sandals and boots. If our feet were the same size I'd never have to worry about buying shoes. I'd simply shop in Aunt

Venus's closet.

A really good coffee smell fills the air. When the coffee maker beeps, Aunt Venus pours the brew. I like coffee okay, but today it's all about having the mug in front of me. Having something to do with my hands.

"Would Her Highness like her own cup of coffee?" As Aunt Venus sets our mugs on the table, she nods toward PS.

"Very funny. Besides, she's sleeping at the moment."

Aunt Venus takes the letter off of the counter and lays it on the table in front of her chair. She's moving methodically and slowly. I'm sure it's an avoidance thing.

She has her hand on the back of her chair, like she's about to slide into it. But she doesn't.

"We need a snack. I think I have some shortbread cookies in the pantry."

My hand juts into the air, palm out. "Stop, Aunt Venus. Sit. Please? I don't want a snack. I want to know about the letter."

Her chair scrapes across the tile floor. After sitting, she places her hands on the table. Her coffee sits untouched, and I wonder if she even wants to drink it.

My nervous feeling has now ramped up quite a bit thanks to Aunt Venus's behavior. Because I know Aunt Venus knows something.

"You're probably wondering why I'm stalling." Aunt Venus sips her coffee after she speaks.

"You're stalling? Really? I hadn't noticed."

"Ann, this isn't my story to tell. It's your mother's. But on the other hand, I don't want you to miss out either."

I sit straighter. "Miss out on what? It says in the letter a man named Antonio Thomas has passed away. That was my father, right? And now he's dead?"

Aunt Venus is flushed, and I don't recall ever seeing her this uncomfortable.

"Your mom loved him so much. I just knew in my heart they were destined to be together forever."

"Considering I never met my father, forever didn't last very long." Wondering how my mom is going to feel, I run my hand over PS. Maybe her soft fur will steady me.

I can't believe the finality of it. That I'll never have the chance to know him. A part of me reasons I can't miss what I never had, but another part of me is sad at what I might have missed.

I will never know my father.

But if this Antonio Thomas was my father, then maybe I have other blood relatives in Florida. Relatives who could tell me about him.

"So you think the letter is legit?" The minute Aunt Venus read the letter and started acting weird, I knew in my heart the letter was real, but I want to hear her say it.

"Yes."

"So, should I go to Florida? Should I try to call Mom? She'll probably have a signal when she arrives at the airport. If I leave her a message now, surely she'll check before she delves deep into the recesses of the jungle."

I think PS senses my stress. She stretches and looks at me, her golden brown eyes barely open.

Aunt Venus cocks her head before giving me the look. "If you even have an inkling you're going to Florida you better not call your mother. Understand?"

I nod my head. "She would try to stop me. Tell me not to go."

Aunt Venus sips her coffee then sets her mug down. "She hasn't talked about this in thirty years. For whatever reason she didn't want you to know your father. I can't say it was the right decision, but it was her decision."

I think about Mom, spitfire that she is. Her beautiful face, short haircut. My green eyes and red hair come from her. Do I look anything like my father? Maybe my olive-toned skin has come from him since both Mom's and Aunt Venus's skin-tone is moonlight white.

"Did you know him? My father?"

"No. I didn't. Your mother and I grew up here in Georgia. When your mother was eighteen she went on a mission trip. She was supposed to be gone a month. But she didn't come back with everyone else. She called me to tell me she was staying in Florida. She'd found a great job, great apartment and a great guy."

"Mom said she started doing mission trips when she was young."

"Your mother has always loved the Lord. But I sensed a change in her while she was in Florida. She told me about Antonio, but I never met him. Then one day she showed up here. You were three months old. Your mother asked me not to ask any questions, so I didn't. I wanted to talk about it, but I soon learned I needed to let her work it out. So here we are. You, me and Trixie."

While this information sheds a little light on the situation, it certainly raises more questions than it answers.

"In your opinion this is real. My father, whom I never met, has died and apparently left me something because I've been called to the reading of his will. In four days. On my birthday no less."

Aunt Venus reaches out to cover my hand with hers. She smiles her sweet smile. "This is real, Honey. And we'll celebrate your big three-o when you come home."

"You want to go on this road trip? You know, for support?"

She gives my hand a squeeze before settling back in her chair. "I have a ton of work to do. Besides, I think this invitation is solely for you."

"Invitation? More like a summons. But PS will accompany me, of course."

"Of course."

We sound so matter-of-fact. Like my trip is ordinary.

I wish I had the Jaguar XK.

If I did, I'm sure the trip would be fabulous.

Intriguing

REMEMBER HOW I wished I had the Jag? The wish has turned into a need. I need the Jag! I'm slowly driving the streets of Hampton Cove, Florida. I'm less than two miles from the address I was given by the attorney, and I'm surprised I haven't been arrested for driving *under the affluence.*

My car is only five years old, but it might as well be fifty years old. The houses aren't houses. They're mansions. Big, beautiful, so not-what-I'm-used-to. My mom left this kind of lifestyle?

Maybe not. It was thirty years ago. And my father was unemployed when I was born. But even if he did have money, it wouldn't have impressed my mom.

I can still hear her telling me not to hoard and store up treasures.

I'm sure there are plenty of treasures in these houses. I'd also bet there are a lot of Jimmy Choo shoes in the closets of these homes.

Nervous beyond belief, I follow the directions my portable nav is speaking to me. PS is oblivious to what is going on. As usual, she's asleep in her bed on the floorboard.

"It's almost time to wake up, PS. We have less than a mile to go before we arrive at the address."

I'm still driving slowly when I come to a cul-de-sac. Three concrete driveways shoot off the circular edge while the middle of it boasts a nicely landscaped area with a beautiful white gazebo. A couple of fancy-looking benches sit among the palms and other bushes and flowers I can't name. I wonder if anyone really leaves their elaborate homes to come and sit in the gazebo in the cul-de-sac.

Seems highly unlikely to me. Unlikely, yet intriguing.

I jump at the dinging noise my GPS makes before the computerized voice starts speaking. "You have reached your destination."

My destination, my foot. I don't know what I have reached. Turmoil, mystery? Although luxurious, it's still scary.

I round the probably-never-used sitting area until I see the mailbox with the numbers I'm looking for.

Swaying trees, with their green leaves, block the view of the house. Being this close to the water I assume there's always a breeze. A circular drive beckons me. Taking a deep breath, I steer my car onto the drive, fighting everything that screams for me to pull away from this place as fast as I can. I manage to stop mid-way down the concrete path.

A short stone walkway leads to a small wrought iron gate flanked by two of the biggest palm trees I have ever seen.

It takes me a couple of minutes to gather my things before I walk up the stone path, PS in her carrier in my left hand, my small purse and backpack slung over my right shoulder. Some habits are hard to break. Living out of a backpack for years might have had a few benefits. Learning how to pack light being one of them.

But I don't think I'm anywhere near equipped to handle what's inside this house. What I'm going to need you can't put in a backpack.

The breeze feels nice. It almost makes the heat seem non-existent, and carries that you're-in-Florida-near-the-ocean scent. Candles can try to recreate it, but they fall short. There's nothing like the real thing.

The gate creaks slightly as I open it. It clangs shut behind me causing me to jump. I turn to the right where three broad steps lead me to a path to the front door. Two concrete lions greet me on either side.

This place is very symmetrical.

I continue a short distance and hang a left to the front door. Using my free hand I ring the doorbell. An ominous sound, really it's not foreboding at all, echoes through the house. Prelude to an emotional slaughter?

I'm being overly dramatic, I know. But at the moment I'm not feeling like a confident grown woman who crunches numbers for multi-million dollar businesses. Or used to, I guess. Right now I'm feeling like a little girl who wants to hide in the corner.

The lock on the door clicks.

My heart races.

Taking a deep breath, I paste on a smile.

The door swings open.

My heart pushes so far into my chest I wonder what's keeping it in. The most beautiful woman I've ever seen stands in front of me. I wonder if her smile is pasted on her face too, or if it's genuine.

"You must be Ann. We've been expecting you," she says. "Come in, please. Can I help you with anything?"

She holds out her hand apparently willing to take some of my baggage. But I'm not willing to give it up. "No. I'm fine."

"Is that," she bends a little, her gaze locking onto PS's carrier, "a cat?"

"She is. I hope she's not going to be a problem. I didn't have anyone to keep her."

A slightly mischievous look passes on the woman's face. "Oh, no. She won't be a problem at all. What's her name?"

Somehow I don't think she's telling the truth, but what do I know? "Her name is Princess Sari. I call her PS."

"How clever. Hello, PS."

As she ponders my Princess I take in the foyer. It's beautiful and bigger than my whole condo. Luxury and richness hang in the atmosphere. I'm surprised my medium income lungs can breathe.

PS seems to have captured the attention of the woman with the brown hair. She looks to be about my age, brown eyes, tanned skin, nice figure.

And remember, she's beautiful.

Momentarily, she straightens and holds her hand out.

"I'm Stace. It's nice to meet you."

"It's nice to meet you. Stace?" I ask, shaking her hand.

She shrugs her shoulders. "Stace is short for Anastasia, an extremely cumbersome name."

Cumbersome? I would give a pair of JC shoes for a name like Anastasia. If I had a pair of JC shoes, that is. What would she think if I called her Anastasia? "I think Anastasia is a beautiful name."

She looks at me with a puzzled expression. "Thank you. But I don't like it. Come on, I'll show you to your room. How many more bags do you have?"

I shake my head. "None. This is it. I mean, I'm only going to be here for a couple of days, so I didn't pack much. Oh, but I do have a disposable litter pan in the car. For PS. I'll grab it after I'm settled in."

"Nonsense. The help will get it for you. Is your car locked?"

I laugh. "No. It's highly unlikely anyone around here would want to steal my old ride. The litter pans are in the plastic bag in the back seat."

"Great. Come on."

We wind our way up the staircase. At the top of the stairs, to the left, is a sitting area. A huge Zebra-patterned rug sits on top of the polished hardwoods. Sleek, modern furniture fills the space. It looks like a great place to hang out and read if you could ever get comfortable on the couch. The white couch that looks like no one has ever sat on it.

We continue down a hall.

"Here we are."

I follow Anastasia into a room on the left. She sweeps her arm through the air. "You have a great view."

A great view and so much more. A beautiful four-poster bed graces the room. Soft white fabric drapes across the frame. The same fabric hangs down by each post. A slight breeze from the open French doors causes the draping to billow slightly.

And the view! Blue water, sunshine and palms, a city in the distance. You can see forever. "I'm speechless. This is amazing."

"Well, we're glad you're here. While you settle in, I'll go see how the help is coming along with your cat's accessories."

Ooh. She can't even *say* litter pan. "Okay. Thank you."

I set my backpack, purse and PS's carrier on the bed. I free PS, and cradling her we stand at the balcony. An ornate black wrought iron railing keeps me safe, but it certainly wouldn't stop PS from jumping. We are up pretty high, so I don't think her chances of surviving are great.

She's purring which means she's found a sense of peace I haven't. I back up a few feet and sit on the end of the rounded bed. The brown comforter is going to look fabulous with PS's white fur on it. Maybe I can find a blanket to lie across the bed.

My thoughts drift to Anastasia. Who is she? She looks familiar. Not celebrity-like familiar. She looks like someone I know. But I can't pinpoint anyone. She's definitely at home here. Does she live here? Could she be related to me?

No. She's much too beautiful to be related to me.

I go to the bathroom to grab a towel to lie on the bed until I can find a blanket. The bathroom is bigger than my condo, also. Browns and corals combine for a beautiful color scheme. The tub is big enough to swim in while about twelve people can fit in the shower.

Shaking my head, I make my way back to the bed, lay the towel on it, then set PS on the towel. She immediately starts giving herself a bath.

Anxious and perplexed at this whole situation, I unzip my backpack then pull out a few items. I shake out the dress I brought to wear to the reading of the will. Closing my eyes I remember that my black pumps are still in my car. Oh, well, I'll get them later. The empty closet has plenty of hangers so I hang up my dress. Since I had rolled it, the fabric doesn't have too many wrinkles. I'm sure they'll fall out before I need to wear it in the morning.

"Hi. I'm back. Here is your bag. And here, I saw these shoes in the back seat. I thought you might need them."

Anastasia has the huge white plastic bag in one hand and my shoes in the other. I walk to her.

"Thank you. I appreciate this. But I thought you were going to get the help to do this."

She smiles as she hands over my things. "I am the help."

AFTER ANASTASIA gives me a blanket to protect the bedspread, I shut the French doors, leaving PS in my room.

Because Aunt Venus didn't pick up when I called, I left a message on her phone telling her I arrived safely. I can't wait to talk to her and tell her about this place.

Now I'm sitting in a luxurious kitchen. I will my mind to find another word to use, but luxurious is just so appropriate. Even though the kitchen is nice, it could use a little color on the walls. It's certainly not cheery like Aunt Venus's kitchen. This kitchen is more industrial with its big appliances and stark white décor.

And luxury.

Anastasia sets a glass of lemonade in front me as she slides into a chair next to me.

I still can't believe she's the help.

"So, what are you wondering? Why I'm in shorts and a t-shirt instead of a uniform? Come on, tell me what you're thinking."

"I don't know what I'm thinking. Because I have so many thoughts jumbling around my mind they're all crashing into each other and nothing is making any sense."

"That's a great big sentence to avoid answering my question."

I pick at a non-existent speck on the glass table. "It's the truth."

"I have a college degree. In business management. I work at a nail salon and I'm saving my money to open my own salon one day."

"Nice." I'm not really surprised. Anastasia seems like a lady who knows what she wants. She certainly doesn't seem hesitant in any way. And her nails are beautiful.

"Mama has been the housekeeper here since she was in her late teens. She always hires one or two girls to help her out. One of them quit about a month ago, so I'm filling in."

"So, who lives here?"

Anastasia's gaze cuts sideways. She almost frowns, but not quite. "Well, Mama still lives here. She has a suite downstairs. But since Antonio died, the house is empty."

"You mean no one is living here?" All this space and beauty going to waste? It seems unthinkable. Just like bombarding her with questions about Antonio.

She smiles. "You are, now."

"Ah, I'm only here for a couple of days. One of them being my birthday."

Her expression turns to surprise. "Really? When?"

"Tomorrow."

She reaches out, covering my hand with hers. "Me too. Tomorrow is my thirtieth. And I'm hoping my guy, Jimmy, will have something fabulous planned if you know what I mean." She pulls her hand off of mine then uses it to tap her left hand's 'ring' finger.

"Oh. You're expecting to become engaged?"

"Expecting? No. He says he's not ready for marriage." She laughs. "Hoping? Yes. Maybe it's more like praying. Praying he'll change his mind. Fast."

"Well, I'll be praying right along with you then." My hottest prospect for marriage, Jason, walked out about six months ago. But I've never been in a hurry to marry. I think Mom and Aunt Venus have skewed my vision of that institution.

"How about you? No ring, so probably no husband. How about a boyfriend?"

I shake my head. "No. I prefer to enter my thirties single without any prospects."

Stace laughs. "You're funny. Is tomorrow your thirtieth, too?"

"It is. Strange how these things happen, huh?"

Her expression turns serious. "Very strange. But tomorrow isn't until tomorrow. Tonight Mama is planning a huge dinner. Seven o'clock."

I have been up since two a.m. It's now almost three p.m. I really hadn't planned on an event this evening. I wonder what huge dinner really means. Lots of people or lots of food. I'm in the mood for neither. I'm physically and mentally exhausted. "I may need to lie down for a little while. It was a long drive."

"I figured as much. Why don't you go on up. Oh, and we dress for dinner, so . . ."

"So, no shorts and t-shirts?"

"Not tonight."

It's a good thing the dress I brought has just been cleaned. It looks like it's going to get a work-out while I'm here.

Impression

"ANN, YOU'RE LATE. Are you almost ready?"

Anastasia's voice reaches me as I'm sitting in the bathroom on the floor in front of the vanity, scanning the cabinets for super glue. I didn't think I'd have much luck. A thought that's proving to be true.

"I'm in here." Maybe Anastasia can help me.

"What are you doing on the floor?"

I look up. Then I want to crawl in the cabinet. Anastasia is wearing a turquoise summer dress. On her feet are silver and turquoise sandals which look very expensive. And beautiful. Her toenails are even a light blue shade, complimenting the sandals and dress.

My feet with their three month old pedicure of a winter red instinctively bury further under my rear as I stay seated.

"Ann?"

I guess I have to answer. "My shoe broke. The heel came off so I was looking for some glue to glue it back on."

I hold my black pump in one hand, the heel in the other. "See?"

"Oh. That looks like a problem. Let me take a look."

She holds out her hands and I give her the shoe parts. I then decide it's not practical for me to crawl in the cabinet. I also can't sit on the bathroom floor all night, so I stand.

Anastasia shifts her gaze from my broken shoe to me.

"What gives? I said dinner party, not funeral."

I smooth my black, short sleeved, just-below-the-knee length dress. "I didn't know anything about a dinner party. This is the only dress I brought with me."

Her gaze drifts up and down the length of me. "Six and six, right?" she asks, pointing to my body and feet.

"Yes."

"Don't leave this room. Please. I'll be right back."

She tosses my shoe along with its heel on the bed before leaving. I sit on the bed between my shoe and PS. I look down the front of my dress making sure I don't have any white PS hairs clinging to me.

So the words dinner party means people. Who could possibly be here? Anastasia is not dressed like the help this evening. She's dressed like a hostess.

This is all so confusing.

My door opens. I can hardly see Anastasia through the jumble of material she's carrying.

Actually it's only two dresses. She has two pairs of strappy sandals dangling from her arm, high heels jutting toward me.

"Okay, pick one. Coral sundress with tiny black polka dots or this very cute chiffon flowery print."

Both dresses are beautiful. "I'll take the coral."

"I knew you would. Here." She hands me the dress.

"Where did these come from?"

"From me. I wanted to help Mama with dinner, and I couldn't decide what to wear. So I brought a couple of choices."

"Thank you. I'll go put this on." I head for the bathroom.

"All right. The shoes are on the bed. See you downstairs. Pronto."

Even though I know she's gone, I still dress in the bathroom. I'm a pretty modest person. After slipping the dress on, I hang my 'funeral' dress back in the closet.

The coral dress is soft. It fits me well. I don't recognize the name, but I'm sure it's expensive. It just feels like it is.

I walk to the bed, stopping about a foot away. The sandals sit on the bed, proud and tall. I know, without a doubt, they are JC's.

Stepping closer, I can see the white label with those lovely words, Jimmy Choo. Anastasia has left me a pair of JC shoes to wear for the evening.

Is this how Cinderella felt? Fluttery heart and all smiles?

My foot tingles, I swear it does, when I slip the shoe on. My bad pedicure clashes with the elegant shoe, but I don't have time to do anything about it. I'm already late for whatever it is that is happening downstairs.

After buckling the strap around my ankle, I quickly put the other shoe on. Coral suede JC platform sandals now adorn my feet. Cautiously, I take a few steps around the bedroom. It's like I'm walking on air.

I'm not sure what kind of impression I'm going to give to whoever is waiting downstairs.

But I'm sure it will be the wrong one.

AS I REACH THE bottom of the stairs, laughter drifts from the back of the house. I believe that's where the living room is. The back wall of the room has four sets of French doors which open onto a covered veranda. Of course people would be gathered there. If I remember correctly, a bar graces the room on the left. There is nothing about this house that isn't elegant.

Except me.

The laughter becomes louder with every step I take. I'm not sure I'm ready for this. Whatever it is.

I step into the room expecting to be bombarded with unknown faces. There are only three people in the room.

Anastasia is one, a man hovering very close to her makes number two, and another man, heart-stoppingly attractive, makes number three.

"Ann. Finally." Anastasia is walking towards me. She grabs my hand.

"Wait," I whisper to her. "Thanks for the outfit. And the shoes. You don't even know. These are like the champagne of shoes for me."

She leans close. "It's nothing. I'm glad everything fits. Our secret."

I have so many questions running through my head as we walk toward the bar. Each question seems to breed another one.

"Wow," the dark-headed-hovering-over-Anastasia-guy says. He's pointing his index finger at me, then Anastasia, then back to me, so I'm not really sure what his 'Wow' is all about.

"Hi," the other guy says. "I'm Brett Hamilton. It's nice to meet you."

I shake his hand. "Ann Thomas."

"And, Ann, this is my Jimmy, my love," Anastasia says.

"Yeah, I'm Jimmy."

He doesn't hold out his hand. He just has a look about him that indicates I should be thrilled to meet him. My other observation? Jimmy talks loudly.

He nods his head towards me, but he's looking at Brett. "Do you see this? They look like twins."

I know he's not talking about our clothes, so therefore I'm not following what he is saying at all.

"No comment." Brett's gaze lingers on me, but he doesn't seem interested in the conversation.

I turn to Anastasia to find her looking at me. If her expression is a reflection of mine, I'm sure I look puzzled. And her eyes are saying crazy, so mine probably are, too.

"Ladies," Jimmy starts. "Except for your hair color you look exactly alike. Come, look in this mirror?" He points to the huge mirror behind the bar.

"Jimmy, my love. You've obviously had too many martinis. You're cut off."

Anastasia gives me a he's-crazy look before cuddling up to him, which leaves me standing next to Brett.

Long, straight sandy hair which brushes his collar and light green eyes accentuate his extremely handsome face. Put those features together with a nice physique and I'm definitely interested.

I mean as interested as I can be considering I'm only in town for another twenty-four to forty-eight hours.

I wonder who he is and why he's here.

Matchmaking doesn't seem like Anastasia's style. There must be another reason.

"Would you like a drink?"

His voice has a nice sound to it.

"Thanks, but no. I don't drink very often."

He holds up his glass. "I'm drinking soda water and lime."

The water does look refreshing. "I'll have one of those."

With the fresh air wafting in off the veranda, the gorgeous view of the water, and the company of the beautiful people, it does seem appropriate to have some sort of fizzy, cold beverage in hand.

Brett steps behind the bar, busying himself with making my drink.

Loud Jimmy speaks. "Ann. You said your name is Ann, right?"

I smile at Jimmy. "Yes. Ann."

"Thought so. I don't make too many mistakes, right, Babe?" He winks at Anastasia.

"You're almost perfect, Jimmy."

"You know it, Babe. But Ann, Babe, can't you guys see the resemblance between you? It's kind of freaking me out."

Anastasia grabs onto Jimmy's arm. "You're seeing things. Let it go. Come out here with me for a minute."

She mouths the word sorry to me as they head out on the veranda. Her turquoise blue dress swirls around her.

Brett comes from around the bar, handing me a mirror image of his drink.

"So what's up with Jimmy?" I ask. "Do you think Anastasia and I look that much alike?"

"Anastasia?"

"Oh, well, Stace."

"Yeah. I always forget her real name is Anastasia."

"I think the name Anastasia is beautiful. I would never shorten it."

"I've known Stace a long time. Jimmy? I've only met him a couple of times. Stace has been seeing him a while though, I guess."

It doesn't escape me that he hasn't answered the question whether we look alike or not. The whole thought is crazy. Anastasia is so beautiful. I don't look anything like her.

Since he probably doesn't want to embarrass me by saying we look nothing alike, I decide to let the gorgeous guy off the hook. "What kind of work do you do?"

That should be a safe enough subject.

"I'm a CPA."

My heart double-beats. "Really? I'm an accountant. A numbers kind of girl."

His eyes widen. "Nice. What kind of firm do you work for?"

Visions of the pink slip float through my mind. "Actually, I'm out of work right now."

"I'm sorry to hear that."

Laughter drifts in from the veranda. Anastasia and Jimmy are standing by the rail, heads close together. They're not quite kissing, but it's apparent they are very comfortable with each other.

"Stace swears she's in love." Brett takes a sip of his drink after his statement.

"Does that bother you?" Might as well ask and be done with it. Is he pining for the beautiful girl?

"Not like you think. Stace is like my little sister. I want to see her happy, yet I'm not sure Jimmy is the ticket."

More laughter from the veranda.

"She thinks he's the ticket. She wants a ring for her birthday."

"I'm sure she does. She hates the thought of being in her thirties and single. But Jimmy's not the marrying kind. I think she's taken in because he whips out his credit card every time she wants something. He better not hurt her."

Brett Hamilton's protective nature inches into my heart. "Broken hearts are never fun."

He smiles. "Are you speaking from experience?"

Lack of experience is more like it. Something I'm not ready to admit to the guy who, if he is still single, has probably broken a lot of hearts. "This conversation could turn depressing. I say we change the subject."

"I say I hit a nerve."

Anastasia's sweet perfume engulfs our space. "And I say it's time to eat," she says.

Her timing couldn't be more perfect.

I follow Anastasia and Jimmy to the dining room. Brett walks next to me. We must appear stiff compared to Anastasia who is clinging to Jimmy's arm. She even rests her head on his shoulder while they walk. That takes talent.

Glancing at Brett, I realize I could do the same. His shoulders are at the perfect head-resting level.

He pulls out my chair for me. Protective and a gentleman. He must have some flaws. I'm sure they'll come to light soon.

A girl who looks to be in her early twenties comes in and pours water in our glasses before placing salads in front of us.

The conversation is clearly dominated by loud Jimmy with Anastasia coming in a close second. I wonder if Jimmy paid for the dress and shoes I'm wearing. That thought is a little unsettling.

As unsettling as it is, it still can't make the shoes feel any less fabulous.

The same girl returns to clear our salad plates as we finish.

Anastasia hands her plate over. "Thank you, Chloe. The salad was perfection."

"You're welcome. Your mother made the dressing herself. A secret recipe, she said."

"I'm not surprised. Mama is a genius when it comes to food. I can't wait for the rest of the meal."

The clinking sound of the dishes fades as Chloe leaves the room. As wild as Jimmy was earlier about how Anastasia and I looked alike, he hasn't mentioned it once since we've been in the dining room. Maybe Anastasia clued him in on how embarrassing it would be for me for anyone to disagree.

Not that I'm dissing myself. There's cute and then there's beautiful. Like exotic verses pretty. Kind of the same, but totally different.

A woman enters the room, eyes downcast, carrying a platter of meat garnished with delicious looking vegetables. The smell of the food makes me realize how hungry I am.

This must be Anastasia's mother.

Just before she reaches the table she looks up. Her gaze locks with mine.

Her mouth opens in a gasp but no sound comes out.

The platter crashes to the ground as her hands fly to her face. She shakes her head, backing out of the dining room, muttering words so softly I'm not sure I'm hearing right.

It sounds like she is saying, "It can't be. It can't be." What can't be?

"Mama." Anastasia runs after her mom as Chloe rushes in, towels in hand.

"I'll take care of this," the young server says as Brett, Jimmy and I push back from the table.

Jimmy follows Anastasia, while Brett and I stand, observing the literal hot mess on the floor. Steam rises from the meat, while my stomach growls in an inappropriate manner.

"Go now," Chloe says as she drops to her knees and begins to corral what was supposed to be our dinner.

We tip-toe our way through the splattered liquid and shards of food.

I'm precariously trying to keep the shoes free of food. My foot slips slightly as we are almost out the door.

"Careful." Brett steadies me, his strong grasp not unnoticed. His warm hands reveal how chilled I had become. "We don't need another casualty. The dinner was bad enough."

His grasp loosens as we walk to the living room.

I already feel like a casualty.

I just don't know what caused the war.

Inheritance

I SIT ON THE end of the bed, once again in the funeral dress. I'm barefoot. The morning breeze blows gently across my skin.

Happy thirtieth to me.

My backpack is packed. I plan to take off after the reading, spend my birthday night in a hotel room somewhere in north Florida. PS and I will celebrate in style.

Take-out and television.

When I came downstairs this morning there were muffins set out, juice in the refrigerator, and the coffee had been brewed. Chloe popped in for a minute. We didn't say anything other than the usual morning greetings. Hello, how did you sleep, here's breakfast, and let me know if you need anything else.

So I ate by myself.

Anastasia said she'd be back this morning to drive me to the lawyer's office. I'm not sure if she's just driving me, or if she's attending the reading.

One fact remains. I still don't have any shoes to wear. Unless I wear my flip-flops. Anastasia took her Cinderella clothes and shoes with her last night when she left. It's probably a no shirt, no shoes, no admittance type of building, so I'll have to wear something on my feet.

PS is purring loudly. She seems to like it here. She better enjoy this comfortable bed, because it's back to the floorboard for her in a few hours.

Shoving my feet into my flip flops, I grab my purse and head downstairs. Anastasia should be here in a few minutes. Once downstairs, I sit on the veranda, enjoying the comfortable temperature that allows me to sit outside. The Atlanta weather won't be this nice when I return home.

This mansion of a house sits along a canal. There's a grand swimming pool nestled between the house and the canal. Too bad I won't have time to enjoy either. I also notice for the first time a boat docked in front of the house. So many luxuries, so little time.

"Morning."

The serene calmness of the view is interrupted by the non-Anastasia voice. The voice is Brett's. My unprepared heart beats a little faster as he sits next to me.

Great. The gorgeous guy gets to see me in my funeral dress and flip flops. He is not dressed casually at all. Dark blue suit, pale blue shirt, awesome black, silver and navy striped tie. Somehow the image of him being a CPA doesn't really mesh. He's too gorgeous to be so smart. But his suit pulls it together.

"Good morning. I was expecting Anastasia." That's not really what I wanted to say. But I guess it's better than 'good morning, CPA's don't normally look like you, therefore I'm a little flustered.'

"Sorry to disappoint. She asked me to pick you up. She's running late."

I wouldn't call Brett a disappointment. But with his arrival the hope of Anastasia lending me another pair of shoes disappears.

So I guess I'll wear my flip-flops.

"Would you like any coffee or breakfast?" I look around for Chloe.

"No thanks. We need to leave."

He holds my chair, and once again reminded of his gentlemanly attributes. I scoop my purse off the table.

His gaze travels over me. Not in a bad way. In a sincere kind of way.

"You look nice."

Everything about him says he's genuine, not making fun.

"Thank you, I think."

He smiles at me. His clean, masculine scent surrounds him.

"What do you mean you think? Can't take a compliment?"

We start walking toward the front. "Yes, I can take a compliment. I'm feeling a little under-dressed at the moment, though."

I hold my flip-flop clad foot in out in front of me.

"I wouldn't worry about it. You'll blend in just fine."

Ah. In one sentence he's touched on my dilemma in life.

I'm blendable.

We walk to his car which isn't a Jag. No, it's a pick-up. Black, well-used, but nice. Big cab, four doors. Nothing rich and luxurious like his attire, though.

And since he's a gentleman, he opens the door for me. A pair of black soccer cleats and some sort of text book are tucked up under the dash.

"Sorry about that," he says, as he reaches around me. He tosses the cleats and book behind his seat, then tries to brush away the stray grass.

I might not have stopped him if I were still wearing the JC's, but since I'm in the flip-flops I hold out my hand. "You don't need to do that."

He shrugs his shoulders before helping me into the truck. His hand grips mine in an effort to steady me as I step into the cab. His grip is firm yet gentle. His hands remind me more of an outdoor type of guy instead of the hands of a man who works in an office all day.

I can't tell if the cleats are his size or not. They look like they could be. But that doesn't explain the text book.

He starts driving.

"I have to make a quick call," he says, sliding his finger around his phone screen.

After a couple of moments he starts speaking. "I know you're in class, but I also know you check your messages at lunch. Your math book and cleats will be at the front office. Go get them. No excuses. I'll talk to you after school."

Setting the phone in his lap, he continues to drive offering no explanation. I'm sure it wouldn't be good manners to ask any questions.

He glances at me. "I'll have to run by the high school right after the meeting. Maybe you can catch a ride back to the house with Stace."

"Sure. I don't mind."

He clearly doesn't want to offer an explanation. But his phone conversation raises questions in my mind. Does he have a child? Black cleats could belong to a boy or a girl. This sheds a light on the gorgeous guy I hadn't even considered. He's not wearing a ring, but I guess that doesn't mean anything. Although if he had a wife or a significant other, why didn't he bring her last night?

Cold air whistles out of the vents, blowing his hair slightly. The thought of him being attached pings at my heart. A crazy emotion. I barely know Brett Hamilton who hasn't shown even a half of a percent of interest in me. We are obviously a business arrangement, not a social one.

I don't have time to ponder any more questions because we are parking in front of an office building.

Brett definitely knows where we're going. We take an elevator up to the third floor. Moments later we are standing in the waiting area of a lawyer's office.

A blonde receptionist wearing extremely pink lipstick sits behind a desk. She smiles and picks up the phone. "Good morning Mr. Hamilton.

It's nice to see you again. I'll tell Ted you're here."

"Thanks, Gretchen."

Brett and I walk past the desk. "Wait here," he says. "I'll be right back."

Brett disappears down a hallway.

Crystal chandeliers hang from the ceiling. Plush furniture invites me to sit. Greens, golds, browns and reds mix together for a very classy, in-style look. Some of the throw pillows have little tassels dangling from them.

I settle into the more than comfortable couch. This whole situation is suddenly becoming real. My palms are a little sweaty. I have that I-wish-I-was-anywhere-but-here feeling running through me. I have no idea what is going to be said once we are called to an office.

My mind has been distracted by meeting Anastasia and the weird dinner last night. The JC shoes were a nice distraction, also. Then Brett's mysterious phone call occupied my thoughts during the drive.

But now there is nothing to deter the craziness running through my mind.

I don't guess Anastasia is here yet. I wonder if Jimmy will come with her. Maybe pop the question in the lawyer's office?

Brett returns and sits in a chair across from me. He smiles my way. "It's going to be okay. Don't look so nervous."

"I wish I could believe you. I don't even know why I'm here. And nobody wants to talk about it."

"Hi, Brett. Good to see you."

Brett stands.

"Ted," Brett says while shaking his hand, "Good to see you. It's been a while."

"It has. And this must be Miss Thomas."

I stand, subtly trying to wipe my hand on my dress before taking his hand in mine. "Hi. Yes, I'm Ann Thomas."

"Ted Reynolds. Nice to meet you. Why don't you two follow me? We're ready to start."

TED OPENS THE door while Brett hangs back, letting me enter the room first.

The biggest desk I've ever seen sits at one end of the room. Four chairs are placed in front of it. Two are already occupied. One by Anastasia and the other by her mom. I really can't see her because

Anastasia is blocking the view, but I know it's her.

Anastasia mouths the words 'sorry' to me for the second time in two days. I'm not sure if she's apologizing for her mom being here, or for lying to me saying she was running late.

She was obviously early.

Brett places his hand on the back of the plush chair next to Anastasia, indicating I should sit. So I do.

He sits next to me, looking out of place except for his expensive suit. His well-built frame somehow crams into the fancy chair, making it look non-existent.

Ted walks behind the massive desk. I would say the huge chair would swallow him up, but Ted's a big guy. Not big in a bad way, big like he could have been a pro wrestler. He kind of doesn't match the elegance of this place, either.

His desk top is shiny, bright and neat. Very few papers grace it. A pen holder and phone are the only other items on the desk. It seems like a waste of space.

I look at Anastasia. She mouths the words 'happy birthday' and smiles. I mouth 'you too.'

I still can't take a really good look at her mother. Anastasia has strategically placed herself so any contact, visual or otherwise, will be minimal.

What is already a strange situation in my mind becomes a tad bit stranger.

"Good morning." Ted speaks with a lawyer kind of official voice.

"Morning." Brett and I speak at the same time, while Anastasia and her mother mumble out a greeting.

Ted clears his throat again. I hope he's not catching a cold.

"We all know why we're here, today, so I'll start."

I want to raise my hand and my voice to tell Ted I have no idea why I'm here.

Ted starts reading. Strange verbiage and terms that aren't used in everyday life spout from his lips. I don't hear anything of interest until he says the word inheritance.

Inheritance?

He keeps reading, flipping pages as he finishes. "Now for some facts."

He leans back in his chair. I'm waiting for him to clear his throat, but he does it so quietly I almost miss it.

Sitting straight once again, he places the papers on the desk.

"Antonio was legally married for ten months to Trixie Hudson. They had one daughter, Angelina Thomas."

He stops talking before looking at me.

Who is Angelina Thomas?

Ted lowers his head to peer at me from above his reading glasses. "That would be you, I presume?"

A foreboding sensation crawls along my skin as I shake my head. "My name is Ann. Ann Thomas."

"Yes, it came to Mr. Thomas's attention that your name might have been changed, but your given name is Angelina Thomas."

My thoughts are jumbled. It seems Ted is speaking in a foreign language. My father was definitely this Antonio Thomas and my real name is Angelina? Did Mom have my birth certificate changed?

"Therefore, throughout this process you will be known as Angelina."

He pauses. I take this opportunity to look at Anastasia. She's staring straight ahead.

"Antonio Thomas also recognizes he has another daughter, Anastasia Castillo."

My hand covers my mouth to stifle my surprise. I have a sister? A half-sister?

A loud gasp indicates Anastasia is as surprised as I am. "What?" she asks. "Are you serious?"

I'm not sure how much more my heart can take. I don't even know who I am at this moment. My name has been changed. I have a sister I never knew about.

I'm thankful I'm wearing my flip-flops. They make my exit out of the office quick and uneventful.

I actually make it out of the office, down the stairs, and outside without incident. The ever-present gentle wind fills my lungs. Finally I'm able to breathe.

Within moments I feel a tap on my shoulder. I pretend I don't notice. Brett's presence is comforting, but I don't know if I'm ready to talk.

I can hardly think.

"I imagine you're shocked."

His voice, a whisper in my ear, resounds loudly through my brain. "Shocked doesn't begin to cover it."

He gives my shoulder a gentle squeeze then comes around to face me. Like staring at the gorgeous CPA is going to make my thinking any clearer?

I'm afraid of what else he is going to tell me. Is he a long lost brother or something?

Thinking of Brett as a brother, half or not, depresses me beyond my understanding. Which is crazy.

I now know why Anastasia and I are here.

What about Brett?

Inconceivable

"LET'S SIT FOR a minute." Brett's voice has the power to sooth, but I'm not sure it's going to work considering my current mental state.

He leads me to a bench outside the front doors. Even though the sun shines warmly down on me, I rub my arms. I debate the source of my chill bumps. The situation or Brett's touch.

He has to be warm in his suit, but his demeanor remains cool and calm.

"I wasn't sure how much you knew. Apparently you don't know a lot."

Rubbing my neck doesn't ease any tension. "I don't know anything."

He leans back. "With the way you seemed buddy buddy with Stace last night I wasn't sure."

"She met me at the door with a smile, then told me she was the help. I'm so confused."

"We have to go back inside. But I'll quickly tell you what I know."

"Thanks."

"Hey, and Ted bills by the hour, so you don't need to keep running out."

I look at him to see how serious he is. His killer smile greets me. I momentarily think I can handle any news if it's given to me by him.

Then I rein my thoughts in. I need to know how he plays into this.

"Okay. Stace's mother, Lovey, has worked in the Thomas home her whole life. She was madly in love with Antonio. He seemed to return her affections. Then comes Trixie Hudson, your mother. She sweeps Antonio off his feet. Trixie finds out she's pregnant. Antonio marries her. What no one knows is that Lovey is pregnant as well. By Antonio."

He starts to speak again, but I hold up my hand. "Wait. Give me a minute to process this."

"You've got ten seconds. Remember the words 'by the hour.'"

My fingertips press hard against my temples. Mom, who always chooses God over me, became pregnant before she was married? To a man who impregnated another woman? Even if Mom didn't know about Lovey, aren't those kind of guys easy to spot? And I have a half-sister. Beautiful Anastasia is my half-sister.

This is unbelievable. "Okay. Go on. I think."

Standing, he shoves his hands in his pockets. "All of this came to light when Trixie and Lovey were in the hospital at the same time giving birth. I think you were born fifteen minutes before Stace."

My breath hitches at the absurdity of it all. Could Antonio have planned his demise any more perfectly? "Thirty years ago today."

Brett nods his head. "You're right. Today is Stace's birthday."

"And mine."

"And yours. Happy birthday?"

"I don't know. You tell me."

"I'm not sure. I do know that Antonio acknowledged both of your births. He swore to your mother that it was over with Lovey, so your mother stayed married to him. But when you were about three months old, your mother caught him with Lovey. Trixie took you and left. No one ever heard from her except through lawyers. Antonio was devastated. He never married again."

My voice catches. "You sound like you were there."

"I wasn't. But my dad was. He was Antonio's accountant. My dad died five years ago and I took over."

A glimmer of hope strikes through the craziness. Brett's not related.

The hope is replaced with despair. No wonder Anastasia's mother hates me. And maybe Anastasia and I do look somewhat alike, although I don't see it. After all, we are sisters.

A car alarm rings through the air. Almost as soon as it starts, it stops. My gaze remains fixed on the ground, unfazed. If only my inner alarm could be silenced so quickly.

Brett snaps his fingers in front of my face. "Ann. Ann."

I look up. "Angelina."

"What?"

"My name is Angelina. Ted told me so."

He rubs his forehead before shaking his head. "We need to go back inside. Our few minutes is up. We need to hear what else the will says."

I stare at him, disbelief running through me. "You mean to tell me you don't know?"

"Not really. I know some numbers, but how they're broken down I have no idea." He holds his hand out, an indication he's willing to help.

My legs are shaking, but I take his hand and manage to stand steady on my feet. "Lovey hates me."

We start walking.

"This isn't about Lovey. This is about you and Stace. Just remember that."

I run the mantra through my head as we head to the office. The click of the knob as Brett turns the handle shoots through me like a bullet. I feel like I've been shot. I take a deep breath.

Brett once again places his hand on the back of my chair. I sit, more cautiously than before. I can't get comfortable. My shaking limbs won't let me.

Ted seems fidgety now. His eyes don't quite meet mine when he speaks. "I'm sorry for how this information is being relayed, Angelina. It must seem impersonal and cold. I wish this could be done differently. But unfortunately, it can't."

"It's okay."

My voice comes out so softly I'm not sure if he hears me, but he nods his head.

"I only read a portion of Antonio's will today. In thirty days from now, all three of you, Angelina, Anastasia and Brett, will meet here again to discuss the remaining part of his wishes. Ms. Castillo, you are welcome to accompany your daughter as well."

Great. Another trip down here in a month. What if I have a job?

"Angelina and Anastasia have the potential to inherit a vast sum of money. The exact sum will be disclosed at our next meeting. Until then, here are your instructions."

He focuses his attention on me. "Angelina, a bank account has been set up in your name. There are no checks with this account. Just this debit card."

Ted opens a drawer and holds up a gold card, the logo unreadable to me from this distance.

"This card is the only access to your bank account. Antonio has deposited slightly over one million dollars in this account. It earns no interest, has no fees."

If I felt shaken before, I'm not sure how to describe what I'm feeling now. Fog swirls around my brain. A vacuum seems to be closing in on my mind.

One million dollars?

"You have three weeks and three days to spend one million dollars. That will leave plenty of time for all the transactions to run through the bank before our next meeting on May fifth, when we will read the rest of the will."

I'm literally gulping air into my lungs.

"There are stipulations," Ted continues. "You must spend the money on yourself. You can buy nothing for anyone else. You can't have any single item purchase over ten-thousand dollars except for a car. You may only buy one car and you can't spend over fifty thousand dollars on it. Remember, no one receipt may total over ten-thousand dollars. If you go into a dress shop, your total purchase has to be ten thousand dollars or less."

I guess Ted is still talking. My accountant brain is working overtime trying to multiply numbers in my foggy head. Three weeks and three days. That's twenty-four days to spend one million dollars. Minus the fifty thousand for the car. That would mean I would have to spend approximately forty thousand dollars a day.

One million dollars at my disposal and I can't even buy the dream Jag.

"Ted," Brett says. "That's about forty thousand dollars a day, every day."

"It is. I'm glad you've caught onto that. Because you have a part to play in this, too."

"Me?" Brett asks.

"Yes. According to Antonio's will, for accounting purposes, you are the only person, other than the clerks at the store of course, that can touch this card. Angelina is never to have this card in her possession. You must accompany Angelina everywhere to supervise every purchase. No one else can accompany you two on the shopping excursions. And remember, not one thing can be bought for anyone else. She can't buy you a coke, lunch, a ticket to a soccer game, a piece of gum. Nothing. And no online shopping."

At these words my world rocks. I have to spend the next twenty-four days with Brett? Spending forty thousand dollars a day on myself? Am I dreaming? This is inconceivable.

"Angelina. You are to live in the house in Hampton Cove until our next meeting. If you fail this test, not only will you not inherit the estate, Anastasia won't either."

I glance at Anastasia. Her widened eyes indicate her surprise.

It was at that moment my world went black.

"I HAVE NEVER fainted before in my life. I swear."

"At least your color is coming back."

"I'm surprised my face isn't blue. You can turn the air down a notch."

Brett and I are in his pick-up truck. Even the fainting spell couldn't garnish anything heartfelt from Lovey Castillo. So after assurances I was fine, and assurances from Ted the meeting was indeed over, Brett had no choice but to take me back to the mansion.

Or whose-ever house it is. I guess if I pass 'the test' Anastasia and I will own it together. I'm still not sure as to how all this is going to come down.

"I need to run by the high school. Then, since you seem to be feeling better, you and I are going to go somewhere and have a talk."

"I'm excited. Is that card burning a hole in your pocket?"

"That card is going to ruin my life."

With those words spoken, he turns into the high school and parks in front of the main doors. "I'll be right back," he says, leaving the car running. I guess he doesn't want me to overheat. He probably thinks I'll faint again.

I want to know who wouldn't faint after being told the father you never knew was a multi-millionaire, your name isn't what you thought it was, you have a half-sister fifteen minutes younger than you, and there's a woman whose hatred of you stems from the fact that she thinks your mother is the reason her love destiny was never fulfilled.

I think a short fainting spell is right in line with appropriate behavior under such circumstances.

There are so many unanswered questions. So many things I do not know. Although now I know Brett isn't related to me. That's a plus.

But I still don't know who the cleats and the math book belong to. At this point, I'm too confused to try and figure it out.

The door opens. Brett pitches his jacket and tie in the back seat. He slides in, then takes a moment to roll up his shirt sleeves.

I'm watching him, mesmerized. I wonder if he knows how good he looks.

Probably not.

"Thanks for waiting."

Like I could have done anything else.

"No problem."

"This isn't the first time Ricky has done this. He thinks if he doesn't have his books he won't be responsible in class."

At least I now have a gender and a name. "Ricky?"

"My little brother. Not literally. I'm in a big brother type program mentoring young men. I met Ricky two years ago. He's a good kid who never knew his dad. He has a great mother, Paula, who wanted Ricky to have a male influence in his life."

So this Ricky and I have something in common. But I never got the male influence. "It sounds like a great program to be a part of."

"It is. Which is why you and I are going to have issues. Ricky has a soccer tournament coming up. I'm taking him. As in out of town. I pick him up from practice sometimes. I have other commitments as well."

I sit up straighter, my defenses on alert. "Remember. I didn't write the will. You cannot blame me for this. You can't."

"Do you like Mexican food?" he asks as he whips into a parking lot. I wonder if I said no would he leave. Probably not.

"Yes."

"Good."

After we're settled in a booth with our waters in front of us, chips and salsa at our disposal, he brings up the conversation we didn't finish.

"I'm not blaming you. Really I'm not. But I can't be your keeper for the next . . ."

"Twenty-four days."

"Yeah. Twenty-four days. We have to think of a way around this." He slaps the gold card on the table.

"Put that away," I hiss. "What if we lose it? We're in big trouble."

"It's out here as a reminder. That's all."

Brett is being ridiculous. "I'm serious. Put it back in your pocket. It makes me nervous."

"You're nervous? What about me? I don't know about you, but I have a life. One that can't be placed on hold because of an accounting stipulation in a will. At least you're unemployed."

His cold but true statement clashes with the festive Spanish style music that fills the air. A mariachi band has started playing for tips a few tables down. Hopefully they'll stay away from our table.

"So who do you work for?" I ask.

"Myself. But not much longer."

The music sounds louder as the band has moved down one table. At this rate they'll be here shortly.

"What do you mean?"

"Antonio was my dad's client. When my dad passed away I guess you can say I inherited his practice. Over the last two years, I've been slowly fazing the clients out. Antonio was the last one. Once this estate is settled, I'm no longer a practicing CPA."

"Oh, so you'll be unemployed like me? That's what you're striving for?"

He takes a bite of a chip. "No. I'll be able to do what I've been waiting to do my whole life."

At this point I have no idea what this man is going to say he's been waiting to do his whole life. I can guess one hundred times and probably not get it right. So I don't even try. "And I take it supervising women shopping isn't what you're aiming for as a career."

He laughs. "Funny. And right. Not my thing."

"Then what is your thing?"

I watch as a smile appears on his handsome face. His shoulders relax like a weight has been lifted off of them.

"I'm going to be a missionary. I'm leaving for Peru next month."

My gaze shifts outside, hoping he doesn't catch the disappointment I probably can't contain. The mariachi band moves in front of our table. I see Brett whisper to them before slipping some cash in one of the guitars.

Even a flavorful version of the happy birthday song ringing through the restaurant can't lift my spirits. Learning Brett's life dream has propelled my heart into further depths than when I thought he might be my half-brother.

At least then I would have been able to love him.

Intertwined

"HERE YOU ARE. Home, sweet home."

Brett shifts his truck into park. The trees are still blowing like when I first arrived yesterday. Is it possible only twenty-four hours have gone by?

But today I know where the walkway leads. I know what lies behind the massive front door. Mystery, turmoil, and craziness.

"I appreciate the ride." I no longer want to keep my gaze fixed on Brett. I'm not going to think about how his clothes fit him really well, or how handsome he is.

Why waste my heart? Like my mom, he'll be gone more than he's around. He'll be focusing on people he's never met more than he focuses on me.

At least I know what I'm not getting into.

He walks beside me to the front door. The breeze keeps sending his scent my way. A nice scent, which is good, because it looks like I'm going to be spending a lot of time with Mr. Hamilton. On the other hand it might be easier if I didn't find everything about this man attractive and pleasing.

"Why don't I come back after dinner and we can make some sort of a plan?"

The tone of his voice makes it sound like he'd rather be doing anything else. I get it.

"Sure. But that means today goes by and I haven't spent any money. You wouldn't even let me pay for my own lunch."

"What kind of man would let a woman pay for her own birthday lunch?" His gaze lingers on me, making me feel special.

I remind myself it is my birthday and I should feel special. Except now I'm sharing my birthday with a half-sister I just found out about. Somehow the betrayal of it all dings the special factor a little. "Very gentlemanly, but tomorrow, if I want to stay on track, I'll need to drop eighty grand. We'll have to remember to put that in the plan."

I know I'm coming off sounding ungrateful, but this is too crazy to be real, yet it is. It's very real. And unnerving.

"Okay, we'll put it into the plan. See you around eight."

He rests his hand on my shoulder. Not sure for what reason. It wasn't like an 'I'm sorry' kind of touch. It was more like a reassuring touch. Reassuring me he'd be back at eight.

Staring into his green eyes takes the focus off his well-put-together face. He seems genuinely concerned for me. But that doesn't change my situation.

Or his for that matter.

He can't wait to be rid of me.

"So," I start. "You're just going to throw me in the lion's den?" I nod toward the mansion.

"Lion's den?"

"Lovey lives there, remember? She'll probably poison my food or something."

Brett laughs. "Don't let your imagination run away with you. Lovey won't poison you. Her fight was with your mother, not you."

"My mom. Yeah."

"I bet you can't wait to call her and give her an earful."

"That won't be happening for a while. She's in the depths of a South American jungle until the beginning of May."

"Vacationing?"

"No. Missionarying."

His gaze sparks. "I think now I remember my dad telling me she was a missionary when she came here originally."

This talk is starting to depress me. "I need to go in and try to process this whole mess. I'll see you later."

He removes his hand from my shoulder, then backs up a couple of steps. His keys jingle as he pulls them out of his pocket. "See you at eight."

I'm not sure if the sunlight and swaying trees are playing with my vision or if Brett actually winks at me.

Of course, winks can be friendly gestures. I hear his truck door shut as I stare at the front door. Hopefully what lies on the other side won't be a frontal assault.

By a woman named Lovey, no less.

I'M SITTING ON the veranda where I started my morning. Only a million things have changed since then.

Literally.

I've received several happy birthday messages on my phone. One was from Aunt Venus. I tried calling her back, but had to leave a voicemail. I hope she calls back soon. I really need to talk to somebody.

Somebody I know. Somebody who wasn't a stranger a day ago.

My accountant instincts are trying to kick in. I wish I had my laptop with me. The need to open an excel worksheet to track this spending is overwhelming.

I spend some time downloading and customizing a spreadsheet to my phone.

This idea that I have to spend all the money on myself is crazy. Sure, I've coveted a few pairs of JC shoes, but I don't even know where to begin in this process. And given my track record, I'm not so good at it.

I guess I could buy a laptop. That would kill a thousand or so. Then the software would eat up a couple hundred more. Hey, it would be a start.

"Ann?"

I look up. Anastasia is standing a few feet away from me. She's almost a ghostly version of the Anastasia I met yesterday.

"Hi. Happy birthday to us, right?" Her voice is ever so soft and she looks a little paler.

She walks over then sits in the chair next to me.

"Yeah. This isn't exactly what I planned on happening on my thirtieth birthday."

"Me either." Her lips, which have the capability to produce that beautiful smile, stay in a straight line, giving her a pensive look.

I had forgotten about Anastasia's hopeful ring-on-her-finger event. Although it's still early. Plenty of time left in the day to become engaged.

"Sisters. We're sisters." Her voice is kind of hesitant.

"I guess we are." The reality of it hasn't set in at all.

"Half. Half-sisters."

"Yes, just half," I say, like it lessens the implications.

"Jimmy was right. You know, about us looking alike."

She starts laughing and I join her. Moments later I'm dabbing the corners of my eyes, I'm laughing so hard.

"Come on," Anastasia says. "Follow me."

I follow her inside to the bar. Her color has returned, and she confidently walks to the mirror as she motions for me to follow.

When I reach her we stand next to each other. Both of us have puzzled looks on our faces. Her eyebrows raise. I raise mine.

She smiles, I smile. She winks, I wink.

"This is crazy. Do you see it? The resemblance?" she asks.

I scrunch my face. She's so beautiful. I don't feel like I look like her at all. "I can't say. Honestly."

Her fingertips brush her cheekbones. "We have the same bone structure. That came from Antonio for sure."

My breath catches. Now is the time. I mean, things can't get much crazier, can they? "You knew him."

She stops touching her face and turns to me. "Yes. I knew him. But not like a father. I can't believe he never told me. And Mama never told me. So really, we're kind of in the same boat, Sis."

"You were around him your whole life," I challenge.

"As a man who employed Mama. That's it. No heart to hearts, no father-daughter dances. And he left *you* the money."

There is attitude in her voice. "Seriously? You're going there? He left me a test. If I pass, you inherit money."

"You better pass. Do you know how to spend money?"

"I know how to manage money. I'm an accountant, remember?" My mind swirls with everything that has happened in the last twenty-four hours. "Do you have a picture of him?"

She crosses her arms. "You've never seen him, have you?" she asks.

"No. Infants can't remember and I guess that was the last time I was in his presence."

"Wait right here," she says before rushing out of the room.

I lean against the bar turning away from the mirror. Away from the supposed resemblance of Anastasia and me.

In the past I had Googled the name Antonio Thomas in Hampton Cove, Florida. There were several choices. All of them required additional money in order to learn more information.

Once again, loyalty to my mom won out, and I never pursued any of them. Especially since I would have had to spend my hard-earned money.

"Here we go," Anastasia says as she walks back into the room. She joins me at the bar, lays down a small photo album and pushes it toward me.

The pink and lace print cover leads me to believe this is Anastasia's album. Not her mom's.

I slowly open the book.

A photo of a young girl, about twelve maybe, stares at me. She's standing on a beach, the waves behind her. She's holding a sand dollar.

"That's me," Anastasia says. "Antonio took me to the beach that day. A rare occurrence. But, turn the page. Somebody offered to take our picture."

Willing away feelings of jealousy, I turn the page. "Oh," I say. It comes out with my breath that I had been holding.

"He was kind of beautiful, wasn't he?" she asks.

Without asking, I pull the photo out from behind its plastic barrier. I trace his handsome face, his dark, wavy hair. My skin-tone came from him.

"It's sad you didn't know," I remark.

"You, too."

Setting the photo down, I leave Anastasia standing behind the bar and head back out to the veranda. Maybe the fresh air will clear my mind. Something needs to. Between the lawyer, my new *family*, and Brett, being knee deep in unbalanced corporate bank statements seems like child's play right now. I'm used to my mind spinning around numbers until they balance out.

Emotions and feelings?

Much harder to deal with.

Especially when so many unknowns have intertwined.

At least I know what he looks like, now. I sit on the wide concrete railing, resting my back against one of the columns. It's hard to settle comfortably against the stone, which sums up how I'm feeling. Even the expansive view of the bay doesn't seem to relax me. The water is calm, steady, so unlike my heart.

"Look," Anastasia says as she stands next to me. "I'm confused, too. But it's my birthday. I love my guy, and I want to be engaged. It's what I've been thinking about for days. I was sad when Antonio died. Sad because he'd taken such good care of Mama. I had no idea how sad she was. And it was their choice not to tell us. We have to take this information and go from here. But first I'm going out for a birthday dinner with my love."

The one thing I notice as we're close together is our skin coloring. Anastasia is a little browner than I am, but hey, she lives in Florida. "We both have his skin tone."

"We do. I'll see you tomorrow. I'll come by in the morning after breakfast. I'm assuming you'll still be here? The will said you had to stay and I don't think Brett, the keeper of the card, is going to follow you to Atlanta, is he?"

"I'm staying. I don't have a choice."

"Wish me luck?" Anastasia holds up her left hand, curls all her fingers except the 'ring' finger, which she waves at me.

"I'll be praying," I say.

"Thanks, Sis."

Her 'Thanks, Sis,' lingers in the air as she leaves.

Sis.

I have a sister.

And my mom knew this. She deprived me of a relationship with my half-sister. Is this why she hauled me around the world? Hiding from Antonio? Hiding *me* from Antonio? Okay, I know the whole situation would have been awkward had we ever just showed up here. But I know now. Did my mom think the whole thing would simply go away eventually when everyone had died?

Well, only one person has died and thirty years of secrets have been let loose in Hampton Cove.

Apparently Antonio hadn't been satisfied with the way things had turned out. So he decided to turn them upside down after he was gone.

Just like a man.

I DISCOVER A cozy library in the mansion. It seems like a nice place to hang out until Brett arrives for our eight-o'clock meeting. Built-in bookshelves line two walls, a comfy tan couch graces the middle of the room, and a baby grand has perfectly nestled itself into a corner.

Running my hands over the keys, I start playing. But then the words of the Psalm flood my mind and I abruptly stop, willing the words and tune away. Mom has no idea the impact her sing-song Psalms have had on me. They've never left me.

I might go as far as to say they've haunted me. At least that's how I feel at times.

"You play?"

I jump slightly at the intrusion of the voice.

His voice.

Brett stands next to the piano. I'm grateful for his interruption. "You must have a key."

"Inherited it from my dad." A small smile appears on his face.

"I'll have to remember that." My heart will have to remember, because seeing Brett does things to my heart. But then I recall his missionary dreams, and the zinging thrill of seeing him unzings.

"Here," he says as he pushes a box towards me. "Nobody should go a whole birthday without a cake."

I take the box as a nervous energy races through me. Opening the white cardboard lid I see a small cake, decorated with white frosting and yellow flowers. A green icing 'happy birthday' cramps its way around the cake top under the flowers. No name. Generic.

But no less thoughtful.

My name wouldn't have fit anyway.

Angelina.

"Thank you." I stand, hoping all thoughts of a child's song will leave when I step away from the piano.

Thankfully that chapter of my life is over.

A few minutes later we are sitting on the veranda, coffee and cake in front of us. "Chocolate cake. Good choice." I slide my fork into my mouth, the moistness of the cake causing me to savor the flavor.

His slice sits uneaten, but he does sip his coffee.

"I'm glad you like it," he says.

Brett seems disconnected. His body sits in the chair next to me, but his gaze is way out on the bay. I really want to talk about tomorrow, but I don't feel like the conversation will be well received.

So I'll start a conversation about something else. "Anastasia is hoping to become engaged tonight."

Brett's body stiffens a little. Such a slight reaction, that had I not been looking for one, I probably wouldn't have noticed it. But it was there.

"I've said it before. He's not going to ask her to marry him."

I smash the crumbs from my plate onto my fork. "What makes you so sure?"

"Things. He's not the marrying kind. He likes to play the field. And he told me he has no plans to marry Stace."

I set my fork on my plate, crumbs and all. "That's kind of cold. He said that to you? Did you ask or did you volunteer that information?"

Brett turns toward me. "I basically asked him what his intentions were. I was going to warn her, but then with Antonio's death and everything else happening I never got the chance. Now, it's too late. He'll probably give her a gift card for her birthday and she'll freak. I have my phone at the ready like every big brother should."

He taps his phone which sits on the table.

"Big brother to Anastasia and Ricky? You're a busy guy."

"Sometimes. And trust me when I say it's a whole lot easier being Ricky's big brother."

Pushing my plate towards the middle of the table, I settle into my comfortable chair. The bay air blows soft and warm, every once in a while carrying Brett's scent on it, which combined with his green eyes and his insistence that Anastasia is like a little sister to him makes him everything I've ever looked for in a guy.

Yet he's a missionary.

Can fate be any meaner?

His phone vibrates and he picks it up. He slides his thumb around then works his thumbs across the screen. Texting.

"Here it is," he says. "One big brother 'it'll be okay' talk coming up. I hope you don't mind. She asked where I was. She should be here in a few minutes."

"No, I don't mind. When she arrives, I'll make myself scarce."

"I'm sorry about this. We haven't had a chance to make a game plan for tomorrow."

I shrug my shoulders. "Really, how much do we have to plan? You drive me to the shops. I'll find things I like. It sounds simple, doesn't it?"

"I guess."

"I hope all the packages will fit in your truck."

He chuckles. "You have fifty grand to spend on a vehicle. Why don't you buy a big SUV? Then we'll have plenty of room."

The thought of spending fifty thousand dollars on a car causes me to slightly hyperventilate. The upside? If I bought a newer car I could ditch my ride and not be embarrassed riding in the neighborhood. "I wouldn't know where to start. What do you know about cars?"

"Not a whole lot. I own a six year old pickup. I can think of other things to spend my money on."

"Yeah, well, I need to spend money. A lot of it and fast."

"Point taken. We'll drop by a dealership in the next couple of days."

"Is there a Jaguar one close by?"

He looks at me with raised brows. "You've got champagne taste, don't you? Maybe spending this money won't take as long as I thought."

If he only knew.

The sound of a door slamming, then heels clicking, stops our current conversation, but starts a new one.

"She's here," Brett says. "And those shoes are hitting it hard."

"I'm outta here." I push my chair back and stand.

Brett cocks his head. "It sounds like she's running."

Footsteps are quickly making their way to us. There is no time for me to make my escape. I guess I'll have to deal with the tears and anger.

Oh well, she is my sister.

"Brett!"

Anastasia's voice carries through the house. I watch as she bursts into the living room, her pretty pink dress clinging to her in all the right places. I can tell the second she sees us on the veranda.

"Brett, Ann. I'm so glad you are both here. Look, isn't it gorgeous?"

She thrusts out her left hand then crosses the short distance to Brett and me. The biggest diamond I've ever seen on a real person in real life captivates my gaze.

"I'm getting married!"

Ironic

I LOOK AT Brett who still has his gaze locked onto the big diamond. I want to give him a what's-going-on look.

"Well?" Anastasia says. "Aren't you going to congratulate me?"

"Congratulations," I blurt. "Your birthday wish came true."

"Yes, it did. And it was the most romantic dinner, with flowers, candles and a guy playing a violin. Jimmy got down on his knee in the middle of the restaurant. I'll never forget it. Never."

Brett sidesteps a little closer to me.

"That's great, Stace." The tone of his voice indicates he's either jealous or concerned. I'm going with concerned.

"And," she says, her big brown eyes shimmering with tears staring straight at me, "I want *you* to be my maid of honor."

Stunned I continue to stare back at her. "Me?" I ask, flashbacks of the movie *My Best Friend's Wedding* running through my head. When Cameron Diaz asked Julia Roberts to be her maid of honor mere moments after meeting her, I said that would never happen in real life. Okay, I've known Anastasia a little longer than mere moments, but not much.

But now I know how Julia felt. I can't say no. I mean, she's my sister.

I guess right now the half part isn't important. There are more Anastasia eye-tears. You know the ones that brim at the edges, but don't ever manage to quite spill over. I'm too shocked to conjure up my own eye-tears. I'm surprised I'm still breathing normally.

"I'm sure Ann would consider it an honor to be your maid of honor. Wouldn't you, Ann?"

I look at Brett. He has no idea what I'm considering. His expression is trying to tell me something, but I don't know him well enough to decipher his face. But I go along with it. "Sure. I, *Angelina*, would love to be your maid of honor."

Now her eye-tears do spill down her cheeks, mascara free, and she grabs me and hugs me. But only for a millisecond. Then she backs up. "I have to go tell Mama. She's going to be thrilled. She's been waiting to plan a wedding for ages now."

I stand next to Brett as the pink whirlwind that is Anastasia flees the room, her excitement along with that flowery scent she wears, still hovering. There is so much energy I think the furniture would jump to life if it could.

"He's never going to marry her, huh?" I pretty much whisper the words, not wanting them to carry anywhere near Anastasia's ears.

"I'm shocked."

"Shocked or jealous?" I have to ask.

His look tells me I shouldn't have. "You know how I feel about her. Something isn't right."

"It certainly seems right to her. I know I don't know Jimmy, and he's very loud, but I saw him staring at her last night with a look that said pure adoration. Love. It was in his eyes."

"You should have stopped at the beginning of your sentence. You don't know Jimmy. I'm glad you agreed to be in the wedding. If you hear or see anything that you think is odd, let me know. Please."

The moon casts shadows across the veranda, across Brett's face. He seems intense regarding Anastasia. Ricky too, if I remember the stern tone in his voice when he was leaving that voicemail for him.

There's more to Brett Hamilton than I'm seeing.

I'M SITTING ON the bed petting PS. A knock on the door startles me. Brett left over an hour ago, Anastasia right after. That leaves only one person in the house that I know of, which leaves me a little on edge.

Lovey.

Surely *she's* not standing on the other side of the door. I open it cautiously, and sure enough she's standing there. She's shorter than I realized, but still beautiful. Still stoic.

Still unnerving.

"Hello." I break our stare fest.

She half-smiles and I see Anastasia in her. "Hello. I don't think we've been properly introduced, except in that lawyer's office and that certainly wasn't proper at all. I'm Lovey Castillo."

She doesn't offer a hand or a hug, but her voice is warm. "I'm Ann. Or Angelina. Take your pick."

"You look like an Angelina in my opinion. You also look like your mother. How is Trixie?"

It quickly comes to my attention there is far more separating us than a door frame. A chasm of emotions and years of untold details will be hard to bridge. For now, I'm sticking by the saying *Less is more.* "She's fine."

"I'm glad to hear that. Can we be expecting a visit anytime soon? As the housekeeper, I like to be kept apprised of any visitors. And since Antonio is gone, this is your place."

Just like Anastasia, eye-tears appear. Her voice is soft, yet mournful in a way. Is she mourning Antonio's passing or the fact that the place is mine?

Even though the place, or palace as I would call it, isn't legally mine. Yet. And since I haven't spent even a dime of the money, I'm not on the fast-track to acquiring it. "I wouldn't call it my place. I'm a visitor. And no, my mom won't be joining me. She's traveling right now."

"Is Trixie still doing her God trips, or has she stolen someone else's man and gone on the run?"

The chasm has now become a whole lot wider. I may not be my mom's biggest fan, but there's no need for the downright meanness Lovey is spouting. "She's a missionary."

"There, there," Lovey says, starting to reach her hand out to me. But apparently Lovey realizes how wide the chasm is also, because she pulls her hand back. "This must be very hard for you. I wanted to let you know if you need anything at anytime, I'm here. I have a suite downstairs if you ever need anything from me or Anastasia."

Ha. So I'm not the only one who calls her Anastasia. That's probably the only thing Lovey and I have in common. But I was raised right and Mom taught me how to be polite. "Thank you for your offer."

Lovey backs up a couple of steps. "Well, goodnight then."

"Goodnight."

She turns and walks away, her frailty becoming much more apparent. Her walk is more slow than brisk. Although that may be her emotions walking.

I shut my door then make my way back to the bed. PS sits like a sphinx. Regal with her paws underneath her and her stable expression.

She doesn't flinch as I sit. My mind is jumbled with Lovey's visit. The woman who hates my mom is offering to be there if I ever need her. Something my mom has neglected to do.

I start humming the tune to one of my favorite Alanis Morrisette songs. *Isn't it ironic?*

The words, though trapped in my mind unspoken, are very loud.

Jimmy-loud.

I BARELY GULP down a cup of coffee after a night of broken sleep before Brett's presence invades the kitchen.

"Are you ready?" he asks.

If I had my back to him, I would think he was onboard for our day. But since I am viewing him straight on everything about him contradicts his tone. His stance in his well-worn denim jeans exudes annoyance. His left hand holds his phone while his right hand works it. His foot clad in those boots taps the tiled floor, while his facial expression indicates the day isn't starting well. A black T that has the words 'a remedy' scrawled across the front of it rounds out his look.

"I guess so." I finish off my coffee and set the cup in the sink.

His attention deviates from his phone. It focuses on me. "Did you sleep at all?"

My hand automatically brushes the top of my head. My hair feels smooth. Nothing sticking up. Maybe the fact I pulled it back in a ponytail has him confused. I even dabbed a little make-up on this morning.

Obviously I didn't dab enough. "I slept off and on."

"You look tired, that's all."

At least today I'm not giving off the wrong impression. I am tired and I look tired. Fine with me.

It's a good thing Brett is a missionary and off limits to my heart. If he wasn't, I'd feel obligated to go back upstairs where I'd conceal something and brighten up something else. "I promise I'll keep up with you."

He eyes my feet. "Are you wearing those flip-flop things? We have a lot of walking to do."

"I planned on being here two days, remember? I didn't bring much of a wardrobe. It's either these or my broken black pumps. Take your pick."

"I guess you have a point. Our first stop then will be the shoe store."

I can't help but smile. My guilt trip come true. "Fine with me."

"The sporting goods shoe store. You need a decent pair of tennis shoes."

"No Jimmy Choos?" I can't deny a little relief settles in my veins.

"Jimmy's what?"

"Jimmy Choo is a name brand shoe. A very nice and expensive shoe. Sorry the name hits so close to home." Even the shopping trip is invaded by Anastasia and her fiancé.

"The Jimmy shoes will have to wait. Practical tennis shoes come first. Let's go."

I settle in the front seat of his truck. There are no cleats or math books to maneuver around today. No, only eighty thousand dollars to maneuver.

If I let myself think about my situation I'd be overwhelmed. So I'm not. I'm only going to take it one dollar at a time.

A hundred and twenty five dollars later I'm wearing very cute, yet practical, tennis shoes with white ankle-length sporty socks. These are a necessity. Brett said so.

"Feel better?" Brett asks as we start walking toward other shops.

"My flip-flops would have been fine, but I do admit, these have somewhat of a cushiony, comfort factor about them the flip-flops lacked."

"Trust me on this. Your feet are thanking me."

"If you say so."

"I say so. Tell me when you see a place you want to shop in."

The sun is shining and the sidewalks aren't too crowded yet. We're at an outdoor mall with several shops. I have no idea where to begin.

Across the street I spot a shoe store. A part of me wants to head right over. Another part hesitates.

"How about that shoe store," Brett says pointing across the street.

He must have seen me looking that way. We cross the street and moments later, as I'm about to open the door, his voice stops me.

"Ann, do you have your phone?"

"It's Angelina, and yes I have my phone."

He looks at me matter-of-factly. "Let me see it. I'm going to put my number in."

My right hand dips inside my purse, then I hand my phone to Brett. "I'm assuming you're doing this in case we somehow become separated?"

"No. Although that does have its merits. My thought is you can text me when you're done shopping, and I can come in and swipe the card."

My feelings try not to be hurt, but I must confess they are a little. I mean I knew the guy wouldn't want to shop all day. What guy does? But somehow the shopping doesn't seem nearly as enticing with me on the inside of the store and him on the outside. But I play it off like it's nothing. "Where are you going to be?"

"Not far. I'll see if there's a coffee shop close by. I still have things to do to get ready for Peru. I'll be doing emails and work from my phone, so just hang tight if it takes me a minute."

"Oh, okay."

"And if you don't find anything in this place, just text me with the store you're in. I'll find it. Here. I'm under Hamilton and Son. It's the business line."

He holds his phone up like his words haven't impersonalized this situation enough.

"All right, Mr. Hamilton. I'll text you when I'm ready to make a purchase."

I enter the shoe store feeling more alone than ever. Chill bumps sprout at the air-conditioned atmosphere. I rub my arms, my mind journeying in a million directions. Million. How long will that word invade my thoughts?

Spotting the sandal section I make my way toward it, the shoes I'm passing blurred by Brett's rejection. I was under the impression that I handled rejection better than this. I've had enough practice. Maybe it's the fact that I'm out of practice. My last boyfriend, Jason, left over six months ago. That's it. I haven't dated much in the last few months, so the chances of being rejected were narrowed significantly.

At least I feel a little better now that I've determined the reason for my reaction to Brett's indifference towards me.

Besides, I do have to remember I'm a business assignment to Brett Hamilton, CPA. Other than Anastasia's upcoming wedding, whenever that will be, Brett and I have nothing personal happening.

A pair of silver sandals catches my eye and I pick one up. It's a JC of course.

"Would you like to try those on?"

A Barbie Doll-looking associate is standing so close to me I swear I can smell her makeup. Her nametag says Hazel, but I'm not buying it. Must be a shoe store stage name.

I eye the shoe again. It won't hurt to try it on. And I do have to spend money. A lot of it. "Sure. Size six, please."

"Certainly. And let me know if there are any others that interest you."

Adrenaline ramps inside of me. It's real. This crazy scenario is not a dream. I *have* to spend money. "I will. I'm in a spending kind of mood all of a sudden, so I'm sure I can pick out a few more pairs."

After quickly perusing more sandals, a baby blue colored leather chair beckons me, so I sit. I untie the shoe I just tied about twenty minutes ago. I slip off the sock, thankful my foot hasn't had time to smell like anything besides the soap I used this morning while showering.

I wiggle my toes in anticipation of the pretty silver sandal.

"Here you are." Hazel hands me the right shoe along with one of those little hose slip on things before placing the shoe box at my feet. "Did you find anything else?"

Her words may be offering to help, but her movements and expression indicate she's not that thrilled with her work. She moves a little slowly and her gaze is always drifting. No eye contact. And her smile is an auto-smile.

"I did. How about every sandal you have a size six available."

"Which sandal?" she asks as I'm suddenly worthy of eye contact. Wide-eye contact I might add.

"Every pair. Size six."

"All right. Uh, I'll be right back. It might take me a minute."

"No problem." It'll probably take her a lot longer than a minute. I'm wondering if she gets paid on commission. I thought all these high-dollar store clerks were paid on commission.

Note to self for future. Find stores where you know associates are paid on commission. The process may go quite a bit faster.

I've just slipped the strap in place on the silver sandal when a pair of stable, brown pumps appear in my downward view. I slowly lift my gaze and see a woman who is older than Hazel and probably the manager of the store.

"Yes?" I ask.

"I'm Marie Tallent, the store manager."

Ha. Spot on. I stand. "Hi. Ann, um, Angelina Thomas. Nice to meet you."

Marie's gaze is suspicious and she's not quite frowning, but close to it. Crazy considering the store she manages could possibly be the recipient of a huge sale.

"Hazel tells me you want to try on every size six sandal in stock."

"Try saying that three times in a row, huh?"

Ms. Tallent isn't amused. "Is this a joke?"

I knew spending money would be difficult for me, but I didn't think it would cause a problem for the stores. "No. It's not a joke. I have to spend eighty thousand dollars today and thought I'd start with a few pair of sandals. Can you help me out, or do I need to go somewhere else?"

Once again I'm feeling like Julia Roberts. Only this time it's the Pretty Woman scenario when she's trying to shop on Rodeo Drive.

Marie's gaze locks onto mine, and I guess mine convinces her I'm serious.

"I'll tell Hazel to bring you those promptly."

"Thank you, Ms. Tallent."

I walk over to the foot mirror. The silver sandals fit perfectly, and they feel pretty good, too. But, I am not doing any more sandal shopping until I get a pedicure. My toes are ruining the look of the beautiful shoes.

Out of the corner of my eye I watch Hazel and Ms. Tallent bring box after box out, setting them next to my chair.

I sit back down. One hand unstraps the silver sandal, while the other pulls a black and white sandal out of a box. "Pretty," I say. "Very pretty and cute."

It doesn't seem like that much time has passed before the to-buy stack is now four stacks. When I see I only have one more pair to try on I text Brett.

TIME TO PAY FOR THE DAMAGE. :)

Moments late my phone buzzes back. ON MY WAY.

Ah. Brett knows how to be polite as well.

I debate on the last pair of sandals. I'll probably never wear them. They don't fit as well as the others, so I pass.

Hazel starts taking the boxes to the register. As I tie my tennis shoes it hits me how insane this really is. Will I ever wear these sandals? There are more than five pairs of JC's in the bunch. Last week at this time I couldn't afford one pair.

My heart starts racing as I try to conjure up some inner peace at this transaction that will take place when Brett arrives. Thousands of dollars worth of shoes will be in my possession.

My face feels hot and flushed. This isn't right. This money could be much better spent. As much as I don't want to live in a third-world country I don't mind sending money to them.

I sit wondering if there is any way the will can be changed.

A soft overhead ding indicates Brett is here.

"So, you found some shoes?" he asks as he walks up to me.

"I did. A few pairs. But this is ridiculous. All this money for shoes. What if I donate my part to charity? Can we change the will?"

Brett looks puzzled. "I'm a CPA, not a lawyer, but Antonio's will was very specific. My gut feeling is if it could have been changed, Ted would have told us."

Hazel is still carrying my purchases to the counter as Ms. Tallent starts waving her wand in front of the boxes one by one.

"Wait, wait, wait," he says, his gaze taking in the scenario. "All these? Where are we going to put them?"

"In your truck."

"Will they fit? Honestly, Ann, I realize you have to spend some money, but we have to be practical until we can buy another vehicle."

I smile as I watch Ms. Tallent try to focus on her job instead of our conversation. "I think you rang that one twice," I say. "Could you check please?"

Ms. Tallent's annoyed expression glances at the cash register. "I'm sorry. I'll take it off."

She pushes a few buttons. Hazel is busy bagging the boxes after they have been wanded.

"That'll be eight thousand, seven hundred dollars and thirty-six cents."

Ms. Tallent looks like she's sweating as she speaks the total.

Brett already has his wallet out. He whips out the gold debit card and swipes it. "We're going to a dealership tomorrow. You're buying an SUV."

As he's shoving the card back in its protective sleeve he looks at me.

"Pin number?" he asks.

"Pin number? You think I know the pin number? I'm not even allowed to touch the card."

"Well, the machine here is asking for a pin."

"Try running it as a credit card." I'm speaking calmly and softly for a Georgia girl who any minute now could be terribly embarrassed.

Brett takes the card out and pushes a couple of buttons before swiping the card again.

He turns to me. "Won't work. It's asking for a pin."

"Well," I say, turning to Ms. Tallent. "It seems there's a slight problem with our card. Can you give us a minute?"

Interesting

MS. TALLENT'S look says she'd like to give us a few things, a minute not being one of them. "Certainly."

Brett and I walk to the front of the store. "I'm calling Ted. Why didn't he give you the pin? This is crazy."

Brett's hand is on his hip and his phone is pressed against his ear. "Ted, please."

I can't help but glance toward the counter. Hazel has stopped bagging the shoe boxes while Ms. Tallent peruses the receipt still in the register, probably trying to figure out how much of a pain it will be to void the transaction.

"Voicemail." Brett's voice is whispered and irritated.

He connects again to Ted lawyer's office. "Gretchen. This is Brett Hamilton. I really need to speak with Ted. Is he in the office today?"

He shoves his hand in his pocket. "Court. Great."

I smile at Hazel and Ms. Tallent. Like everything is going okay. Like our phone conversation hasn't just revealed the keeper of the pin is unavailable.

Brett is shaking his head. "The thing is, Gretchen, I really need to speak with him. You could say it's an emergency."

He pauses. "Sure," he says, standing a little straighter. He turns his attention to me, a hopeful look in his eyes. "Write this number down, please."

I grab a pen and a receipt out of my purse and jot down the number as he tells it to me.

He takes the paper from my hand and repeats the number into the phone to Gretchen. "Thanks. I appreciate this."

"Okay," Brett says to me as he starts sliding his finger on his phone. "She gave me his cell number. I'm texting him. Maybe, just maybe, he will be able to respond."

"I hope so. Ms. Tallent and Hazel are looking rather put out."

"Personal friends, now?"

"I've been in here close to two hours trying on every sandal they have in my size. I know their names."

A group of three girls enter the store wearing extremely short shorts and skimpy tops. Designer purses dangle from their shoulders. I lower my voice and whisper to Brett. "They don't look old enough to drive let alone have a job. How can they afford to buy anything in this store?"

"Daddy's plastic." His voice isn't so low. In fact his insinuation couldn't be any louder or clearer.

"You know, I didn't ask for this. I didn't even know who my father was. And I'm only doing this for Anastasia. I could care less about the money."

Bold and untrue words, but they sound good.

Brett looks a little confused, but only for a moment. "I wasn't talking about your situation. Your daddy's plastic is totally different from theirs."

He really doesn't sound sarcastic. "Thank you for acknowledging that."

"Their cards probably work."

I stare straight-faced at his grin. Dazzling as it is, I'm not finding much to smile about.

Brett's phone buzzes. "Ah," he says. "Gretchen will be calling in a minute with the pin."

We hang out for about ten minutes until his phone rings. "Hi Gretchen." Moments later he puts his phone back in its case. "Got it. Let's go pay for all those shoes."

I don't feel as relieved as I probably should. Maybe a small part of me, tucked deep inside, doesn't want to know the pin. Doesn't want to purchase the insane amount of shoes boxed and bagged behind the counter just waiting for someone to be able to press the four pivotal numbers after swiping the card.

Hazel, who had drifted off toward the expensive purse girls, has now reappeared behind the counter. Ms. Tallent is trying not to scowl.

"I think we're ready now."

"Let's hope so." Ms. Tallent pushes a couple of buttons. "Slide the card, please."

Brett does. Then after pushing the all-important numbers, things start happening on Ms. Tallent's side of the register. Within seconds she rips the receipt off and hands it to Brett.

"Thank you."

Hazel starts setting the huge bags on our side of the counter. The expensive purse girls stare at Brett and me as we haul the bags to the front door.

"I'll be right back with the truck."

Brett leaves me standing just inside the door, bags surrounding me. Bags of gorgeous, expensive dream shoes. Shoes that I never imagined would be on my feet.

Shoes that the reality of owning isn't nearly as exciting as the dreaming was.

"AT LEAST YOUR closet is big," Brett says as he hauls the last bag into it.

"The closet. Not *my* closet. And it's overly big. Almost as big as my condo in Atlanta."

Brett starts handing me shoe boxes, and I start stacking them against the wall.

"Are you actually going to wear all these shoes?"

"At some point. Not today."

He smiles. I like how his smile makes him even better looking than he already is. Just what I need.

"You know," I say. "You act like this is my doing. That I want to be out spending this money like this. I'm being forced. You can see it's not my normal behavior." I point to my flip-flops now cast aside, looking homeless next to all the shoes that have boxes.

He nods. "That is exactly my point. You have no shoes to wear, yet given the means you go out and buy useless shoes."

The need to defend Jimmy Choo rises quickly. "These shoes are far from useless. They're just not to be worn with shorts. Or at least I don't wear them with shorts."

Visions of tall, leggy beauties strutting around in shorts and stilettos fill my mind. Definitely not me.

Brett scratches his head. "Okay. Useless may be a hard word. Impractical might be better."

"Say what you want. They are beautiful shoes and I can't wait for an opportunity to wear them."

"Which I'm sure won't be far off with Stace's wedding. " His gaze catches mine. "Don't forget you're my eyes and ears."

"Are you sure there's nothing more to your concern than you just don't trust Jimmy? Something I should know?"

His tall, firm stance indicates he's not hiding anything. "Like I said yesterday, I don't want her to get hurt."

I hope his protective nature is just that. Protective. Not spurred by another action. Like love.

Although it really doesn't matter to me. I'm not his type of girl.

We have moved outside the closet into the arena bathroom. Why we choose to stop and converse here I don't know. Although the bathroom is very elegant and spa-like, the bedroom with its balcony and beautiful bay view would make a better place to have a conversation.

My gaze catches a movement out of the corner of my eye. Before I can speak, PS waltzes up to Brett's leg, swishing her puff-ball body and tail all over his jeans. Maybe white cat hair will enhance the well-worn look.

"Uh, hi cat."

His tone is very pet-unfriendly.

"Her name is PS."

"Strange name for a cat." He moves to the left. So does PS. Apparently she really likes the feel of his jeans.

"It's really Princess Sari, but I call her PS."

"PS is much better than Princess anything."

Brett's phone rings. As he answers it, I bend down and pick up PS. I carry her into the bedroom and set her on the bed. She settles on her blanket.

I may have reservations about being here, spending this money, and being a maid of honor, but the one thing I don't question is the view and the continual soft breeze. Both are calming, serene and can take my mind off any number of issues.

Brett walks into the bedroom. "I need to go pick up Ricky. He sprained his ankle. I'm going to take him to have it looked at."

"Oh, okay," I say, trying not to think about the approximate thirty thousand I didn't spend today to meet the forty thousand a day quota, of which I'm already forty thousand dollars behind.

"Come on. You can ride with me and meet Ricky."

"Are you serious?" Is Brett trying to involve me in his personal life?

"Yes. As long as it's just a sprain we can go spend more money before the shops close tonight."

That explanation my heart can understand.

And accept.

The one that ran through my head when he first spoke the words scared me.

I don't want to be in his personal life any more than absolutely necessary.

I JUMP OUT of the truck when I see Brett and Ricky exit the school. A black backpack dangles from Brett's elbow. It keeps slapping against his hip as he tries to support Ricky.

"Here, let me take that." I nod my head toward the backpack.

"Who's she?"

I look at Ricky and am met with a cold stare from big, dark brown, almost black eyes, barely visible under a swoop of thick, black bangs. That same genuine can-never-get-from-a-bottle black colored hair frames his face in a shaggy cut.

"This is Ann."

My gaze cuts to Brett. "Angelina, actually. It's nice to meet you."

"What are you, a nurse? Is that why you're here?"

His words sting, because they clearly say I don't want you around.

"Ricky, this is a friend of mine. Please treat her with respect," Brett says as he opens the door to the back seat.

"Sure. So she can slam me like your last *friend*? And now I'm relegated to the back seat. I see how it is, man."

"I'll take the back," I volunteer. This kid oozes animosity, and I'll do what I can to stop the leak.

"No, Ann." Brett shakes his head.

He helps Ricky into the back seat of the truck. "And you, watch the mouth. She isn't like my other friend. Totally different scenario. Just hang with me here."

With those words Brett shuts the door to any reply Ricky may have had.

Running his hand through his hair, Brett looks at me apologetically as he opens my door. "Sorry about that. He's eighteen, but at times acts like he's twelve."

"It's all right." I maneuver into the truck, grateful for the leather seat which will stop any daggers Ricky may try to shoot my way.

"SHE ISN'T going to eat dinner?"

The she would be me. Apparently Ricky has decided against communicating directly with me. Instead he has decided to act like I don't exist. He's probably thrilled that Brett is dropping me off in front of a row of shops. Expensive shops.

"Ann is going to eat later."

I guess Brett has decided to communicate for me as well as refuse to use my new given name.

Ricky's ankle is sprained. The doctor wrapped it and told him to take it easy for a couple of days. Which is when his next soccer game is. Nice.

Brett stops the truck at a sprawling outdoor shopping mall entrance. He puts the truck in park and climbs out. The next thing I know he's opening my door.

"I'll be back in an hour and a half." He extends his hand. To help me out, of course.

"About time. I call the front seat."

Ricky's voice is loud. Like Jimmy's.

"Nice meeting you," I say as the manipulation of the seating arrangement takes place. And no, it wasn't nice meeting him at all, but remember, I've been taught to be polite.

"Yeah." Ricky's response isn't quite so loud this time.

"Have fun shopping," Brett says as he shuts Ricky's door.

"I'm sure I will." It's been such a fun day so far, to think it won't continue on would be crazy.

I stand in the same spot until I can no longer see the truck. I'm not really excited about shopping, but I must.

"Excuse me."

I turn at the sound of the voice which belongs to a teenage girl. A cute girl. Pretty smile, red hair, like mine, and warm-looking hazel-colored eyes. She has her hair pulled back into a pony-tail. Her denim capris and white top fit her nicely. I have no idea what this girl could want with me. "Yes?"

"Was that Ricky Cantrell in your truck?"

That's what the girl could want with me. "I don't know his last name, but his first name is Ricky. Do you know him?"

"A little. We had a class together last year. I've seen him in the halls this year, and we go to the same church, but we haven't talked very much. Is he okay? His ankle I mean?"

I think the girl's concern is genuine, but I also think she has a bigger agenda than finding out if his ankle is okay. "Yes, it's just a minor sprain. He should be back to normal in a couple of days."

"That's good. I hope he'll be able to play against Regal. They're our rivals."

"So you're a soccer fan, huh?"

"Not really. I'm a Ricky fan, though, you know?"

Young love. "I see. What's your name?"

"Lauren. Lauren Davis."

"Hi, Lauren. I'm Angelina Thomas."

"Oh, I love your name. Very cool!"

If I had met her last week that part of the conversation would have been totally different. Hi Lauren, I'm Ann. Boring. "Thanks."

"So how do you know Ricky?" she asks.

"I'm sorry to disappoint you, but I don't really know him at all. My friend Brett, who was driving the truck, now he knows Ricky pretty well."

"That guy driving the truck is hot. Is he your boyfriend?"

Teens in Hampton Cove are direct. "That would be no. He's a friend. In fact, I only met him this week."

"Oh. I see. I guess."

Disappointment fills the air. I can't help but be a little curious. "What's wrong?"

"Well," Lauren tries to dig her sandaled toe into the concrete. She avoids looking at me. "I was kind of hoping, you know, that you might help me get Ricky to ask me to the prom."

Whoa. If she knew how Ricky felt about me, she would realize me influencing him to do anything would be impossible. "I'm sorry, Lauren. But like I said, I don't know him."

"But the hot guy does. Can't you help me at all? I really want to go with him, you know? And I know he doesn't have a date. Yet."

"Surely there must be somebody else who can help you. What about the kids at school? Doesn't he have a friend that you can ask?" Really, I'm searching for every avenue here.

"Are you kidding? There's a guy code I'm not touching, and my girlfriends all have a crush on him. They would sabotage me, smiling every step of the way. Besides, it would be so awesome to show up with him. You know, kind of like surprise everyone."

I'm trying to convince myself her excitement isn't contagious. But her cuteness, combined with her fun personality is hooking me. She seems endearing, and why she would want to hang out with bad attitude Ricky is beyond me. But he may not have that attitude at school. It may be directed solely on me. That's a nice thought.

"Please?" she asks.

Visions of Anastasia asking me to be her maid of honor rush through my mind.

Interesting.

How have I gotten myself involved in these things? In such a short time? We'll, I haven't said yes to Lauren yet.

"All right. I'll help."
Now I've said yes.

Important

Lauren left after she stored my phone number in her phone, and procured that promise of help from me. She seems like such a sweet girl. But there is probably more to Ricky than I know. I'll have time later to talk to Brett about him. And this situation. Brett doesn't know it yet, but he is the one who will help Lauren.

I shouldn't be worrying about Lauren and proms. I need to spend some money. Eyeing a purse shop a couple stores down, I go in, and am surprised by how long it takes me to select purses which I think will go with the barrage of shoes I bought earlier.

I text Brett with the name of the store so he'll know where to pick me up. The lady behind the counter is giving me strange looks. After all, she's holding several thousand dollars worth of purses for me. So I keep browsing like I'm still shopping, trying to waste time.

"Excuse me."

I turn. The sales lady is standing right behind me. "Yes?"

"I wanted you to be aware of the fact that we close in fifteen minutes. It's going to take some time to ring up what you have already asked me to hold for you."

Her middle-agedness looks tired. Like she's ready to go home.

"Thank you for telling me. I've already texted my ride. He should be here shortly." I hold up my phone.

"Do you want me to start ringing the items?"

Visions of Ms. Tallent and her scowling face behind the cash register this morning run through my mind. It's obvious now that spending uber amounts of money does cause people to be put out. "You can. But my ride is going to be actually paying for my purchases."

Middle-aged Millie's eyebrows shoot up. A really quick reaction, considering how tired I imagined her to be.

And that's the only reaction I get. She makes her way back behind the counter, seemingly in no hurry to do anything. She doesn't start waving her magic wand over the purses. She simply stands there.

The bell on the door jingles and Brett walks in.

Saunters in.

Swaggers in.

There are several verbs one can use to describe his entrance. In my mind I try not to liken him to the proverbial Knight in Shining Armor. Coming to save the day with the debit card and his good looks. I swear middle-aged Millie suddenly looks a lot perkier than she did moments ago.

And she knows nothing about the debit card.

"Hi there," he says to me. "Are we ready to pay?"

"More than ready." I nod my head toward Mills.

"Let's do it." He walks toward the counter while pulling the debit card out of his wallet.

Ten purses and six-thousand dollars later we walk out.

"That wasn't much money," he says, shoving the bags into the back of the pickup under the bed cover.

"It was the best I could do."

"Just that much more to spend tomorrow. Let's go. I need to take Ricky home, and it looks like it's going to rain."

The ride to Ricky's house is uneventful. No snide or sarcastic remarks were made. I'm not sure if Brett threatened him, or if Ricky just didn't have anything to say. At one point I glanced at the backseat and thought his eyes were shut.

Sure enough, while Brett helps Ricky into his house, thunder rumbles. A flash of lightning slashes across the sky. By the time Brett returns, big, fat raindrops start pelting the truck.

"Just in time." Brett fastens his seatbelt then backs out of the drive.

The swooshing sound of the wipers, rapidly moving across the windshield, fill the cab.

"Ricky's a nice kid. He plays soccer, has a part-time job. He's been accepted to Florida State. Don't let your first impression set in."

Knowing all about first impressions, my heart can't help but soften somewhat toward the teenager. "He was kind of quiet on the way home."

"He ate a lot of food. Plus he was tired."

"Ricky has a fan."

"You?"

I laugh. "No. Although I'll take your advice and give him another chance. A girl from his high school saw me with you guys. She wants Ricky to take her to the prom. And she asked for my help. So, I'm turning that over to you."

Now he laughs. "She what?"

"Yeah. I guess she has a big crush."

"Like I said, he's a nice kid."

The rain lets up a little. The gray clouds, barely discernible in the dusk, scoot across the sky. The lightening seems to have abated. We've transitioned from the busy populated streets to more back roads. A stretch of abandoned lots loom before us, tall grasses waving side to side illuminating through the light the headlights shine on the side of the road.

"So does that mean you're in?" I ask.

"No. I'm concentrating on driving through this wet mess."

"Well, think about it, okay?"

"Don't you think we have more important things to think about?"

I want to call him a stick in the mud but I don't.

He's right.

I have more important things to think about now than I ever have before.

And besides, Ricky doesn't even like me.

I wonder how important that is.

THERE ARE NO traces of the previous night's rain as Brett and I head out to purchase a car. But there are traces of an argument brewing about what kind of a car I'm going to buy.

"But I really want a Jaguar. It's my dream car. I don't care if I have to buy a used one. Really, I don't."

"You only have a fifty thousand dollar budget. It wouldn't be a smart move when you can buy a brand new SUV."

"Ha. I never thought I'd hear the word only before the words fifty thousand dollar budget."

Brett stops at a red light. He turns towards me. His eyes have the power to mesmerize me. They really do. But I can't let that happen. This man's hopes for a positive life change involve a backpack. A direction I'm not headed in again.

Ever.

"Think about it like this. You buy an SUV now. You fill the said SUV with the purchases required to inherit a vast estate. You inherit the vast estate then buy the dream car. All brand new one hundred thousand dollars of it."

I sit in the passenger side once again aware of how right Brett is.

Really? Does the man always have to make sense? If I pass 'the test' I will be able to buy my dream Jaguar. At least Brett thinks I will. And since he's kept the books for Antonio's estate for the past five years, he should know.

"Here," he says, pulling into a busy dealership. "It won't hurt you to look."

Four hours later, I follow him back to the mansion in my new SUV. White with tan interior, leather seats and a navigation system that will direct me anywhere I want to go.

And only a small hyperventilation attack.

But it does ride smoothly.

My own personal luxury.

At the mansion Brett parks his truck in the driveway. He motions for me to let him drive. I turn over the driving of my new vehicle to him with a frown.

"It's only until you learn your way. Then you can drive anywhere you want to go," he assures me.

"I thought that's what the navigation system is for. To guide me places."

"All in good time. Where to, now?"

Settling into the passenger side, I breathe in the smell of the new car. But the new-car fun smell, that doesn't last very long anyway, is diminished by the Brett scent. Not a bad thing to take back to Georgia with me when I go. "I need some clothes. Normal, everyday clothes. I only packed for two days, remember?"

"Why don't you recycle that orangey dress you wore at the almost dinner the other night. It looked nice on you."

I knew that night would give false impressions. "That was Anastasia's dress."

If my remark surprises him he doesn't show it.

"That was nice of her, I guess," is all he says.

"I think she was embarrassed by my clothing choice for the evening. I mean, how was I to know I was supposed to bring party clothes?"

"How about this," he says, pulling into a popular department store parking lot.

"Perfect. I should be able to find something here. I shop in these stores in Atlanta."

He pulls up to the curb. "And we'll be able to bring home whatever you buy in your new SUV. I'll see you in a little while. I'm gonna run across the street to the coffee shop and work."

"Run or drive?" I ask.

"Funny. Text me if I don't find you by the time you're finished."

I hop out of my brand new SUV, then watch it drive away.

I really don't like shopping for clothes. You have to try everything on, and the whole process becomes annoying very quickly.

Today is no exception.

Except I feel I ought to be ashamed of myself at being annoyed. I mean I have so much money to spend. Can a woman really be aggravated at spending so much money?

This one can.

IT'S NOW FRIDAY.

I was able to talk to Aunt Venus, finally, this morning. I think she was in shock at the information I relayed. I texted a picture of my new car to her, and told her I'd text her with any more important purchases. She couldn't begin to imagine how my mom is going to react.

I, on the other hand, have squelched my mom's possible reactions for now, and will continue to do so until it's impossible not to. My stomach already churns with this insane spending.

And I have spent a significant amount of money. Even though I haven't totally evened out what I am supposed to have spent, Brett and I are walking through the parking lot at the high school to watch Ricky's soccer game. Ricky is apparently a-okay to play today, and Brett thought it would be a nice break from the retail stores. Personally I wanted to go back to the mansion, but Brett insisted I broaden my horizons and sweat.

That's how I see it.

I mean it's south Florida, it's April, it's afternoon and it's hot.

"Watch out," Brett says.

Too late.

I lift my foot. A string of gum dangles between the bottom of my shoe and the black asphalt parking lot.

"Great. These are two hundred dollar sandals." I rub the bottom of my shoe on the asphalt trying to rid myself of the sticky mess.

Brett laughs. "Apparently price doesn't guarantee immunization from gum in the high school parking lot. By the way, you look nice."

I glance down at my designer denim shorts which won't fall off thanks to a belt which cost me more than a car payment. And I could trade my emerald green capped-sleeved shirt for a decent microwave. "I should. I'm wearing about six-hundred dollars worth of clothes and shoes."

"Well, try not to drip any mustard down your shirt when we eat our hot dogs."

"I told you, I'm not eating concession stand hot dogs. I'm not that hungry."

"You don't know what you're missing. When Ricky graduates I'll probably come here just for the hot dogs."

"I thought you were going to be half-way across the world in a couple of months."

His eyes narrow, in a contemplative kind of way. "I will be. But I'll be back to visit."

Thoughts of him leaving bring about a strange reaction. With my mom departing so often, I thought I had steeled myself against feelings of withdrawal. Feelings of abandonment.

Apparently those feelings have stayed close to the surface, or Brett has brought them up from the depths from which I thought I had buried them.

Either way, I don't like my reaction. It ranks right up with the sticky-gum mess and potential mustard drippings.

Brett gives the lady at the entrance some cash, and we settle ourselves on the concrete bleachers. High-dollar shorts meet dusty, grimy cement. You gotta love it.

Brett and I don't talk, but I listen to the chatter surrounding us. Parents, students, little brothers and sisters. Shouts of laughter, cries and whines of little ones, mingle with the conversation of concerned parents. An occasional gust of wind shifts around the hot air.

"There's Ricky. Number fourteen."

Brett points to the middle of the field where the players are warming up. Through my very cool-looking and expensive sunglasses, I spot the numbers on the back of the black jersey. Ricky is quickly maneuvering around, showing no signs of the sprain from a couple of days ago. "He's pretty fast."

"Yeah. He's one of the best players on the team. Coach would be sweating it if he had to miss a game."

"What position does he play?"

"You know something about soccer?"

"No."

"So if I told you he plays forward, would you know what I'm talking about?"

"Not really."

"He plays forward. Which means he's up front trying to score the goals."

"I thought they all tried to score."

"If they have the opportunity, any player can score. But the guys in the back are basically defense. Helping the goalie stop the shots from the other team."

"Oh. I'm sure I'll catch on when they start playing."

"I'll quiz you at half-time while we're eating our hotdogs."

Not wanting to egg him on, I don't say anything. "Does Ricky's mom come to the games?"

"Every now and then. She's usually working. That's why I make sure I come to as many as possible. Plus, they're fun to watch. I played a little soccer in my day. When I go to Peru I'm going to organize a soccer team. Get the boys involved in something to keep them off the street."

I'm already uncomfortable in these high dollar clothes, in the heat, on the concrete seat. I might as well make myself totally miserable. "So what's the draw for you wanting to leave here? Aren't there plenty of boys, like Ricky, who need somebody like you in the United States?"

He doesn't answer right away. His gaze indicates he's watching Ricky, but I'm not sure what that mind of his is thinking. The boys run to the sideline. The game must be close to starting.

Brett's gaze catches mine. "It's what I feel I'm called to do. It's where I feel called to do it. I don't know why God has called me to go so far away, but He has."

When it comes to God people seem to have a lot of vague, unexplainable explanations. His words remind me of many of my mom's words. But I never felt really comfortable talking to my mom about her 'calling.' For some reason, maybe it's because there are no ties with Brett, I feel I can pick his brain on the whole subject. "So how do you know you're called? Is it a feeling? An idea? How do you know it's not your wishes and ideas?"

A whistle blows. Game time.

Brett looks torn between conversing with me and watching the game. Like he would need to give his full attention to one or the other, but he can't decide.

His body turns slightly towards me. His green eyes are hidden behind his sunglasses. I wish I could see them. Their warmth has become somewhat of a security for me over the last few days.

"I can only speak for me. But I get a notion or idea and it won't go away. It's like it's a part of my gut. You know, like a good feeling when I think about it. I try to turn away from it and I don't have a settled spirit anymore. I don't know how much sense that makes, but that's the best way I know how to explain it."

He turns his attention back to the field. I think about his words. Is that how my mom feels? Is everything inside her telling her to leave her only daughter for months at a time to minister to people who she doesn't even know?

Brett scoots closer to me. The cool-smelling Brett Scent invades my space.

"Watch that kid, number eight. The calling is kind of like what's happening on the field. It's like the ball is God, moving forward at a rapid speed. We're following. Sometimes we can catch up with Him, sometimes, because of the choices we make He gets kicked back a little. We need to regroup and keep following Him. If you feel like you're moving forward in life, following God, you have a good feeling inside. You know you're on track."

What he is saying makes sense, but how do you arrive at the point that you can actually see the ball? To be honest the only thing I'm seeing lately is Brett. When I'm not with him, he's in my thoughts. When I close my eyes at night, his face is what I see.

"Look. There goes Ricky."

I watch as Ricky runs, kicking the ball, yet keeping it close to him. I can almost feel his concentration as he makes his way toward the goal. The guy guarding the goal is basically staying in the same position, but I can tell he's ready to move one way or another in an instant.

In one swift motion, Ricky kicks the ball.

Brett stands, so I stand with him.

The ball hangs briefly in the air.

The guy guarding the goal jumps high, but even with his arms up he can't reach the ball which drops into the goal for a score.

Brett starts clapping and I find myself yelling. The crowd is screaming.

I wonder at this feeling of excitement. The energy it creates inside. The euphoric sensation filling me.

Is this the way Brett feels at the prospect of his mission work?

My mom, too?

Because if it is, it's no wonder they can't ignore it.

Impossible

I WAS SURPRISED I didn't run into Lauren at the soccer game. Not that I really wanted to, but I thought, since she was such a fan, I might spot her cheering on her favorite soccer player.

Now Brett, Ricky and I are sitting in a local diner down the street from the school. Ricky ended up scoring the team's only four goals. They shut out the other team, protecting a no-loss season.

Ricky has been civil to me. Not overly polite, but I haven't been the recipient of any sarcastic remarks, either. So I guess this visit is going well. I've been contemplating how to bring up the subject of prom, Lauren. Not sure which opportunity will present itself. The event or the girl. I'm waiting for any lead-ins, but so far there haven't been any.

"Here you go. Mushroom Swiss burger, medium well."

The server slides Ricky's plate in front of him, then follows suit with mine and Brett's. We start passing around the salt, pepper and ketchup. The aroma makes me want to bite into one of the fries, but I know they are hot. Moments later the condiments are settled onto the table, but neither Ricky nor Brett has started eating.

Ricky is staring into space. It's then I notice Brett's head is slightly bent.

He's praying.

I guess Ricky doesn't want to be a part of the prayer, and nobody asked me. Maybe Brett assumed I didn't want to take part.

His not asking unsettles me. Does he think I don't pray?

I shoot a quick prayer up right now before I realize Brett has started eating his burger. Ricky has started too, and I'm still sitting here.

"Hi, Ricky."

Lauren is standing beside him dressed in the blue-polo and khaki slacks uniform of the diner. This is why she wasn't at the game. She's working.

"Hi."

Ricky barely shakes his dark hair out of his eyes before speaking to her. He doesn't really look at her, but instead keeps his attention on his meal.

"I heard you had a great game today. I wish I could have been there."

"It was all right."

Again, his focus is his plate. He doesn't seem very interested in her at all. My task is looking a bit difficult.

"They called me in at the last minute. And I really need the money, so I came in."

"Yeah, I didn't even know you worked here."

"I started a couple of weeks ago. You know my dad got laid off a while back. My mom only works part-time, so money is tight and they told me they aren't giving up cash for anything extra. So, if I have any hope of buying a prom dress, I knew I had to earn the money myself."

"Prom? Prom is lame and stupid. Only losers go to that," Ricky says.

My task is now impossible.

Lauren shakes her head. "It's not lame and you know it. Half your friends are going. And they're not losers."

"They're just stupid. No way am I letting some girl talk me into dressing up and dancing."

Another blue shirt, khaki pants girl walks up to Lauren. "Table five needs you."

"Okay." Lauren turns to Ricky. "Well, I'll catch you later."

"Sure." Ricky hesitates just a moment. "Who are you going with? To prom?"

Lauren's eyes widen a little.

I shake my head. He has no idea that his question has now given her a glimmer of hope.

She smiles, everything about her demeanor changing with his question. "I'll let you figure that out."

I watch Ricky watch Lauren walk away. He has more of a dumbfounded expression on his face. Like he knows something has transpired, and he has no idea what it is, yet he's vaguely aware it all has to do with him.

"Whatever," he says before taking another monster bite of his burger.

I look at Brett whose interest doesn't seem at all piqued by the whole prom conversation.

It's obvious I'm going to have to be the one who continues this prom talk.

"So, Ricky, would you think about going to the prom?"

He shoves a fry in his mouth. Then another.

Brett sets his burger down. "Ann asked you a question."

"Angelina," I remind Brett.

"I don't want to talk about prom. It's lame." Ricky squirts more ketchup on his fries.

I take a drink of my water. "I wonder who Lauren is going with. She seems pretty excited."

Ricky looks at me, and because of his long bangs I almost miss his reaction. Those eyes narrowing in an I-care-but-I-don't-want-you-to-know-I-care type of look.

"She can go with whoever she wants. It doesn't matter to me."

"Maybe she doesn't have a date yet. Maybe she's waiting on someone to ask her," I add, because I need to plant that seed.

Ricky doesn't respond at all. He just keeps eating.

Brett jiggles the ice around in his drink. "If you decide you want to go, let me know. I'll help you rent the tux, buy a suit, whatever guys wear now."

An ally? I try to catch his gaze, but he's too busy focusing on Ricky. "Bro, I'm not going."

"Fine," Brett says. "But let me know if you change your mind."

Ricky has no idea Lauren is counting on somebody to change his mind.

And that somebody is me.

WE DROP RICKY at his house. Brett drives a couple of blocks then stops the truck in front of a vacant, corner lot. He exits the truck, so I follow. The lot has sporadic shoots of grass mingled in with the dirt and rocks.

"We come here and play soccer sometimes. Ricky'll gather up some of the kids. It's not a very good soccer field, though." Brett kicks a rock and we watch it bounce across the dirt.

"I bet they still have fun."

"Yeah, I guess. I wish they could have something more."

"We all want something more, don't we?"

"I think we have a desire to be the best we can be. God puts that in us. We certainly don't want to become complacent. Settling for what the world gives us isn't fulfilling. It's not who we are meant to be."

My heart stirs and rebels. It stirs because his words sound familiar.

They are similar to my mom's talk. She's always talking about how we aren't of the world, we're just in the world. *We're in the world to make a difference and we can't make a difference sitting in our living room on the couch.*

I can even hear her tone.

"I want kids to grow up knowing their ideas are important," Brett continues. "Knowing they can do and be whatever they want to be. Knowing nothing is out of reach. But most of these kids can't see past the dirt of their front yards. They don't dream very big."

"You can't singlehandedly change the world. It is what it is."

"Maybe I can't change everything. But I can change what I can."

I walk over to where he is standing. "You're making a difference in Ricky's life, I'm sure."

"All I want is to give him a vision of what his future could be."

His shoulder brushes mine. I like the feeling, but I don't want to. Brett's thinking is too much like my mom's. Always thinking of others, even when the people around them need them.

I feel like Ricky and I now have a bond. Brett has no idea the loss Ricky will feel when Brett leaves. Brett thinks he's doing the right thing. And he may be.

But Ricky is here, and from what I can see he's counting on Brett. "How long have you been hanging out with Ricky? A couple of years, right?"

"Yeah. Almost two years."

"Think you can convince him to ask Lauren to the prom?"

Brett turns to face me. "Why would I want to do that?"

"Because she asked for our help."

He taps me on the nose with his index finger. "She asked for your help. Not mine."

"Well, I'm asking you."

Stepping back a couple of steps, he shoves his hands in his jeans pockets. "I did see him sneak a couple of looks around the restaurant after Lauren left our table. Did you notice?"

I breathe at the space he's created. "No. I can't tell where he's looking. All that hair covers his eyes most of the time."

"I also noticed his face was a little flushed when she was talking to him."

He certainly seems in tune with Ricky's emotions. Too bad he's not connecting with the important one. "If it comes up, put in a good word for Lauren. It won't feel like it's coming out of left field now that we all were able to interact."

He shrugs. "I'm not sure when an opportunity will arise. It's not like we talk about proms or girls."

"He's at that age. You need to talk about girls. Otherwise, who's going to do it?"

"Things are different now."

"You may be right. But keep your ears open. Prom is soon."

"I hope Lauren isn't counting on Ricky taking her. Disappointment is never fun."

Brett seems so clued in about a lot of things. I wonder why he doesn't have a clue how much he's going to disappoint Ricky?

I know all too well the feelings Ricky will experience.

That's why becoming close to Brett Hamilton isn't even an option in my book.

It's impossible.

Insane

"OKAY, DON'T forget. Dress fitting nine o'clock in the morning."

Anastasia is hanging out with me in my bedroom. I had to shower after sitting at that soccer game in the heat. The night air feels cool.

"We need to pick a really expensive dress," I say. "And shoes. And jewelry."

"You can't outshine the bride. You'll buy what I pick out."

Even though she's laughing I can tell by her look she's somewhat serious. But she needs to be serious. I could never out-shine Anastasia.

Never.

She's petting PS. "How's the shopping going?"

"It's slow. Brett always has to do something with Ricky. I don't know about this whole agreement."

"You bought some shoes, though."

"I did. It was fun, too."

"I'm glad. I'm sure you can hit a jewelry store or two and spend a lot of that cash."

Anastasia sounds normal. But I'm wondering if part of her feels some resentment towards me. If the situation were reversed I'd probably be resentful of her.

But she doesn't act like it. I guess because she still stands to inherit a lot of money—and she doesn't have to work for it.

Yes, shopping is work. This kind of shopping.

It's pressure shopping.

And I'd much rather be hanging out getting to know my half-sister, than wondering around malls and shops all day. And I'd much rather be hanging around Anastasia minus Jimmy. I still don't see what she sees in him.

Anastasia and I haven't had much time to talk. Let's face it. I'm stuck shopping and she's planning a wedding.

"We've set a wedding date." Anastasia's smile is so big.

"You have? When?"

"Saturday, May seventh. Five weeks from tomorrow."

The whole concept is insane. "I thought you wanted a big, extravagant wedding?"

Anastasia's brows arch. "I do and I am."

I shrug my shoulders. "All right. I'm just thinking that's a lot of work to do in a short period of time."

"It is. But I have to have Brett at the wedding. He leaves the next day. I think we can get it all done. I've already ordered the invitations. They'll be here in a couple of days. Will you help me address, stamp and mail?"

She is moving ahead full force. "Sure," I answer.

"Great. Mama has bad handwriting. I really don't want her touching them. At all."

"Let me know when you need me."

"It's so nice having a sister. I'm kind of mad I just met you. I think we could have had fabulous teenage years together."

"Really?"

"Yes. You don't?"

Anastasia and I are very different. I see her being terribly bored with me during the teenage years. Besides, I spent the first couple in some jungle with a backpack and my mom. "I guess I picture myself more the tag-along type. You probably would have been frustrated with me."

"No I wouldn't have. You're so smart—Well, maybe, huh?" She laughs. "You could have helped me with my homework."

I point to her clothes. "You could have helped me with my style."

She leans back against the headboard, crossing her arms in front of her, and shifting her gaze to the upper corners of the room. Her eyes blink several times causing me to wonder if I'm about to be the recipient of more Anastasia eye-tears.

"I'm still mad at Mama for not telling me," she states.

I sit cross-legged on the end of the bed, once again aware that I have yet to get that pedicure I'm in desperate need of. "I'm still mad at my mom for a lot of things."

"Have you talked to her?"

"No. She's in South America. She's supposed to be back in the states at the beginning of May. Then we are having a chat."

"At least your Mama is far away and you have a chance to process some of this before speaking with her. Mama and I had that horrible car ride home from the attorney's office. I thought I was summoned there because she was the housekeeper for so long that Antonio wanted to take care of us."

"Who did you think I was when I showed up here? At the mansion."

Her gaze lingers on the view a moment or so before she answers. "I thought you were his daughter. By who? I had no idea. He never really dated. I thought he had some mistress stored away forever and you were the result."

Okay. She's honest. "I guess I was stored away forever—just not by a mistress. By an ex-wife. And they got married because they had to. She was pregnant. I wonder how knowing that would have affected my psyche growing up."

"I hate to speak ill of the dead, especially since he was our father, but Antonio was kind of a dog. Sleeping with both our mothers at the same time? I'd kill me some Jimmy."

Her words linger unsettled inside my heart. "I hear what you're saying, but other than his being a *dog*, what was he like? Mom would never talk about him. Ever. I know nothing."

She briefly closes her eyes, like she's remembering. "I wish you would have asked me before I found out he was my father. I see everything differently now."

I'm disappointed and try not to let it come across in my voice. "I understand. Kind of. How about some general insight? Was he funny, serious? You said he didn't really date, but did he have friends?"

We sit in silence, PS's purring the only sound other than the occasional caw of a passing bird. I don't want to push her, but I am curious.

This man gave me life.

"He didn't date, but he had a few friends. He threw small parties."

I smile at her. "You inherited those genes."

Her fingers play frivolously with the tassels on the over-sized throw pillow, like we are talking about our favorite novel instead of the man who gave us life. "Maybe. He was always smiling, and here's where I may be jaded by the information we learned at the attorneys. His eyes always looked sad to me. At the time I didn't think the word sad, I thought more like haunted."

Her big, brown eyes lock with mine as understanding settles between us. An understanding that fills a part of the void I've felt throughout my life. An understanding that can only be filled by a sense of belonging to something. Being important to someone.

Being a part of a bigger picture than a well-meaning aunt and a wayward mom.

Not only do I have a sister, I am a sister.

"DON'T MAKE ME wear this dress." I look at Anastasia with what I hope is a pleading expression. The bold red color of the dress clashes with everything about me except my skin tone. But even that's not enough to make me like this monstrosity.

The layers upon layers of red silk and tulle resemble an apple exploding into some form of a Cinderella gown.

Not pretty.

"It is kind of loud," Anastasia says as she walks around me. "Mama, what do you think?"

"It's a no," I blurt out before Lovey can speak.

"It's something to consider." Lovey's voice almost purrs like a cat when she speaks.

"Of course, you're right, Mama. We can consider it."

They can consider it all they want. I'll refuse to wear it. The dressing room is only two steps away and I'm there in three seconds. As I pull the hideous apple-colored gown off, I'm staring at the other dresses waiting for me to try them on.

"Do you need some help?" Our sales consultant's voice carries through the door.

"No. I'm good."

The red dress goes back on the hanger. I flip through the others looking for something that I like. Finding nothing that strikes me, I turn to the price tags. Might as well go with most expensive one.

Pulling the top ticket item to the front, I stare at the sea-green dress. Although the slinky-looking dress is 'my' color, it looks pretty low cut and has no back. It is form fitting and has a sash that looks like it hugs the hip line.

Then there's the flower that rests on the right hip. It's kind of big and gaudy looking.

Oh well. This is my sister's wedding.

My heart likes the sound of those thoughts.

"It's beautiful!" Anastasia says as I walk out for her inspection. "Don't you love it?"

Not really, I want to say. Although it's not as low cut as I thought, the big flower flouncing off my hip isn't working for me. "It's okay."

"The color looks great on you."

"The color is fine. I'm not sure about this." I tap the flower.

"I like it. It's different."

"It's a dress that will make an impression," Lovey purrs.

This is one of the most awkward positions I have ever found myself in. "What about the other women in the wedding? Your bridesmaids? Are they wearing this same dress? I'm just the guinea pig to try it on?"

"There are no other women. You're it."

Stunned, I look at her. "Really?"

"Promise. I'm really liking the dress."

"Anastasia doesn't have many girlfriends." Lovey rests her hand on Anastasia's shoulder. "Other girls are jealous. It's hard to have friends when one is so beautiful and loving."

"Mama, please." Anastasia steps away from clingy 'mama.' She fingers the bow on my dress. The flower is shot with gold threads which compliment the gold glitter-like pattern embedded into the sea-green material.

She looks up at me. "This will be my wedding motif."

Her fingers still caress the flower so I ask, "The flower?"

"Yes. Flowers. Green and gold. It's going to be beautiful! Where's our sales girl. I need a sample of this material."

Anastasia and her mother start fluttering about looking for Sally, our girl. I'm left standing on the raised platform feeling like the chick on top of the wedding cake that is missing her groom.

"Well, well. Don't you clean up nice? Very nice."

Chill bumps run up my arms at the sound of Brett's voice. I turn. "I thought I was supposed to text you when I was ready to pay?"

"I was in the neighborhood so I thought I'd come in and see how long you were going to be. I like the dress."

I can't tell if he's being genuine or sarcastic. "I don't."

He looks around. "Does the bride like it?"

"The bride and her *Mama* have decided it's the motif of the wedding."

"Oh. Lovey's here?" He moves closer and lowers his voice. "This must have been a fun morning."

Brett doesn't seem to have an issue being close to me. Because I don't affect him. I, on the other hand, am greatly affected by his close proximity. He's gorgeous on the eyes and his scent must be called Driving Women Crazy.

Doing my best to rid my mind of Brett thoughts I step away toward the dressing room.

"Sis, wait. Sally's here."

It takes a moment for the 'Sis' to register. But yes, that's Anastasia calling me. I turn to see Anastasia, Lovey and Sally coming toward me at a fast pace.

"Sally needs to take down all your information so we can order that dress," Anastasia says.

Sally motions me down off the cake-top podium then proceeds to pull, poke and prod the dress before coming to stand before me with a serious look on her face. "This dress fits you perfectly. No alterations needed. That's good news, isn't it, Hon?"

Sally takes a couple of steps and grabs a clipboard off a table. "Okay, you can take that dress off. I'll note the size then. And I'll need your name and address. Basic information."

Sally talks with a somewhat annoying tone and she talks fast. She scribbles as I relay all my important information to her.

The dressing room is a haven. I hear Anastasia talking to Brett. I'm not sure Lovey talks to him.

My hundred dollar jeans and T-shirt are much more comfortable. I grab the green dress so Sally will have all the information she needs.

Anastasia taps me on the shoulder as I hand Sally the dress. "You'll have fun finding a pair of shoes to go with that dress. The sky's the limit, huh?"

"Yes. I guess I will. I hadn't really thought about it." What am I coming to when I have the need and the means to purchase a pair of fabulous shoes and the thought doesn't cross my mind until someone mentions it?

Brett looks at his watch. "We're off to a late start. Are you ready?"

"I have to pay for the dress."

Sally glances my way. "I'll have your ticket in a second, Hon."

I turn to Brett. "It'll be just a second, *Hon*," I whisper.

I guess Lovey is still wandering around the store. Maybe she's looking for a dress to wear to the wedding. After all, besides the bride, the mother of the bride is the next most important female.

Anastasia had bought her dress the day after the engagement. Nobody but Lovey and the bridal consultant have seen it. And nobody will until the day of the wedding. She may be my half-sister, but she has some strange ways about her.

"Here you go, Hon," Sally says as she hands me the ticket. "Pay at the front counter. Check back with me in a couple of weeks to see if the dress has arrived."

Brett grabs the ticket before I can. "I might as well take it."

Sally nudges me. "Nice, huh? A gorgeous guy like that paying for your dress?"

Her implication doesn't escape me. "Real nice. Thank you for your help, Sally. Bye, Sis."

Saying that word is still strange to me, but saying that word also warms my heart. Makes me feel like I'm not alone in this world. Gives me a sense of connection like I have when I'm with Aunt Venus.

I hug Anastasia, the feel of her arms around me bringing the I-have-a-sister truth into reality. We don't linger in our hug, but I notice Lovey, whose gaze towards me is skeptical at best, staring at us.

My guess is Lovey isn't happy with our sisterly bond.

I shake off Lovey's gaze as Brett and I make our way to the counter.

We stand in line behind a couple of groups of giggling girls.

"That sales girl thinks you're a kept women." Brett holds up the ticket and the debit card.

"She can think what she wants."

"I hadn't thought about it before. I must look pretty gallant to all these sales ladies who have been ringing up your purchases. You shop, I pay."

"Funny isn't it. You look gallant, I look paid for. What a double standard."

He drapes his arm around me in an unexpected display of affection. "And, the woman I'm paying for is a pretty one."

A couple of the girls in line are now staring at us with kind of dreamy, hopeful eyes. I want to correct their perception of the situation, but to do that would be awkward at best.

Let them think what they want.

The drive to the shopping center doesn't take long. My mind still whirls with the Brett-thinks-I'm-pretty thought as we park and make our way to the stores. A couple of times, when the crowd threatens to split us, I feel his hand on my shoulder keeping me by his side. Close.

"Maybe we should save the shopping for Monday through Friday and skip Saturdays." I say this as Brett has to maneuver us through a crowd of people, mostly teenagers.

His hold on my shoulder tightens slightly. "It is crowded. But we're here, so you might as well spend some money."

I'm so focused on his touch that I almost miss the jewelry store sign to my left. "Let's go in here."

We cut in front of two teenagers who are paying more attention to their phones than where they are walking. "Sorry," I mutter as they look up long enough to scowl at me and Brett.

The proverbial bell on the door jingles as we enter. Chrome and glass cases boast brilliant looking jewelry. Red, green, and blue gems team up with sparkling diamonds. The brilliant jewels rest on cream velvet stands and platforms.

"Good morning, good morning. Can I help you?"

A thin, very pale salesman speaks to us from behind the counter. Black hair and a mustache only accentuate how white his skin is. The dark shirt he wears doesn't help his image at all.

"We're just looking right now," I say, heading toward the counter but trying to move down the row so I won't be standing in front of the skinny, pale guy.

Out of the corner of my eye I see him moving down the counter with us. Yes, we're being stalked.

His kind of nasal-toned voice disrupts the air. "You look like a nice couple. Are you looking for something special?"

A fast way to spend ten thousand dollars I want to say.

"We'd like to look at your emeralds." Brett's voice startles me, but the smile on the skinny guy's face indicates it pleases him.

I turn to Brett. "We would?"

He smiles. "We would."

"Certainly. This way."

We walk across to the other end of the horseshoe-shaped counter. Sparkling, shiny emerald necklaces, rings, earrings and bracelets greet us. Everything emeralds.

Brett's arm once again rests on my shoulder, warming me from the arctic temperatures inside the store. "I thought you might like something nice to wear to the wedding. My treat. Pick out anything you'd like."

I look at him hoping my eyes convey what I'm thinking, which is, what are you thinking?

"I mean it, Darling. Anything you'd like." His voice oozes with sincerity and a fondness that doesn't exist.

A slow flush creeps up my face while commission dollar signs light up the sales guy's. He actually takes on a less-pale tone.

To blurt out "it's really my money" would not only sound stupid, it would sound unbelievable.

Therefore making me look stupid.

Brett is now playing a game, and it's up to me whether I'm going to play along or not.

With my heart fluttering to the point of can-I-breathe, I gently slide my index finger under his chin. His green eyes tell me he wasn't expecting my touch.

His pulse tells me he likes it.

"I do declare, Mr. Hamilton, you never cease to amaze me," I twang in the most southern accent I can manage.

Game on.

Intensity

WE LEAVE THE jewelry store nine thousand, six hundred and fifty-three dollars later. I carry the bag in my hand just like I carry a bag of snacks from the grocery store, just as I walk next to Brett like he's an old friend.

False!

My quivery insides tell me we crossed a line. A thin line, but still a line. Touching him in such an intimate way was not a good idea.

Not a good idea at all.

There's no way I can tell what's going on inside of him, but he looks at me differently now than when we first walked into the store, which in any other circumstances would thrill me.

But these circumstances are skewed.

"Stop here for a minute," he says.

He steps in front of me. Following his lead we enter an alley-type walkway between two buildings, out of the sun into barely cooler temps and shadowy slants of light.

As calm and sweet and almost doting as Brett acted in the jewelry store, his demeanor has changed. Those eyes that moments ago had exuded warmth and caring, now gaze at me with confusion.

They almost have the intensity to back me into the brick wall, but I stand my ground. Literally. I'm not moving into such a precarious position that would leave blowing past him my only way out.

"What was that in there?" he asks.

Okay, besides this guy being gorgeous, this tone of voice only increases his amount of sexy. But it was his game first. All I did was join in. "What?"

"This." His index finger gently makes its way up my throat, under my chin tilting it slightly upward. The only thing that pulls me away from his searching gaze are his lips precariously close to mine.

My knees and I wish we had that wall behind us now.

The game is supposed to be fun.

Flirtatious.

His touch unleashes a passion I'm not prepared for. My heart is also unprepared for the heat in his green eyes, which remind me of my dress with the gold flecks.

More importantly, I find my lips anticipating kissing his.

So when he backs up, taking his gorgeous eyes, his soft touch and the thought of his lips on mine away, I try to convince myself I'm relieved.

But instead I find myself fighting disappointment.

"You don't play fair," he says, his voice now calm and seemingly unaffected by our interaction.

"All's fair in love and war." The instant the words of the cliché leave my mouth I regret them. We are not in love nor are we at war. At least we weren't. We might be now.

This is why I'm an accountant who's not in a relationship. I don't do this well. I don't banter well. Numbers are much easier to deal with than emotions.

"Love and war, huh?"

"Sorry. I didn't mean to say that. It just came out. You know, auto-response."

"Maybe you should think a little longer before you say things. And do things. It could land you in trouble. Let's go. You have more money to spend."

He starts walking, and if I want to stay with my debit card I need to walk with him. I wonder if he knows I'm in uncharted territory by flirting with him. Do I appear nervous? Unsure?

Well, I am, but I don't want him to know that. Besides, his actions indicate that this is nothing more than a game to him. Almost a you-touched-me-so-I-touched-you-now-we're-even type of thing.

We pass a café with outdoor seating. My stomach tells me it's lunch time, but I'm not sure I'm ready to sit down and chat with Brett right now. What transpired between us was really nothing, yet somehow it's changed everything.

I had no idea his touch would awaken a desire to be touched again. Never mind I honestly thought he was going to kiss me.

Heat spreads across my face as I realize I wanted him to.

I slide a glance his way only to find him looking at me. His lips part and move, as if he's speaking, but my mind doesn't register what he says because I'm once again thinking about the kiss that didn't happen.

"What did you say?"

He looks a little perplexed. "I said, tell me when you see a store you want to drop cash in."

Oh, of course, it's all about spending the money. Hey, at least he's staying with me today and hasn't ditched me for the coffee shop to wait while I decide what I'm going to buy.

Just ahead of us I spy a Simply Midnight Lingerie store. I point at it. "There. I want to go in there."

How many times have I wandered in to a SML store dreaming of what I would like to buy?

Now I can actually buy anything I want in there.

"I'm not going in *that* store. I'll wait here." He nods his head toward a bench which is currently occupied by a couple of guys.

"Come on, it's just lingerie. And they have really cute lounging clothes as well. We won't even look at the unmentionables."

"No thanks. Men don't belong in that store."

"Real men don't care. I see them in there all the time." I won't mention they're usually standing around looking like lost sheep, trying not to look at the items hanging on the wall. Or the murals of the women wearing said items.

As we get closer to the door, one of the murals graces the outside of the store. A very beautiful blonde, wearing skimpy pajamas, lounges on her right side. Her body is perfect and the fancy lavender signature in the bottom right corner of the mural scrolls, Jenny.

Jenny's photographer not only captured her beautiful body, but whoever snapped her photo managed to showcase her amber-colored eyes. Eyes which, in my opinion, have a sad look about them.

Not sure why the picture of the pretty girl has affected me, I choose to blame it on Brett's game playing. His touch has stirred up all kinds of emotions in me. Suddenly I have the gift of picking them out in other people? People in photos?

I don't think so.

Still, I'm not sure I'll forget her face or the haunted look of her eyes.

Trying to recreate the fun, casual feeling we had earlier, I smile at Brett pushing the thought of his touch to the back of my mind. "Come on. I promise we'll stay on the safe side of the store. Besides, if I buy something, you're going to have to come in to pay for it, remember?"

He tilts his head to the left. "And you'll probably buy something just so I have to come in."

I laugh. "I hadn't thought of that, but thanks for the idea."

Jamming his hand in his pocket, he motions towards the store with his other hand. "Let's go in and get this over with."

He holds the door for me as we enter the store. I do love these gentlemanly aspects of him.

Upbeat, loud music is playing. A pretty brunette with a headset greets us.

"Welcome. Can we help you find anything today?"

"The way out," Brett mutters, but thankfully she doesn't appear to have heard him.

I speak louder. "We're fine, and no, we're just looking around. Thanks."

She smiles, greeting the people who come in behind us. I wonder what she would have done if I told her we did need help. She'd probably put that headset to use and summon a salesperson.

Brett doesn't walk beside me, he lags behind a little. I can tell he's uncomfortable. His masculine self doesn't know what to do in this feminine store.

And even though we're not in the most extreme feminine section, his masculinity is oh-so-apparent amidst the frill, lace and nearly naked pictures of women.

Suddenly I'm uncomfortable. Or jealous.

"Let's go." I turn toward what moments ago was our entrance, but now conveniently becomes our exit.

"What?" he asks, now matching my stride.

"I don't need anything in here."

I don't wait for him to open the door. Instead I push through, the heat assailing me as I step outside. The fact that the pretty brunette sales girl tells Brett bye in an I-wish-you-weren't-leaving tone, doesn't escape me either.

I mesh right into the people streaming by, moving quicker than I normally do.

"Hey," Brett says, keeping pace with me. "You don't *need* that ten-thousand dollar necklace you're carrying, but you bought it because you have to spend money. Did I miss something back there?"

I look at my jeans and T-shirt. I did not start out my day trying to impress Brett. But now I'm aggravated that I played the part so well. After our little game playing, which I admit back-fired on me, I wish had dressed to impress just a little.

Even though I know I can't fall for this guy.

Even though I know he'll break my heart if I do. But he got playful with me today.

And you know what? I want to play.

"I THINK THIS is the last bag," Brett says as he drops a big shopping bag inside my bedroom door.

I look around the room. Shopping bags have taken over the luxuriously carpeted floor. We started out setting the packages on the bed, which caused PS to scamper into the closet. But the bed quickly became filled, so now the floor is littered with bags of all colors and sizes.

Brett leans on the door frame, legs crossed at the ankles, arms crossed in front of his chest. I so enjoy looking at him.

"Do you still want to order out like we talked about earlier?" he asks.

We decided to skip dinner to spend more cash, so he suggested ordering Chinese food when we got back to the house. Mansion. Pick your abode. "Sure. Putting this stuff away is going to take forever, so I'll do it later."

I close the bedroom door, then we make our way down the stairs into the living room.

"At least you spent a huge chunk of the money. We're almost caught up for under-spending the first few days. That spreadsheet you downloaded has been really helpful." Brett eases his phone out of the case.

"It has. This whole thing is some kind of crazy. I don't need anything I purchased."

"I'll admit the money could be better spent. A lot of people are in need. I'm ordering the Happy Family. What do you want?"

The sinking feeling I hate has returned. You'd think having all the money in the world to spend would be thrilling. But really, it's becoming annoying. I don't understand the father I never met. "I bet it's hard for you watching money that could help in a third world country sit unused on the floor of a million-dollar house. I'll have Orange Chicken if they have it."

"I'm sure they do. What kind of soup, because they always ask." He holds his phone to his ear.

"Hot and sour."

"My kind of woman." He holds up his finger. "Yes, hello. I'd like to place an order to be delivered."

I like how because I order hot and sour soup I'm his kind of woman, but when I spend thousands of dollars on unnecessary things not so much. He truly didn't want to talk about that.

He probably wouldn't believe me if I told him I felt the very same way.

As he places our order, I tune him out. Maybe Brett can tell me about my father. I think I'm a little apprehensive at what I might learn. As a child, my mom whisked me off to countries all over the world. Was it to avoid my father? Why didn't she want me to know him? Or my half-sister for that matter. I could have had a fine life here in the mansion while she traipsed around from country to country.

Brett slides his phone back in the case. "It'll be here within twenty minutes. I had to order an appetizer or they wouldn't deliver. Twenty-five dollar minimum. I chose extra egg rolls. I hope that's okay."

"It's fine."

"It doesn't sound like it's fine."

"I want to know about my father."

Brett looks at me as if I asked him to fly me around the sun a few times. His expression is puzzled. Have I puzzled him because I'm asking, or is he not sure what he should tell me. "What exactly do you want to know?"

He speaks slowly like he's giving himself time to think. It's giving my heart time to beat faster, and my mind time to wander.

I sit on the couch. "I don't know much about my father. Anastasia told me a little bit, but I want to know more. Is it because of Lovey that my mom severed all ties with him? Refused to talk about him? Pretended like he didn't exist."

"Those sound like questions for your mother." Brett settles himself at the other end of the couch.

"Yeah, maybe. But she's halfway around the world tending to other people's needs. Saving other people's lives. Although if she knew I needed a shoulder, I'm sure she'd cut her trip short and come home." Speaking those words makes me fidgety, so I try to get comfy by sitting sideways and curling my legs underneath me.

"Are you sure about that?"

"Yes." I say the word boldly, although my heart doesn't feel the boldness.

"This is probably going to be a shock to your mother, too. Like you pointed out, she kept you from Antonio, wouldn't even tell you who he was. Now you're living in his house and you're on the verge of collecting his estate. You're in the middle of everything she tried to keep you from."

I hug a throw pillow to my stomach, while I play with the tassels. "I'm going to try and process all the mom stuff later. Right now I want

Rich in Love

to know about my father. Everything you know. Good, bad, whatever."

"You have to remember, I've known of your father for a long time, but I only met him about five years ago when my father passed away."

"That's longer than I had. I want to know what he was like, because the info I have on him doesn't make him look like a very grand person, you know?"

"He was a kind man. He liked walks on the beach, sunsets and pastel colors."

I toss the pillow at Brett. "Come on. Quit making fun. I really want to know who he was."

Brett laughs. "Honestly, it's not complicated. He inherited his fortune from his family. They were big in textiles back in the day and sold to a conglomeration for millions and millions of dollars. I'm not sure Antonio ever worked."

"So that's why my birth certificate has his occupation listed as unemployed. Does he have any other family?"

"Not that I know of. He had a brother and a sister. They died in a car wreck about twenty years ago. Antonio was the only heir left. His mother died, I guess about ten years ago, and his father a couple years after that."

"Did he have friends?"

"Female or male?"

"Ha. Whichever." I look around to make sure we're alone. Even though I see no one else around I still whisper my question. "Did he and Lovey ever have a relationship?"

"Not that I know of. At least not in these later years. He always treated her with kindness and respect, just like he did Stace, but I never saw anything real personal there."

"No wonder she's a bitter woman."

"All this explains her reaction to you the night of the dinner."

"Yes." I realize I'm still whispering. "She came to my room the other night acting like she wanted to befriend me. But then she made a rude remark about my mom."

"Like I said before, Lovey is harmless. She just obviously holds a grudge."

The doorbell rings. After Brett pays the delivery guy, we move out to the veranda to eat our dinner. I notice Brett pause for a couple of seconds before eating. His mouth moves slightly. I know he's praying.

I say a quick 'Thank You, God' in my mind before spooning the first bite of my orange chicken into my mouth.

The presence of food seems to have stopped our conversation. I've learned a couple of things about my father, he's never worked, and he was a loner. Anastasia had hinted at the loner aspect, now Brett confirmed it.

And I have the opportunity to be just like him. If I inherit all his inherited money, I certainly wouldn't have to work. And since my mom will probably disown me, I'll be virtually alone, considering Aunt Venus lives miles and miles away.

Brett is leaving as well. But Anastasia and Lovey will still be around. Joy!

Well, real joy for Anastasia.

Lovey, not so much.

Oh, but if I'm the owner of the house can I fire her? Will Anastasia own the house with me? If that's the case Mommie Dearest will be sticking around for sure.

The twinkling lights of the skyline capture my attention for a moment. The air is warm, the food tastes great.

And I have a distracting man sitting virtually next to me. Distracting in the sense that if I let myself, he would occupy a whole lot of my thought time. You'd think with the task set before me, and my newly found half-sister, I would have plenty of other things to think about.

"I guess you like your food. You've gotten quiet. Ten minutes without talking." Brett puts the lid on his now-empty soup container.

"The food's good. The view's good. Just reflecting, I guess."

"I hope nothing I've told you about your father is disturbing you. All in all I think he was a good guy. Just a bit misguided at times."

"It feels weird knowing I'll never know him. How did he die?"

Brett pauses. His face has skeptical written all over it. "You don't know?"

"No. I didn't ask anyone. I guess people thought I knew."

His gaze becomes extremely intense. "So you have no knowledge about the details surrounding his death?"

This is becoming weird, fast. "Brett, you're starting to scare me. How did my father die?"

Irrational

BRETT STANDS. He walks over to the edge of the veranda. His back is to me, which isn't a bad view, either. I scoot out of my chair to join him. I sit on the ledge, and lean my back on one of the columns. Whatever he has to tell me can't be that bad.

Can it?

He crosses his arms. He's about a foot away from me, yet his gaze indicates he's miles away.

My right thumb pushes the cuticle of my left thumb. I'm attempting to stay calm while Brett gathers his thoughts. At least that's what I assume he's doing. He's certainly not speaking out loud.

He turns. His beautiful face combined with my anticipation cause me to breathe in sharply.

"Why did you come here?" he asks.

His question is completely unexpected. "I received a letter from Ted the attorney stating I had to come here. For the reading of the will of a man named Antonio Thomas."

"And your mom was on a plane so you had no idea who Antonio was?"

"I was pretty sure he was my father. I went and talked to my Aunt Venus. She confirmed my suspicions. Why?"

He rubs his chin. "Interesting."

"What's so interesting? Talk to me! You're driving me crazy."

Brett sits on the ledge. I turn slightly, my knee brushing his, and I try to reel my mind in. Keep it focused on what he's about to say.

His hands are clasped tightly around his forearms. If his body actions are a sign of what his words will be, I'm not sure I want to hear them.

But I have to.

"Antonio had recently gotten his pilot's license. He leased plane time with a group of people. The day he died he was at the airport. He had filed a flight plan to Atlanta."

My lungs swooshed and my breath caught. "Atlanta?"

"Yes. He had a heart attack minutes before he was about to take off. He was on his way to see you."

The man who gave me life was on his way to meet me.

Then he died.

It figures.

Tears that I had no idea were coming, fill my eyes. For the second time since I've met Brett he offers his shoulder.

I rest my head against his strength, his shirt a soft caress to my cheek, his scent an anchor for my wellbeing.

If my being is indeed well.

Right now, I'm not sure.

One of his hands holds firmly to my arm, while the other gently touches my hair, his fingers brushing down the strands. It's nice.

Then the reason for all this touching bombards my mind. I stiffen as more tears fall. Why?

"I'm sorry to tell you this. I thought you knew. I thought that's why you came."

His words melody their way through my mind, diffusing the unanswered questions.

"Oh, oh, oh, my. What do we have here?"

Anastasia's voice shatters the atmosphere. Brett stops caressing my hair. I swipe my eyes with the back of my hand, trying to rid my face of any signs of tears and running mascara.

"Stace, don't go getting any crazy ideas," Brett says.

"She's practically in your lap. Is that how you always deliver bad news, Brett?"

Her voice holds a tone like I've never heard from her. The way she spits his name indicates she's mad. But why?

I'm still facing away from her. I know my eyes will be puffy. For some reason I don't want her to know I've been crying.

Her sweet perfume wafts through the air making it thick, uncomfortable. Like her demeanor at the moment.

"Stace—" Brett starts.

"No explanation necessary. I'm intelligent enough to figure this out. Go back to comforting the poor little rich girl."

She stomps her way through the house. It's a wonder we didn't hear her coming. Although her steps probably weren't that aggressive until she saw us.

"I'm sorry." I speak my words softly, not trusting my voice.

"You don't have anything to be sorry for. She can be like that. Fly off the handle in a second."

I place my hand on his shoulder. "I guess from a distance it did look like a pretty cozy scene."

"And for some reason Stace didn't like seeing you and me all cozied up."

"Yeah. There's no way she could see my turmoil."

Brett's hand rubs my arm. "It bothers me that your heart is in turmoil. Especially since I was the cause. I don't like seeing you like this."

He's saying words that cause me to think he cares about me. Could it be possible? I can't let my mind stay in that place. "You didn't cause it. My father did. You're just the messenger."

"I wonder how much Stace knew? She was pretty upset."

His hands settle on either side of my waist. I dab the corners of my eyes with my slightly shaking hands. "She was. I hope I'm not the cause."

"She knew Antonio died at of a heart attack at the airport. It's weird. I am sorry you never got to meet him."

"And it was so close to happening. Even though I didn't know it."

"I guess some things aren't meant to be."

And I would give anything if this wasn't one of those things. "How did he find me? Why did it take so long?"

"I'm not sure when or why. I just know he found your address and he wanted to meet you. He didn't care what your mother thought. He said you were old enough to make your own decisions. If you decided you didn't want anything to do with him, he said he'd live with that. As long as you had all the facts."

I find myself tracing the collar of his shirt with my finger. "What facts?"

"I don't know. I guess that you were his daughter. I'm sure he would have told you the truth about Lovey and Stace."

"This is all such a mess. I'm such a mess."

His right hand slides up my arm, and he pushes my hair behind my shoulders. "You're a beautiful mess."

Pretty? Beautiful? Just words to him, or true thoughts? I just found out I lost my father hours before he would have contacted me. That, I didn't know and had no control over. Brett is another story. I know where his heart truly is. I know he's leaving. I can't let him take my wayward heart with him.

I shift slightly trying to distance my body, my soul.

His face moves toward mine.

I close my eyes before turning my head, burying my face in the crook of his neck. His lips brush my hair. Not what he had intended, I know.

But at this point just knowing his intentions is more than I can handle.

SUNDAY MORNING finds me on the same veranda. But this time I'm alone. Well, I have my coffee.

The sky is overcast, the wind strong. But I don't care. I'm sitting on the ledge where I sat last night with Brett. I swear if I try hard enough I can still catch that scent of his.

But I know that's impossible.

Today my hair is up in a bun. Last night it was loose when I climbed in bed, but I kept running my fingers over the strands Brett's lips had touched earlier. Sleep pretty much eluded me all night. Anastasia's outburst and Brett's attempt to kiss me rivaled the information I learned about my father. My mind kept bouncing to a million places, scenarios and what-ifs.

What-ifs that don't matter now.

Because my father is dead.

"You need more coffee?"

I guess I was so lost in my thoughts I didn't hear Brett's approach.

"Sure." I hand him my cup.

"Be right back."

He disappears, but not before I notice everything about him. His fresh, clean look. His black and white pin-striped dress shirt tucked into his black slacks. His rolled-up shirt sleeves that show off his tanned arms. Black dress shoes exuding class and style.

And this man called me beautiful.

I push fallen strands of my hair off my face. Even though my leggings and tank are stylish, new and expensive, I feel like a slouch.

"I hope I got the cream and sugar right," Brett says as he comes back onto the veranda.

I stand to meet him. "If I can drink my mom's version of my coffee, I can drink anything." I look into the cup as he hands it to me. "But this looks perfect."

"Good. You okay this morning?"

His gaze holds concern. I really don't want him being concerned about me. He has other things to be concerned about. Ricky, Peru. More important things. "I'm doing all right. I didn't even attempt to put away the shopping spree. I'll do it today. Unless, we're going shopping again."

When he left last night he just said he'd see me later.

"Sure. I'm taking Ricky to youth group at three, but we could go out this afternoon and ding the debit card a little. Or a lot."

"All right."

I know I sound less than enthusiastic, but my body and brain are tired. Maybe I can take a nap before we leave.

"Do you want to go to church with me this morning?"

Okay. That question came out of the air. "Church?"

"Yeah. You know that place where people go to worship together. Church."

"I'm really not dressed and ready to do anything. I wouldn't want to make you late."

"Oh, there's plenty of time. It's just after nine-thirty and it doesn't start until eleven. And the best part is, it's right next door. We're practically there."

"Next door? A church?"

"Yeah. It's a house church. A small group of us meet there every Sunday morning. Nothing strange or weird, I promise."

"I know about house churches. They're fine. So there's a pastor living next door?"

"Right house, wrong profession. Stephen Day, the owner of the house, is a wildlife photographer and travels all over the world. He's not home most of the time. His uncle, Roger Day, is the pastor. Stephen turned one of the garages into an area where we meet."

"Nice. Non-denominational I presume?"

"You got it. So what do you say?"

I struggle with my answer. I do miss going to church. But going to church with someone can be a bonding experience. And right now, I don't want to bond any closer to Brett than I already have. "I think I'm going to pass today."

"Sure. It's your choice. I'll leave my truck parked here if you don't mind. I'll be back about one or so."

"Okay." To my relief the intimacy of last night has vanished. Maybe it's the whole church attire and conversation. If I'm honest, God has put a damper on a few aspects of my life.

This aspect, this closeness to Brett, I welcome God to damper anytime.

I SWIPE THE mascara brush over my lashes, the finishing touch to my make-up routine. The mirror still reveals my restless night. All the more reason for Brett to not call me beautiful or pretty today. Really, when he says those things his words unnerve me.

As I maneuver through the make-shift path I made around the shopping bags, I glance at my watch. Brett should be here in about fifteen minutes or so. Which gives me a little time to start putting away some of these items.

I think I'm just shopping jewelry today. A few purchases and we will really make a dent in the balance.

I start digging through one of the bags when the hair on my neck stands, sending shivers along my arms. I glance to the left and sure enough, I have a visitor.

Anastasia is standing in the doorway. The same place Brett stood last night. Whereas the intimacy vanished between Brett and me, it appears Anastasia's mood hasn't changed a bit.

For someone so beautiful, she has no trouble looking mad and mean. The only thing sparkly about her today is that giant ring on her finger.

"Hi." I don't know what else to say.

"I didn't think you were such a taker."

No polite formalities for her. Just straight into attack mode.

"What are you talking about?"

"You come waltzing in here like you own the place, and you don't even know you own it. Then a million dollars drops in *your* lap, and depending on how *you* handle it I may or may not get my rightful inheritance. Next, you trap my best guy friend, my big brother, and steal away whatever time he used to spend with me. And to top it all off, my father died because of you."

Whoa! Any serenity that had been roaming around in my head has completely left. PS scampers off the bed, into her hiding place in the closet. I feel like joining her.

Instead, I sit on the edge of the bed. "What do you mean Antonio died because of me?"

"I heard Brett tell you last night Antonio had a heart attack right before leaving to track you down. I guess the thought of seeing you was too much for him."

Did she really go there? I know she can't read my mind. I'd spent half the night convincing myself I hadn't killed my father. So I don't know whether I'm speaking more to her than me when I say, "That's pushing it and you know it."

She hesitates, like her resolve might be faltering a little. "It's still a fact."

"We can't change the time we have on this earth. God already had a plan. It's how it worked out." This rationalization is the only explanation that keeps the guilt from living in the forefront of my mind.

"I guess it's easy for you to be so cold and religious. Your mama's the missionary and you never knew Antonio."

"None of this is easy for me. Why are you being so irrational?"

"Me? I don't think so. I see what I see. You're the one who has come out of nowhere and inserted herself into my life."

"I was summoned here. Legally. And I'm only doing what the will said I had to do so you can inherit your share."

She places her index finger on her cheek and looks to the ceiling. "I don't recall hearing the lawyer say you need to sit in Brett's lap." Her piercing gaze returns to me. "Care to refresh my memory?"

"I wasn't sitting in his lap." So is she upset because she thinks I killed Antonio or because she thinks I'm stealing Brett from her?

Or both?

I don't say anymore because I don't know how much I want to put out there. Do I really want her to know how upset I was? Do I want her to know I was crying? At this point it seems like any information I give her will be like throwing myself to the wolves so to speak.

Not sure I'm up to being eaten alive.

"You might as well have been. He's a respectable church-going guy. You claim to be a respectable church-going girl. I didn't expect this type of behavior."

"I was having a moment, okay? An emotional moment. Brett just happened to be there and he was trying to make me feel better."

"By holding you in his arms? That's how Jimmy comforts me. Jimmy, my fiancé."

Even the Florida air and the great view from my room can't temper the frustration that is building inside me. It's so obvious she wants to do battle. What happened to the sisterly love we had just yesterday? "Sis—"

"Don't Sis me. It's Stace. And really, you are causing me so much distress I don't think you should be my maid of honor. I can't imagine how stressful the wedding and the preparation would be since you've crossed this line."

My eyes widen as hurt jolts through me. She doesn't want me to call her Sis anymore? And she's firing me from being her maid of honor.

Words I don't really mean, and know I shouldn't say, tumble from my mouth. "Fine with me. I didn't like the ugly dress anyway. That big flower on the hip looked ridiculous."

The look on her face reinforces my thoughts that I shouldn't have voiced those words. It's like the air swooshed out of her.

"I see," she says, backing away from the door. "I'll try to stay out of your way the next couple of weeks while you're here."

She turns and walks quickly away.

Maybe I should have gone to church.

Inevitable

"ANASTASIA FIRED me as her maid of honor."

Brett has just helped me into his pick-up. He leans on the door. "She fired you?"

"Yep. She came upstairs a few minutes ago and told me that I killed Antonio and there would be too much tension if I were to continue in my role as maid of honor. So she released me from my duties."

He shakes his head. "That's insane," he says before shutting the door. Moments later he slides into the driver's seat.

"It's probably for the best. I'm here. I'll do what the stupid will says, then I'm headed back to Atlanta. This way, she'll get her share, I'll get mine and I'll leave behind no ties."

"None?" He starts the car, and it sounds like he revs the engine a little more than needed.

I look his way to find him staring at me. His gaze averts as soon as mine connects. "None."

Not that Brett's been real talkative or present during these shopping trips, but as the afternoon goes on, I notice he seems a bit more withdrawn today. There are no sarcastic comments, no role-playing for the clerks. He kind of keeps a step or two behind me and whips out the debit card when needed.

As if to show my insistence in moving back to Atlanta, I walk into a furniture store. An hour later I walk out, having spent close to ten thousand dollars on a new living room for my condo. It will be delivered when I'm back in Atlanta. Brett was no help in choosing any of the items.

"We've got fifteen minutes before we need to go and pick up Ricky."

His voice has an edge to it.

"Let's go then."

We walk to the car. Now I'm a step or two behind him. His strides are long and fast. No matter what state he's in, he's always a gentleman, so he opens my door.

Moments later we start down the road. "You seem a little short today. Didn't church go well?" I ask.

"Church was fine." His tone is cold, his beat clipped.

"Oh, okay. Great."

I quickly replay our conversation when he arrived at the house. I conclude he might be a little irritated that I can't keep an eye on Anastasia's wedding plans now that I'm not the maid of honor. "Don't be mad at Anastasia," I urge.

"I'm not mad at Stace."

We drive a little while in silence. When we pull up at Ricky's, he's outside waiting. He strides to the truck, climbs in, and we all say our hellos.

"I guess you two are attached at the hip," Ricky says before clicking his seatbelt into place.

Brett smiles and I don't comment. I don't even look back to see if Ricky is smiling or being a smart-aleck. Only the sound of Brett's truck shifting gears as he backs out of the driveway and starts down the road is heard.

It doesn't take long to reach the church where the youth meet.

"We'll pick you up at six," Brett says. "Then we'll grab a bite to eat. Sound good?"

"Sure. Will your 'friend' be dining with us?"

"She will," Brett says before I can refuse.

"Right. See you at six." Ricky opens the door of the truck. "Oh, and thanks for the ride."

The door shuts in not quite a slam, and I watch Ricky saunter to the front of the church where some kids have already gathered. I also notice more girls than guys flock to him when he reaches the crowd.

He high-fives a couple of the guys, his hand jutting up over the girl's heads. I immediately recognize Lauren because she's the first to reach Ricky and the one that stands the closest to him when all settles.

"The prom's just over two weeks away," I say.

"I'm sure if Ricky wanted to go, he'd be going."

We pull away from the church onto the road. I notice after a couple of turns we aren't headed toward the shopping district. We're heading for the water.

Brett parks in a gravely, sandy lot.

"I'd thought we'd chill for a little while. Walk the boardwalk. Maybe feed some seagulls," he says while opening my door.

Warmth engulfs me as I step out of the truck. Not sure whether it's the sun or Brett's touch as he helps me out, I choose to blame the sun.

After all, Brett's been so cool today. This little diversion confuses me. Who am I kidding? Everything about Brett confuses me. From his almost kiss last night, to his offer of church this morning, to his attitude this afternoon.

The ocean is to our right as we walk along the boardwalk. Little shops, restaurants and places to buy drinks line the left. The sound of the surf, seagulls overhead, and snippets of conversation surround us, almost emphasizing our silence. I'm running his moods through my brain.

I have no idea what's running through his.

Probably not thoughts of me.

He motions me to a bench. We sit, not too close together, not too far apart. The space between us definitely undecided. Since we sat at the same time it's nobody's fault. It's just how it played out.

Like life plays out sometimes. Out of our control.

The people strolling by don't hinder the sweet breeze coming off the ocean. Riding in on the wind are smells of fried food and saltwater which combine for a unique scent found only at the ocean.

The fact that I even notice is a reminder that I'm not at home. This isn't familiar territory to me. There's too much that comes to my attention that isn't routine.

Like Brett.

I've worked with a lot of CPA's. I've worked with a lot of handsome CPA's. But none of them has crept his way into my heart like Brett has.

"So, tell me a little about your mother."

Brett's question interrupts my whimsical daydreaming.

"My mom?" I ask, wondering why he would want to hear about her.

"Yeah. How did you feel when she left?"

"Which time?"

"All of them."

The sun's rays seem more intense now. My gaze is drawn to the blueness above. Not a cloud in sight.

I didn't realize how vulnerable I was regarding my mom. I would have sworn my heart was as hard as a turtle's shell. That I'd protected it from the loneliness I thought I'd forgotten. But like the cloudless sky, its turquoise backdrop wide and vast above me, my heart lays open, begging to release some of its aloneness.

"Well, in the beginning it was great. I was able to live with my very cool aunt who had a boyfriend. She was so different from my friend's parents, yet she knew how to keep me in line. She didn't put up with anything either."

"So in the beginning you were okay when she left." His tone sounds hopeful.

"Yes. I was fine with it. I didn't want to go and Mom didn't want to stay."

"How did that make you feel? Knowing she wouldn't stay stateside."

"I don't remember it making me feel any one way. I just didn't understand. I saw her in action my whole life. Giving and giving until she collapsed into bed at night. Struggling to learn languages. Sick at times. I still don't understand. But it's her calling. So I accept it."

Brett sits a little straighter. His gaze leaves my face and stares toward the ocean. He looks like an ad for a men's cologne. His focused gaze, his beautifully angled face looking like it was carved to perfection. His hair just the right length to hint at rebellion.

One girl can't quit staring at him as she walks, causing her to stumble into her friend. They laugh, and the staring girl tries to look serious as they walk off. Brett seems oblivious, but I'm not.

"After that first time?" he asks.

"She would be gone for a while. Then she'd come home. Reenergize I called it. But she never stayed long. I remember in my junior year of high school a guy I really liked asked me to the prom. I was so excited, especially since Mom was home. But when I told her, and she found out the date, we all realized she was leaving two days before the prom. I asked her to change her flight, but she couldn't. She wanted my date to pick up his tuxedo early and come over for pictures. I didn't even ask him. While she was in one of her meetings I asked Aunt Venus to take me shopping. Mom acted like she was hurt when she arrived home and found out that we bought a dress. But I knew she was secretly okay with it. She didn't like doing that stuff. At all."

"So then you became angry?"

"Not really. It just became habit. The way it was. After I got my license I would always drive her to the airport. Much less personal goodbyes happen there you know."

"No, I didn't know."

"Yes. With people watching it's easy to give the obligatory hug then leave. No scene, no fuss. No tears."

"No regrets."

"None."

He puts his hands on his knees then stands. "It sounds like you've become really good at saying goodbye."

I stand. He doesn't smile. His lips are closed. Not ready for kissing like they were last night. "I guess I have."

His left hand runs through his hair as his right hand jams into his pocket. "Come on," he says in that same curt tone he had earlier.

My heart slamming in my chest almost causes me to gasp.

Is it possible I have somehow affected Brett Hamilton?

WE WALK THE boardwalk for a little while longer, neither of us saying anything of importance. My realization brings to my attention that things have changed. I miss his playfulness. His smile.

We head back to his truck in time to pick up Ricky from the church. When we arrive, Ricky jogs over, but he doesn't open the door. Instead, he stops in front of Brett's window.

Brett pushes the magic button and the window slides down. "What's up?"

"Well, um, I was wondering. You know, if it would be all right if somebody else came to eat with us. I mean if it's no trouble. And no jokes, because it's a girl. Lauren."

My mood lifts a little.

"No jokes," Brett says. "And sure. Tell her to come on."

A big smile graces Ricky's face. "Great. Thanks. I'll just be a minute."

He jogs back to the church then disappears inside the front door.

"Well. I wonder what happened there?" I ask, glad to have something to talk about.

"I don't know. Maybe he does like her."

Moments later Ricky and Lauren walk out of the church. Ricky opens the truck door while Lauren slides in.

Brett's gentlemanly manners obviously have rubbed off on Ricky.

"Hi." Lauren's voice is full of enthusiasm.

"Hi," I say. "You remember Brett, don't you?"

"Sure. You guys were all out to eat together at the Diner. But he's not your boyfriend."

I wonder how many shades of red a face can turn in a few seconds, because that's probably what is happening to me right now.

Brett's expression barely hints of a smile.

Ricky jumps in the other side, thankfully breaking the tension Lauren's comment caused.

After seat belts are clicked into place, Brett once again drives out of the church parking lot.

"How about that seafood place over off the Selma waterway?" Brett asks.

"Sure," Ricky replies. "But isn't it kind of expensive?"

"Don't worry about that. Seafood okay with you ladies?"

I nod while Lauren says yes from the backseat.

It's not a long drive and there's no wait, so in a few minutes we find ourselves sitting outside at a table on a deck on the waterway. With the covered porch and ceiling fans turned up high, it's not as uncomfortable as I thought it would be.

It's actually kind of nice.

I scan the menu, having trouble deciding between all the great sounding dishes. I end up choosing a salad and shrimp and grits.

We place our order. Brett orders an appetizer of cheese sticks, one of Ricky's favorites apparently, and before we can even delve into a good conversation, the cheese sticks appear on the table.

"Is this place always so fast?" I ask, placing one of the cheese sticks on my appetizer plate.

"Pretty much," Brett answers. "And you'll like the food. Promise."

"I wonder what the food is like in Peru," Ricky says, looking at Brett. "Do you think you'll be eating goat and crazy stuff like that?"

With a very serious look on his face Brett says, "I heard they eat a lot of slugs, worms. The crawling creatures we consider slimy are thought of as a delicacy in Peru."

Both Ricky and Lauren stare at Brett in fascination. "You're joking, right?" Ricky asks.

"I guess I'll find out. Better savor this cheese stick while I can." He takes a bite.

Ricky looks at Lauren. "He's kidding. He has to be. Nobody would eat a worm."

"People eat snails," she says. "And that's totally gross. Yuck."

"Are you kidding or what?" Ricky's look is practically pleading with Brett.

I sit a little straighter and focus my attention on Ricky. His eyes reveal more than a casual interest in Peruvian cuisine. Like he's asking a bigger question. Like the picture is bigger than what his words are saying.

"Tell you what," Brett says. "While I'm there, I'll photograph my food and send it to you. Then you can see for yourself."

Our food comes, piping hot and delicious. Brett didn't exaggerate at all regarding the food. I notice Ricky isn't eating with as much gusto as he normally does. His fork to mouth speed is medium to slow tonight instead of full on.

But he finishes his dinner. We all pass on dessert because we're so full.

As the waiter clears the table Ricky asks if he and Lauren can take a walk. There is a pier a couple of blocks away.

"Sure," Brett says. "We'll join you after we take care of the check."

"Thank you for dinner Mr. . . ." Lauren starts.

"Brett. Call me Brett. And you're welcome."

Ricky and Lauren scoot away from the table. I notice Ricky touching Lauren's shoulder as they walk to the door.

"I can pay for mine," I say, wishing I could pay for everyone's dinner. But that would be breaking the rules. Voiding the will.

"Your dinner tonight isn't going to break me."

"I know that. But at least I'll have spent some more money."

"This isn't going to make a bit of a difference. I'm paying."

I quit arguing with him, and I don't protest when the waiter shows up. Brett hands him his card.

"You know," Brett says after the waiter disappears, "It might not be a bad idea for Ricky to hang out with Lauren. It's obvious she really likes him, and it appears he's a bit taken with her. It might be good for him to have somebody to turn to when...you know."

I know where he's going with this. What he didn't say was when he left. But Brett doesn't understand. I had somebody when my mom left. My Aunt Venus loves me so much, and she took such good care of me.

But she wasn't Mom.

And Lauren isn't Brett.

Different people feed different needs in our lives. Most of the time they aren't interchangeable.

But I guess it makes Brett feel better about abandoning Ricky by easing his mind with this rationalization.

"Do you think he'll ask her to the prom? That's what she's hoping."

Brett tilts his head. "Not sure. He was pretty adamant about not going. But maybe I can change his mind."

"Well there's not too much time left. He better decide quickly."

Brett nods as the waiter brings back his card and receipt.

"Let's go," he says, pocketing the receipt. He puts his card back into his wallet, then pulls out my chair.

We start walking down to the pier.

"So, what do you think that question about what they eat in Peru was all about?" I ask.

"Curiosity?"

"You think that's it?"

"Why not. Seems like a natural enough question. Why? What are you thinking?"

"I don't know. The whole conversation seemed a little odd to me."

"I'm not down playing what you're saying, but I've been around Ricky for a couple of years. He is always asking questions. I think my answer freaked him out a little, don't you?"

"Yes. Just a little."

"Maybe someone in Peru will help me fix up a worm like a food dish and I'll send him that photo."

I laugh. "If you do, let me know. I need to make sure I'm with him when he sees it."

"So, you plan on keeping in touch with Ricky after I leave? I thought you were headed to the ATL."

My heart jars at the words I had carelessly thrown out. It seemed like the thing to say. Again, not thinking before I speak. Now I can almost see Brett thinking ahead, planning on people hanging out with Ricky after he leaves.

First Lauren. Now me.

When will Brett realize that no one can take his place?

"I doubt it. That boy doesn't seem to care for me. I thought it would be fun to see his face, that's all."

Ricky and Lauren come into view. They are leaning against the railing looking into the water. Brett comes up behind Ricky and taps him on the shoulder.

Ricky jumps slightly then gives Brett a why-did-you-do-that look. Brett smiles. I'm glad he's smiling for some people.

"See anything good down there?" he asks.

"Na. Just water."

Ricky turns and leans against the railing. Lauren does the same.

"Thanks again for dinner. I really enjoyed it," Lauren says.

"Yeah," Ricky chimes in. "Thanks. You always know how to come through, man."

"Glad I can be of assistance." Brett pulls his sunglasses out of his shirt pocket and puts them on. "Ready?"

"Yeah, sure." Ricky nods towards Lauren.

Brett and I fall into step behind the young couple. They are laughing and joking as they walk, while Brett and I stiffly maintain a cool distance between us. I'm reminded of my first night in Hampton Cove where Brett and I followed Anastasia and Jimmy into the dining room.

Even though so much has changed since that night, some things are still the same.

As soon as we pile into the truck, Lauren speaks. "I'm texting my mom now, Brett. You can drop me off at the church. She'll pick me up there."

"All right. I don't mind taking you home, though."

"That's okay. She doesn't mind."

Lauren's voice sounds a little closer than it did earlier when we were in the truck. I turn slightly in my seat and see that she is sitting in the middle of the truck. Ricky has leaned over, I'm assuming, to help her with the always tricky middle seatbelt.

Mine and Brett's distance seems to grow wider as Lauren and Ricky's closeness seems to grow closer.

We pull into the church parking lot. Fifteen minutes later we're still waiting.

Lauren's phone buzzes. "Finally," she says. "It's my mom."

"Hi, Mom. Are you close?"

Silence.

"Oh. Okay. Yeah, I'm sure he won't mind. I'll see you soon."

Lauren's voice sounds different, sad now.

"I love you, too, Mom. Promise." She shoves her phone into her purse.

"Brett, do you mind taking me home. My mom has a really bad headache and can't drive."

Now her voice has an edge to it.

"Sure. Give me directions."

Brett follows Lauren's directions. In less than ten minutes we arrive at her house, a cute bungalow.

"Thanks again," she says. "It was great spending time with you guys."

"Nice seeing you again, Lauren," I say.

"Same here," Brett tags on.

Ricky exits the car before helping Lauren out. He walks with her to the front door. They seem to be having a discussion and it's a couple of minutes before he saunters back to the truck.

"You two seem like you're having a lot of fun," Brett says as he pulls onto the main road.

"Yeah. She's decent for a girl. Her mom is out of it sometimes, though, and Lauren is embarrassed."

"She doesn't need to be embarrassed around me," Brett says.

"Me, either," I add. I wonder exactly what 'out of it sometimes' means exactly.

"By the way, can you help me out like you said a few days ago? It looks like I'm going to prom."

A small thrill shoots through me. Yes. Lauren snagged her guy.

Brett half turns while still driving. "You're serious? You're going?"

"Yeah. I'm not even sure how it happened. But I guess it won't be so lame. A lot of my friends are going."

"We'll go out tomorrow and rent you a tux. Sound good?"

"Sure."

We pull up to Ricky's house in about ten minutes with nothing more said about the prom or Lauren.

"See you tomorrow, man," Ricky says. He opens his door and slides out.

"I'll pick you up from school," Brett says.

"Okay." The back door shuts.

A knock on my window startles me. I look over and Ricky is motioning for me to open my window.

"Are you coming with Brett tomorrow?" he asks as the window slides down.

I look over at Brett who is looking at his phone. "Not sure," I say.

Ricky looks to the ground for a moment before looking up and shaking his shaggy bangs out of his eyes. "I was kind of hoping you would. It'd be good to have a girl's opinion."

A warmness seeps through me. "All right then. I'll be there."

"Thanks," he mumbles, then shoots off towards his front door.

Brett backs out of the drive.

"I guess Ricky's going to the prom was inevitable, wasn't it. Once she had her sights set on him, it was as good as done."

His tone is a cross between bitter and resigned.

"Maybe."

I'm not sure how I feel about Brett's statement, but one thing I do know. If I dared set my sights on Brett Hamilton, I would in no way, shape or form think landing him was inevitable.

Interfering

MY ONE WEEK anniversary of being in Florida starts very uneventfully. I am now able to make my way around a little in my new SUV. Places and landmarks are starting to look familiar.

Of course, I can't shop unless Brett is with me.

We shopped yesterday until school let out, then we went to the tuxedo rental place and managed to rent Ricky a tux for the prom. Then we all had dinner again before taking Ricky home.

This morning Brett had a meeting with the people helping to sponsor his trip to Peru. We agreed to meet at noon at a quaint shopping area a little north of Hampton Cove.

I pull into the parking lot a few minutes early. I'm still a little behind on the daily spending. But I know I can catch up with a couple of full days roaming the stores.

It all seems so useless and wasteful. I don't know if I'll ever wear all these shoes and clothes and jewelry. That crazy expensive necklace I bought to wear in the wedding now will not be worn at the wedding. I guess I can wear emeralds at any time, but Brett and I both thought it would look great with that dress.

Maybe I'll buy a new comforter and sheets for the room here at the mansion. Maybe a white set so PS's fur won't be seen.

Even with the blanket on the bed, the brown comforter isn't fairing so well.

I decide to do a little window shopping until Brett arrives. I'm becoming so used to this warm weather. In a good way. I'm sure I'll miss it when I return to Atlanta. Even in May the ATL still has some pretty cool nights at times.

I'm walking next to the shops when I hear Anastasia's voice.

"Well, if it isn't the poor little rich shopper. Spending our money wisely, dear sister?"

I turn around and come face to face with not only Anastasia, but her mom also. Lovey's scowl looks like it's hurting her face. Anastasia, on the other hand, avoids looking directly at me. They both are carrying large white bags which are overflowing with everything green and gold. Flowers, ribbons, cloths. I'm not sure what all they have, but they have a lot of it. Lovey's forearms look strained.

Maybe the painful-looking expression on her face has nothing to do with the scowl, and more to do with the weight of the bags.

"Can I take that for you?" I offer.

"We don't need your help," Anastasia says, pursing her lips together after she speaks.

"Speak for yourself, Anastasia." Lovey looks at me. "Our car is a little ways up. I'd appreciate your help with this bag."

"Sure."

I barely speak the word before Anastasia stomps off. Lovey and I follow behind, unable to catch up to her if we wanted to.

"That girl is headstrong and impulsive," Lovey says.

As much as I'd like to, there is no way I'm voicing my agreement with that statement.

"That comes straight from her father," Lovey continues.

It takes all I have not to stop the momentum of my steps as she mentions Antonio. Lovey has a knack for bringing up hot-topic subjects. Again, I'm not touching this one.

"I'm still trying to see Antonio in you."

I wonder what kind of reaction Lovey is looking for from me. Do I take her bait to continue this conversation? As much as I'd love to know if there was anything Antonio-like about me, I still don't trust Lovey. Could I even believe her if she revealed anything?

"You would have added an element of elegance to the wedding," she says. "A much needed element considering my daughter's poor choice for a groom. I'm sorry she changed her mind about you. Now I have to put up with a cousin brasher than Jimmy, if that's possible. And she looks terrible in the dress."

Lovey must need an outlet for her pent up frustration. And I guess she chose me.

"I'm sure everything will turn out great," I say.

"That would be a first for me," she responds.

Unable to muster up too much sympathy for Lovey, we arrive at their car. The trunk is open and Anastasia is already in the car. I place the bag into the trunk then make sure the trunk is closed properly.

"Thank you," Lovey says.

"You're welcome," I reply.

No more words are exchanged and I quickly scoot back onto the sidewalk before Anastasia 'accidentally' backs into me.

In less than five minutes I've learned more about Lovey than I have the whole time I've been here. Not that I understand her anymore than I did, but she obviously doesn't like Jimmy.

She has an appreciation for elegance.

And even though he must have broken her heart, she's open to conversations about Antonio.

Is there something in the Hampton Cove air, or is it a coincidence that both Ricky and Lovey have not acted totally hostile toward me in the last twenty-four hours?

My phone buzzes with a message.

Brett's here.

The awkwardness that carried us through Sunday dissipated somewhat last night during our outing with Ricky. But that point of naturalness we had for a short while has disappeared.

I text Brett back.

Minutes later I see him walking towards me. I shut my eyes and for a moment I picture his walk in slow motion. The way his arms move as he places one foot in front of the other. His hair blows away from his face and heads turn as he walks by.

I open my eyes as the reality of Brett stands before me. Once again his sunglasses hide his eyes. I'm not sure I ever wished for rain before, but I might now.

"Morning," he says.

"Good morning," I reply.

"That remains to be seen." At least he smiles slightly after speaking.

"Let's get started then," I say, and he and I start hitting the stores. One after the other. I'm buying, he's taking the purchases to my SUV.

Late in the afternoon we walk past a clothing store that caters to teens. One of the posters features a guy with thick hair like Ricky's almost covering his eyes. As we pass the entrance I slow my walk. An idea is forming.

I stop and turn around.

"Why are you going in here?" Brett asks as we enter the store.

"I'm looking to change my style a little," I say over the extremely loud music playing overhead.

"Really? A little? And hey, the girl's section is this way."

He points to the left.

"I'm not looking for the girl's section."

He looks confused, but I walk to the guys half of the store. Visions of Ricky and his style flash through my mind. I start looking at shirts. Pants are out. No way we wear the same size.

But shirts are different.

I'm sure he wears a medium shirt. He's lean, but tall. Not too tall, but he's not short.

I pick out a couple of shirts and drape them over my arm. Light colors seem to be Ricky's choice. He especially likes to wear white shirts. I think he knows they show off his great skin coloring.

"What are you doing?"

Brett stands behind me.

"Would you hold these, please?" I ask as I find another style I think Ricky will like.

Pulling out a couple of the new style, I hand them to Brett and continue to the next rack.

"These clothes aren't for you."

"Sure they are."

He places his free hand on my shoulder. "This could void the will, you know."

I like the feel of his hand so I don't step back. Besides, he's taken the sunglasses off. Even though the store doesn't boast great lighting, I can still see his eyes. Which in truth is probably to his advantage and not mine. "Not if I actually wear them. Or some of them. I can't possibly wear and use everything I'm purchasing."

He takes his hand from my shoulder. "All right. And I might like seeing you in one of these shirts."

I turn and start digging through the next set of clothes before he can see how he flusters me. After picking out a few more shirts, I head toward the cash register, but stop when I see a rack of socks.

"Thinking about wearing guy socks, too?" Brett asks.

"Yes. I am." I grab as many pairs as I can carry, then dump them on the counter where you pay.

The guy behind the counter looks at me strangely, but counts the pairs then rings them up along with the shirts.

In the scope of things not a lot of money is spent. But my heart feels lifted a little.

We walk out of the store and head to my SUV.

"This is nice, what you're doing," Brett says.

"What? Buying some different clothes?"

"You and I both know these clothes aren't for you."

I keep silent as we walk.

"He'll appreciate them," Brett continues.

"I'm trying really hard not to be wasteful. You know, I think I want to go to an electronics store. I need a few games. A WII, maybe an X-Box. Oh, and I hear that Guitar Hero is a lot of fun. Maybe you can ask Ricky and his friends what games are hot right now."

We reach my SUV.

"Will do," Brett says then smiles. He puts the bags into the already full car. "Not much more room in here."

"I know. I'm through. For today."

He pulls his keys out of his pocket. Mine are already out and at the ready since I had to unlock the door.

"How would you like a chance to wear one of those dresses and fancy pair of shoes you bought?" Brett asks.

"Where, when and with who?"

"Tonight, not sure and with me. I think we need to talk, and I don't want it to be in between stores or over a hurried lunch."

Visions of our last attempt to converse at the mansion run through my head. "Or where we'll get screamed at by Anastasia?"

"Exactly."

"Okay."

He jingles his keys in his hand. "See you tonight then."

"See you."

I jump into my SUV so I don't become distracted by watching him walk to his car. Because yes, watching him walk is distracting.

Mesmerizing.

I back out of the parking space wondering what Brett wants to talk about. It's probably nothing specific. It's definitely not about us, as in together.

Oh well, whatever it is, at least I'll be wearing all the right things.

WHILE BRETT doesn't have a suit on, he does look very nice in his gray slacks and black polo shirt. As if we phoned each other for the color scheme, I chose a gray dress with black pin stripes. The dress is sleeveless has an empire waist. The material flows to my ankles making me feel all soft and slinky. I chose to wear a pair of flat silver sandals. All the walking today had me cringing at the thought of putting on heels.

My curiosity piqued, we travel away from the water and away from the town. We are in more of a residential area.

He turns onto a road that boasts nice houses. Not mansions like where I'm staying, but nice houses none the less.

After making a couple of turns he pulls into a driveway.

"Here we are. Chez Hamilton."

I feel my eyebrows raise as I look at him. "This is your house?"

"It is."

"It's beautiful." I'm now accustomed to him opening my door, so I take in the front of his house as he makes his way to my side of the truck. Beautiful stucco, wrought iron railings, incredible landscaping make for a home anyone would love to live in.

"Do you do all this landscaping yourself?" I ask, admiring the closely clipped grass and pretty flowers that line the walk-way to the front door.

"Yeah. But I'm hiring a lawn service while I'm gone. I haven't decided if I'm going to sell or rent. I need to see how it all goes before I make a decision."

"My mom never owned a house. She stays with my Aunt Venus when she's home."

"I don't want to sell right away. There are companies that will rent your home for you and take care of everything. That's an option, too."

"I guess." All this talk of him leaving has the potential to put a damper on the evening.

"I hope you don't mind that we're not going to a restaurant. I thought it would be nice to have dinner here. I've made a salad, and I can slay anything on the grill."

"Sounds yummy."

He unlocks the door then opens it, letting me go in first. Glistening hard wood floors, contemporary furniture, and a very homey feel greet me. The walls are painted a warm beige tone, while splashes of rust, orange and yellow adorn the throw pillows and pictures on the walls.

"Oh. What a nice place. It's got a great feel to it."

"Well, it's not a multi-million dollar place, and while I do have a terrace, there's no water view. Just a plain, boring tree-line view."

"Hey, I'm used to no terrace at all. So any view is okay with me."

"Perfect," he says.

I keep walking past the living area. The kitchen is at the back of the house. Granite counter tops and cherry cabinets make for an elegant yet practical look. A cherry dining table sits off to the side with six chairs surrounding it.

Brett scoots around me and opens the stainless steel refrigerator. "Club soda and lime? Or I have regular sodas, water. I have wine if you'd like some."

"No. Club soda and lime sounds great."

I watch him move around his kitchen. Sounds of ice cubes dropping into the glasses followed by the fizzing sound of the soda remind me of that first night I met Brett.

Before I knew all I know now.

I sit at a table on the terrace. Brett had soaked cedar planks, and he is now putting the planks and salmon and seasonings on the grill. As he checks a couple of knobs and centers the planks, I wonder why he wants to leave all this.

He shuts the lid then looks at his watch. "About twenty minutes and we'll be eating."

"Is there anything I can do to help?" I ask.

"No. I'll bring out the salad and bread right before the salmon is done."

"Okay. It's nice out here. And beautiful. Not plain and boring." I smile.

"In itself it's nice, but after the view you're used to seeing, this really doesn't compare."

"I'd be a happy girl with this view. Promise." He has no idea I'm referring to the view of Brett sitting in the chair. Much nicer, in my opinion, than the water view.

We make small talk until the food is ready. After I comment on the delicious food, Brett tells me how he really likes to cook. Right about now I'm wondering two things.

First, why am I here tonight?

Second, why is he still single?

BRETT WOULDN'T let me do a thing to clean up. He quickly took the dishes to the kitchen and refreshed our drinks. After he set mine in front of me, he sits back in his chair. Except he scoots it a little closer to mine. We're next to each other, yet facing each other. Close proximity to look and touch.

Great.

"I hope you didn't mind coming here instead of going out?"

"No. It's been great."

"Less distractions."

That's what he thinks. He has no idea what a distraction he is. I'm not sure how I feel knowing I'm not a distraction for him. A little sad, a little relieved. "Yeah," I lie.

"First I have a favor to ask you."

"Okay."

"Ricky and Lauren have been hanging out a lot, and Lauren really wants to come to the soccer tournament this weekend. But her parents can't come and they don't want her going by herself. Ricky asked if you would like to come along and share a room with Lauren. And the more I thought about it the better the idea sounded because we probably can do some shopping. Otherwise that'll be three days without spending any money."

And three days of not seeing Brett. "Will Lauren's mom let her go with me? She doesn't even know me."

"I talked with her. She would like you to call her if you want to go. She said you guys could meet and have coffee or something before the weekend. I went ahead and booked a room just in case. I was lucky there was a cancellation right before I called."

"You were pretty sure I'd say yes?"

"If it didn't work out, I'd just cancel the reservation. Lauren said she could switch with a couple people at work to cover her shifts even though it means she'll be working almost every night next week. But she said it was worth it."

"If her mom doesn't mind her going with me, I guess I can go."

"Great. I'll give you her number before you leave. Just give her a call. Her name is Lane."

"Okay. That's it?"

He settles back in his chair, the expression on his face taking on a serious look. "Not exactly. I wanted to ask you about your travels when you were younger."

"Now I see how you operate. Fatten me up, and then go in for the kill." I'm sure he won't let me joke my way past his curiosity, but it gives me time to process his request.

"I will admit to a little premeditating."

"I will admit to a little hesitancy."

"I know it's not your favorite subject to discuss, but I have my reasons."

He has no idea how I would love to talk to him about anything but this topic. "First, tell me what you remember about your childhood."

"My childhood?" he asks. "I thought I was going to be asking the questions."

"Just go with me here."

"My childhood. Let's see. I remember my school, my friends. My parents. Playing soccer."

I nod. "You know what I remember? Faces of kids. No names, just faces. No friends, just faces. No conversations, just pointing gestures and faces. And school? My mom had some text books, and she homeschooled me when she had the time. I had to be privately tutored for a year before I could enter school in the states."

"You're a smart woman. Somebody did something right."

"While other kids were learning math and history I was learning scripture. Pick a Psalm. Any Psalm."

"What?"

"Pick a Psalm. Psalm sixty, verse one? Psalm one hundred, verse five? What's your pleasure?"

"Psalm one forty. Verse twelve."

Visions of dirt floors, sweaty bangs, and homemade instruments take over my mind. In my mind I start singing the Psalm from the beginning just like I did when I was eight. When I get to verse twelve I sing aloud, but softly. "'I know that the Lord will maintain the cause of the afflicted, and the right of the poor.'" Only now do I look at Brett. "Very appropriate, Missionary Man."

"So you can sing the whole Bible? In the King James Version?"

I laugh. "No. That's funny, though. Not the whole Bible. I know almost all the Psalms. Maybe not every one word for word, but I know the gist of most of them. And as far as the rest of scripture, I know a whole lot. And the King James is the version my mom loves."

"Your singing voice is beautiful."

"It's not really that good. I don't run people off, but I'm far from being able to sing a solo. It was a great way to learn, though. Singing."

"It is. Another great way is reading."

"I agree."

"I want to show you something. I'll be right back."

He walks into the house as I ponder what it is he's going to show me. He does seem a little deliberate tonight. Like coming to his house and dinner are just the prelude to something more important.

And that something has to do with mission work.

Hearing the door click, and catching a whiff of the Brett scent indicates he's back. Moments later he sits across from me and lays a book on the table. It looks like a journal, and it has papers shoved in it, their corners and edges creased and crumbled, like they were jammed in there.

"This," he taps on the journal-looking book, "changed how I look at life."

"Go on," I say, even though I'm not sure I want him to go on. I have no idea what is inside the book, but if it changed his life, then it must be pretty powerful.

He lays his palm protectively on the top of the book. As if the book had the power to open on its own, and his palm squelches that from happening.

"I remember feeling the call to missions when I was young. But every time I tried to talk to my parents about it all I got was lectures on being responsible, having a steady income. I graduated high school, went to college, then earned my CPA. All the while getting pats on my back from my mother, my dad. If I heard, 'good job, Son' once, I heard it a thousand times."

"So you kept a journal?"

He shakes his head. "Uh, no. After my mother passed away my dad changed a little. Not for the better or worse, he was just different. He started talking about phasing out his portion of the business, giving me his important clients. Before I knew it I found myself in the office alone most days."

"What was your dad doing?"

"I guess reminiscing. I found this journal after he died."

"Is it your mom's?"

"No." He slowly opens the journal. "It's my dad's. I found it in his desk drawer. Not hidden or anything. Just in there. I guess he started it sometime after my mother died."

Not wanting to intrude into the personal aspect of the journal, I don't look close enough at the writing to read it. There are lots of scrunched up words written in one long paragraph in black ink. There are also magazine pages, ads of sorts. Boats, lakes, cabins. All kinds of outdoor scenarios.

After Brett shows me the magazine pages, he places them in the back of the journal before looking at me.

"These are all the things they wanted to do, but never did. These words," he points to the hand-written journal pages, "are words of regret. Words of unfulfilled dreams."

I don't know how to respond. I know what he's saying on one level, but I'm not sure what this has to do with me. Not sure why he wanted to share this with me.

"Apparently," he continues, "They wanted to go on a cruise. To

Alaska. They wanted to buy a cabin in the mountains to escape the summers here in Florida. They wanted to do so many things together but they never did. My dad writes in one spot that they kept saying 'there's always tomorrow.'"

He shuts the journal. "Well, their tomorrows ran out. This book is the book of putting off until tomorrow."

"Maybe they never had the money to do those things."

"They had the money. And the time."

"It must have affected your dad for him to start that journal. Have you read it all?"

"Yes."

"So this is a side of your dad you never knew."

"Didn't even know it existed. But I do know one thing. I'm not going to let my dream die with words in a book. I'm going to live my dream."

My heart wants to reach out to him, but since it can't I take his hands in mine. "Do your dreams include children dying while you watch because you're not able to do anything about it? Do they include saying goodbye to people you've formed friendships with, maybe even loved? Do you dream about being the outcast among a whole village of people? Trust me, not everyone was happy to see my mom and me and the teams we were with."

His thumbs gently caress my fingers. "Can you honestly tell me you don't feel you made a difference in anyone's life while you were traveling with your mother?"

"Traveling? That makes it sound like we were on a constant vacation. Mission work is not vacation."

"I have no aspirations that it's a vacation. It's a way of life. And you didn't answer my question. You probably made a huge difference in people's lives."

"Not big enough."

Pulling my hands from his, I settle back in the chair, trying to remove myself as far from him as I can.

I know he's now more resolved to leave than ever, but a part of me wishes he wouldn't go. He can love Jesus here just as much as he can love Him in Peru.

Guilt stabs at me as I finish that thought. And I know what that guilt means, what feeling is on its way.

That feeling I didn't want to experience now or ever again.

But it's here.

Conviction.

Its presence is as strong as it was long ago. Before most children knew what conviction meant, I was experiencing it often. And as you became convicted and changed your ways, the feeling didn't come as often. When it did you knew the Lord was speaking to you. I prayed and thought constantly about certain things.

And now I'm being convicted about trying to change Brett's mind about Peru.

Lord, why do You have to start interfering now?

Imminent

I WAKE UP feeling rather annoyed with God. Not only did I dream and wrestle with the Psalms songs all night, but now that word conviction won't leave my mind.

Lord, it's not that I don't believe. It's not that I don't love You. I do. You know my heart. But I need for that to be enough for You. No more sacrifices. I gave You in my childhood more than most people give You their whole life. Please understand this.

PS purrs loudly next to me on the bed. I stroke her soft fur wishing I could sleep as peacefully as she is right now.

God has to understand where I'm coming from. That's all there is to it.

And I will not let Brett Hamilton into my heart any more than he already is.

And I won't try to persuade him to stay. Okay God? Are we good now?

After showering and dressing I go downstairs, grab a cup of coffee and wait for Brett. Another day of shopping. But today I'm shopping for things that will have a purpose. After the second reading of the will I'm going to start giving some things away.

The next two days are spent pretty much the same as the first two days of shopping. Brett working from coffee shops or my SUV, while I pick out loads of things to spend money on.

I'm not sure what my father thought would happen between Brett and me. I assume there was a reason he had Brett be the keeper of the debit card. I'll probably never know the reason. At least not in this earthly realm.

It's late Thursday night, and Brett is driving me back to the mansion. He doesn't like letting a woman drive him around, so I give him small victories like this.

It helps make up for the times I side-step his missionary questions. Or give him answers he doesn't want to hear.

We don't take this load of packages up to my room. We park them downstairs in the room I've come to call the piano room.

"Lovey will probably complain because she can't get to those bookshelves to dust them," Brett says.

"Well, they can be dusted after me and all my stuff leave. I can't imagine them becoming too dusty between now and then."

"You just can't wait to leave, can you?" Brett asks.

"You should know the feeling. Right?"

"I'm leaving to go toward something. You're leaving something behind."

"Really? What?"

"This house? Your half-sister?"

I love how he leaves himself out of the equation. "You know perfectly well, Missionary Guy, possessions don't mean anything in The Kingdom. And my half-sis isn't exactly speaking to me right now."

"I told you she'll get over it. And if you inherit this house you'll have to do something with it."

"So are you saying I'm inheriting this house? Alone? With Anastasia?"

"I don't know, but either way at least part of this will be your responsibility."

"I'll sign my half over to Anastasia. I have a place in Atlanta, remember?"

"Of course I remember. And remember we're going to Raven's Beach tomorrow. Pack light. Just soccer games and dining out at sports bars all weekend. And shopping."

"Yeah."

"I appreciate you coming along so Lauren can come to the tournament."

"What else do I have going on? All that's happening around here are wedding preparations, which I am not a part of."

It would be good to be away from the wedding buzz of the house. Lovey and Anastasia are in and out of here constantly. We are civil to each other, but that's about it.

Anastasia does have an energy about her. But sometimes she seems too energized. Like she's trying to make up for something.

"I'll be by at noon. We'll go pick up Ricky, then Lauren. Then it's about a two hour drive north."

"All right. Sounds good."

Brett leaves, and I sit at the piano. My fingers run over the keys, the tune to the Psalm I quoted to Brett a couple of nights ago. It's like I've unleashed a monster.

I wonder how I'm going to lock it up again.

FRIDAY NIGHT finds us sitting in the stands of game one of the soccer tournament. Ricky plays three more games tomorrow, and depending on the wins and losses, we'll either go home Sunday morning or Sunday afternoon.

It's warm. We're inland, a few miles from the ocean. There's talk about eating at a restaurant with an ocean view tonight.

"I bought my prom dress," Lauren says. "Do you wanna see a picture?"

"Sure," I reply.

Lauren starts scrolling around her phone. "Here. Look."

I'm staring a picture of a girl wearing a really short, body-hugging strapless dress. It's a beautiful shade of slate blue, but I still can't believe how short it is. "Beautiful. I love the color."

"Thanks. My friend and I were fighting over which one of us was going to wear it. We saw it at the same time and both wanted it. But I won."

"Good for you."

"Actually she didn't have enough money to buy it."

"Whatever works, right?"

"Yeah. And I'm on the lookout for some great sandals that will match perfectly. So excited. You're going to be around to take pictures, aren't you?"

I turn to my left to look at Brett who isn't paying one bit of attention to our conversation. I turn back to Lauren. "I'm not sure what's going on regarding that. I guess I'll let you know."

"A bunch of us have rented a limo. So be at my house by six two weeks from tonight. Almost to the minute!" She shows me her watch. Two minutes until six.

"I'll see what I can do."

Note to self. Buy a camera before prom night.

The game continues, and Ricky's team wins easily six to one. Once again Ricky is the top scorer. After a quick team meeting, we all drive back to the hotel so the guys can shower and change.

Ricky is sharing a room with a team mate. Brett has his own room, and Lauren and I are sharing.

Since the weather alternated between hot and rainy, Lauren and I shower and change as well. The whole team meets in the lobby where we are given directions to the restaurant.

Once there, all the teens sit at the same tables, which leaves us adults to mingle. Brett knows a couple of the parents from being at the games. He introduces me as his friend. He also introduces me as Ann, a faux-pas I quickly correct. People give us looks which say 'we know you're more than friends, but that's okay.'

I think my look that answers 'you have no idea what you are thinking about' goes unnoticed.

After dinner, everyone heads outside to a patio area. The wind is strong, and I quickly dig an elastic band out of my purse to tie my hair into a ponytail.

I'm thankful I'm wearing denim capris as I watch the ladies in their short dresses try to keep them from flying up Marilyn style.

Ricky and Lauren walk up to us. The strong smell of Ricky's cologne about knocks me down. Teenage boys don't grasp the less-is-more-notion when it comes to cologne.

"We're going to take a walk along the water, okay?" Ricky asks.

"Sure," Brett answers. "Be back in half an hour."

"Okay."

They take off down the beach with a group of kids.

Maybe it's because we're not 'parents' but we seem to be excluded from the group conversations the adults are having. There seems to be little cliques among the adult crowd. Some dads are here, but only a few. Mostly moms who seem to be good friends, or back stabbers, not really sure. I heard one woman tell another how cute her haircut was. Then less than a minute after the cute haircut woman walks away the woman who had complimented her dissed the haircut to another woman.

That I don't need.

"Wanna go for a walk?" Brett asks.

Considering my hair is already a disaster I don't see the harm. "Sure."

We set our glasses down. I slip off my sandals while Brett kicks off his Birkies. He's wearing khaki shorts and a white button up short-sleeved shirt. He's rocking his tan and his ever-present pair of sunglasses.

I've seen these women look at him. Stare at him is more like it. And I've noticed a couple of them aren't wearing wedding rings.

We take off in the opposite direction of the kids. The sun is starting to set. Dusk is imminent.

Just like Brett's leaving.

"Psalm eighty-five, ten," Brett says.

The words of the beginning of Psalm eighty-five sing-song through my brain. When I come to the verse in question I try to speak the words without the accompanying tune. "Mercy and truth are met together; righteousness and peace have kissed each other."

"I like that Psalm," he says.

"A good Psalm showing God's faithfulness."

"And promises. So you still believe?"

"I do."

"Every single women's favorite words, right? I do."

"Not the single women I know."

"I've been influenced by Stace, remember?"

"Well, I've been influenced by my mom and my aunt. Aunt Venus has never married, and you know my mom's story. What about you? Why aren't you married?"

"I guess I never found anyone I felt like I wanted to spend the rest of my life with. But back to you. I'm glad you still believe."

"Are you sad to be missing church tomorrow morning?"

"I'll miss going, but I think God understands."

"So you go every week?"

"Unless something like this comes up. Oh, and I wanted to ask you, when we get home tomorrow night I'm meeting with a couple who just returned back from Peru. Would you like to go with me?"

"Thanks for offering, but I think I'm going to pass."

"I guess you hear enough about all things missionary from your mother."

"Yeah. Aunt Venus and I are the recipients of some pretty detailed reports when she's home between countries."

"And you're never intrigued enough to join her."

"Never."

"You said that pretty fast."

"Because it's how I feel."

"It's how you feel or how God feels?"

I stop walking then turn. "I think it's time we start heading back."

Not caring if he's following me or not, I start walking toward the restaurant where I left my three hundred dollar sandals sitting in the sand.

"Somebody has to ask the hard questions, you know?"

Brett has caught up and is matching me step for step.

"I have a mom who asks the hard questions, remember?"

"You probably see it as nagging. I'm not nagging. I genuinely want to know."

I stop walking and turn to him. "Know this. What is in my heart is between me and God. For whatever reason He's called my mom to minister in the far reaches of the world. Apparently just like He's called you. But like my mom left behind a young girl who really needed her, you're leaving Ricky. In the short time I've known you, I see how he has grown to depend on you. He looks to you for guidance. Not sure where Ricky is going to find that when you leave. Or he could end up like me and just do without it."

I start walking.

Brett's hand gently grabs my forearm, turning me toward him.

"I know he's going to miss me."

"Miss you? It's so much more than missing somebody."

"What about you?"

"Me?"

"Yes. Are you going to miss me?"

His fingers against my skin are a reminder of everything I don't want to be reminded of when he leaves. His touches, his smiles, they'll all be a distant memory soon. It's scary how quickly he can turn my thoughts. "You'll do anything to take the focus off of you leaving Ricky, won't you?"

He takes off his sunglasses then shoves them in his pocket, as if his gaze might convey what his words can't. "That's not the question. I know how Ricky is going to feel when I leave. I have no idea how you're going to feel."

His hand loosens its grip on my arm. He places his hand on my shoulder before taking a step toward me. A war is playing out inside of me. Part of me wants to step back and run away, while the other part wants to wrap my arms around him and hold on tight.

He takes another small step towards me. "I'll say it first. I'm going to miss you."

His words whisper their way to my ears, causing chill bumps to race up my arms, which are fighting to stay by my side.

The truth comes crashing back to me, mirroring the waves washing up on the shore. Warm ocean water swirls around our feet like the reality of our lives, before heading back out to the vast unknown.

"Brett," I whisper, staring into his eyes. I take two steps back, watching his gaze stay steady on me. He plunges both hands into his pockets.

"No. I'm not going to miss you. I don't think my heart can take it."

His eyes shut briefly, but not before I see his gaze drop. I take this moment to start walking towards the restaurant.

This time he doesn't catch up with me.

And while this is exactly what I want, it leaves me with an empty feeling. Because like the sun setting and dusk falling, missing Brett Hamilton is a given.

Insatiable

SATURDAY BRINGS a weird day of emotions, flukes and rain. By the time the last game is about to start, it's a given we will be in the finals. The boys are three for three outscoring their opponents by a little to a lot.

Ricky is on fire while playing. I notice how he looks to the bleachers after scoring a goal. Lauren always gives him an air high-five, and he smiles.

Brett might not be far off in his reasoning that having Lauren around will take Ricky's mind off of Brett's absence to an extent. But from experience, I know it won't fill the whole void.

There'll still be an empty chasm in Ricky's heart.

And mine too, if I don't straighten up.

Brett and I are cordial and polite to each other, but it was plain from the first eye contact at breakfast that staying away from each other physically was a must.

We did a little shopping between games. Lauren hung out with Ricky and the rest of the kids. They all seemed to be having a great time.

I'm glad Lauren could come with us.

Late Saturday night, Lauren and I are in our pajamas, each in our own bed. She had been flipping channels, but couldn't find anything interesting to watch on the television.

"So," she asks, "how is it that you and Brett, who is so incredibly hot, aren't dating, but you're fighting."

"Fighting?"

"Uh, yeah. It's so obvious. You two hardly looked at each other today."

"We're not fighting."

"You didn't even hardly talk to him. I mean, hot guy alert, Angelina. Are you blind? Or do you have a boyfriend?"

"We said what we had to say. Sometimes things are complicated."

"I'll say. I'd find it complicated to hang around him and not fall madly in love with him. I mean if I were old, you know."

"Old?"

She smiles. "Sorry. Older."

"Thanks."

"You wanna know something?"

"What," I say, because I know I have no choice but to listen.

"I think both of you secretly love each other, but don't wanna say. He's always staring at you, and you're always trying to look at him. Like with goo-goo eyes."

"I don't even know what goo-goo eyes are. And you can't tell if he's staring at me. He's always wearing those sun glasses."

"Except when it's raining. And it rained all afternoon."

She's sitting on the bed hugging her pillow to her stomach. A bag of potato chips sits next to her.

"It did rain. But he wasn't staring at me," I insist.

"He was. All afternoon." A loud crunch sounds as Lauren puts some chips in her mouth. She has her hair in a scrunchy-bun type thing. Her face has been scrubbed clean, and it's almost like we're having a pajama party.

Nostalgia threatens. These times I never had with my mom. These times I dreamed of as a child.

Aunt Venus loved a good slumber party. My mom, not so much.

And I'm reminding myself of my mom right now. Afraid to put it all out there. Afraid to voice my real feelings.

Afraid of what will happen if I say the words.

But it's not fair to saddle Lauren with my emotional baggage. Best to let her think what she wants.

"It's lights out. We have to be up early tomorrow. First game is at seven-thirty. And we have to check out of here."

"All right." Lauren folds down the chip bag before setting it on the nightstand.

I wait until she settles into the bed before turning out the light.

"Good night," she says as I settle in.

"Good night."

"Mrs. Wanna Be Hamilton."

I don't answer.

Which I'm sure in teen speech that's an admission of sorts.

THE SUN returned Sunday morning. Thank goodness. At least I knew Lauren couldn't track Brett's gaze.

Ricky's team won the tournament. Because there was a short ceremony we didn't get on the road until after six.

We drop Lauren off first, then Ricky.

"Brett, I think my bags are all the way in the back," Ricky says as we pull in his driveway.

"No, I put mine and Ann's in the back. Come on, let's grab yours before the rain starts."

"Okay. Bye, Angelina. Thanks for coming along and rooming with Lauren."

Even Ricky calls me Angelina. Something Brett won't do. "Sure. Bye."

Sounds of Brett pulling Ricky's bags out from the covered truck bed indicated a bit of shifting is going on. Maybe Ricky was right and his bags were tucked deep into the bed of the truck.

A couple of minutes later Brett hops back into the truck. "We're going to have to fly. I told the Williams I'd be there by nine-thirty."

"They're going out of town tomorrow, right? That's why you have to go tonight?"

"Yeah, so if I drop you off I should only be about ten or fifteen minutes late."

The way he says it isn't an attempt to make me feel guilty. But that conviction feeling is washing all over me again.

Really, God?

"I'll go with you."

"No. It's okay. I'll just text them when I drop you off."

"It's all right. I mean it's already after nine. The meeting isn't going to last really long, is it?"

"I don't think so."

"Just head over there. I won't melt."

He laughs. "Okay. Thanks."

This is the longest conversation we've had since Friday night.

This is also the first time we've been alone. I didn't let Lauren out of my sight since I realized how easy it would be to fall for Brett.

We arrive at the Williams's on time.

Just as a storm begins.

Literally.

We barely make it inside the door before the clouds open, and a downpour starts.

"Come on in. Have a seat," a nicely dressed gentleman says.

"Hi, Zach," Brett says. "This is my friend, Ann. Ann, Zach

Williams."

"Nice to meet you, Mr. Williams."

"Oh, call me Zach, please."

"Will do. And I'm actually Angelina."

I swear I hear some sort of a sigh come from Brett, but I ignore him.

Zach shows Brett and me to a couch, where we sit. Moments later a woman comes into the room. She's a very pretty, petite blonde. The couple appear to be in their fifties.

"So, Angelina, are you interested in going to Peru? Is that why you came along with Brett?" Zach asks, in a tone that has a hopeful sound to it.

"No," I answer. "It was kind of a logistics thing. If he had taken me home he would have been late, so I kind of came along for the ride."

"Ann's mother is a missionary. She's in South America right now," Brett volunteers.

"Oh," Zach says. "What organization does she work with?"

"HOW. Hearts of the World."

"That's a great organization. We've worked with them before. They've been around a long time."

"Yeah. My mom has been with them for years."

"That's fabulous. Her dedication is to be commended."

"I'll make sure I tell her when I see her next."

"Before we get too comfortable, let's head into the dining room. We have some maps to show you."

The next hour is spent listening to Zach and Michelle show Brett the map of the city he's going to be living in. They have circled where he's going to live, and have mapped out areas where he'll be working and ministering.

I sit in the midst of the excitement of Peru. I try to remain nonchalant and uninterested, but I must admit my interest is piqued a little.

"Have you been to Peru, Ann?" Brett asks.

"Yes. It was a long time ago. I don't remember a lot and I'm sure things have really changed since I was there." And what I do remember makes my heart sad.

"Were you near Huancayo?"

"We were further south in Tacna."

"Oh, close to the border."

"Yeah. But like I said it was years ago."

"There's still a lot of great work happening in Tacna. Actually before we left Peru just weeks ago, we had a visitor from Tacna. Luis Diaz has been involved with the Christian mission for many years. He is a blessing to us."

Luis Diaz? I swallow hard, hoping no one notices how much the name affects me. Could that be the same Senor Diaz that mom and I worked with years ago? Certainly not. It's a common name. I shake off the nudging that's threatening. "That's good to hear."

"I believe he works with the HOW people. Maybe your mother knows of him."

"She might," I say not letting on I probably know of him. And if it's the same Luis Diaz, he's responsible for changing my life.

This is too weird, God.

I push Luis Diaz to the back of my mind, where he's been for fifteen years.

Zach turns his attention to Brett. "How are the language classes coming?" Zach asks as they start folding the maps.

"They're coming slowly. Between wrapping up my accounting firm and other things, I'm managing to squeeze some in."

When he's had time for classes I'll never know. Must be what he does early mornings. The rest of the time is spent with me and Ricky. At least he has the opportunity to take classes. Mom and I learned on the go.

Of course that may have been her choice.

I try to stop my mind from wandering back to those days spent in Peru. Day's spent with the children there. Of course I was a child, too. I looked at things so differently, as we all do when we were children. Only looking back on that time as an adult brought to light true perspectives.

Or did seeing those experiences as an adult skew the perspective?

Did I have it right as a kid with uncensored views, unlimited trust, and total faith in God because I hadn't experienced anything but living on faith?

This is why I want no part of this life.

This is why I prefer to tell God I love Him, go to church and live in true civilization.

It's far less . . .

Far less . . .

Convicting.

There's that word again.

That word that gnaws at you from the inside out. That word that stops your thoughts, and sometimes your actions, as it grabs hold of your heart.

Go away word!

We say our goodbyes to the Williams. The storm has passed, the rain has stopped, but the air is thick.

Clingy.

Like the dampness has the ability to seep in because a few thoughts regarding a previous life open a realm of vulnerability that had disappeared long ago.

Or so I thought.

"Thanks for coming with me." Brett backs out of the driveway onto the road.

"Sure."

We ride in silence for a little while. The Williams's home is in a nice community, but it's further inland than Ricky's house. It's dark, and the truck's lights reveal we're on a road lined with tall grass and not a lot of buildings.

A pop and a series of thuds cause Brett to pull the truck to the side of the road.

"Great. A flat," he says.

Out here in the middle of nowhere. "At least it's pretty much quit raining," I say.

Brett hops out of the truck. I sit for a couple of minutes, not sure what to do. I'm not the girl who knows a whole lot about changing a tire. Do pick-ups have a spare tire? There is no trunk.

I find Brett squatting at the back of the truck turning a rod.

"This shouldn't take too long," Brett says. "Once I get the spare down I'll make quick work of this. Do you know how to change a tire?"

"Uh, no."

"Want to learn?"

"Sure. I can watch." I'm thankful the rain has quit. I chose today to wear one of the shirts I bought in that teen store. It's a white shirt, kind of thin, and a downpour would show Brett more of me than I want him to see. Not that I'm not wearing a bra, because I am, but I don't really want him to see me in it.

Moments later he has the spare on the ground. He grabs another tool. "This is what you use to loosen the lug nuts."

"Lug nuts. Okay."

He squats down again, and one by one starts removing the lug nuts. His strong arms and muscles make it look easy.

Thunder rumbles overhead. I look to the dark sky. "Do you have a flash light?"

"I think I'll be good."

"Well, let me know if I can do anything."

The second I'm done speaking, the skies open. Big, fat raindrops start falling. I wipe my eyes, probably smearing what little mascara I have left. Instinctively I cross my arms in front of me, very aware of my white shirt which is now plastered to my body.

"Why don't you get in the truck?" Brett suggests.

You think I would have thought of that, but my mind is bogged down with thoughts of a life I imagined I had left behind. I run to the door and pull on the handle. "It's locked."

Still kneeling in front of the tire, Brett doesn't seem to hear me.

"It's locked," I say louder this time.

He looks up at me, then taps the outside of his pockets with his palm. A concerned look crosses his face. He stands.

"See if my side is unlocked," he says.

I run over to his side and find the door locked as well.

Approaching the back of the truck I find Brett working quickly on putting the spare tire on.

"It's locked," I say.

He wipes the back of his arm across his forehead, momentarily pushing his hair out of his eyes. "Haven't done that in a while."

He keeps working.

The downpour slows to a sprinkle. The mugginess keeps the warmth hanging in the air. Having nothing else to do and feeling useless I lean against the truck.

Brett looks toward me.

His gaze fixes on my face, then lowers. He quickly looks away, then focuses on fixing the tire.

I look down. I might as well not be wearing a shirt. The laciness of my bra shows through the thin, soaked T-shirt which clings to my body.

"Is your phone in the car?" he asks not looking up.

"It is. Yours?" I counter, covering my chest with my arms even though he hasn't looked up again.

"Yep."

We've been on this road for close to half an hour now and we haven't seen one car.

A culmination of the weekend emotions, the God interruptions of the last few days, and the overwhelmingly different direction my life has taken recently, threaten to spill over like the clouds dropping the rain.

My wet hair is plastered to my head, my ponytail hangs limply down my back. The darkness of the night combines with the vulnerability of my heart, creating a foreign atmosphere.

Minutes later Brett finishes changing the tire. He stands, wiping his hands on his jeans.

"Okay," he says. "We have to figure something out since not one car has come by."

"You don't keep a spare key hidden in the tire well or somewhere?"

"Used to. I gave the spare to Ricky."

"We could call...."

"Kind of hard with both our phones in the car."

"Yeah." I rub my arms.

"You cold?" Brett asks.

"No." He's the cause of my chill bumps.

"The way you're holding yourself says otherwise."

"It's more like this shirt is now totally see-through and there are things I want to keep to myself. I have another shirt in my suitcase, but the tailgate is probably locked."

He checks. "It is. Here."

I take in a deep breath as Brett pulls off his dark polo shirt. His white T underneath rides up, slightly revealing abs that I've only seen in photos.

"I know it's wet, I'm sorry, but at least if we have to walk you'll be more comfortable." He holds the shirt out with one hand while the other pulls down his semi-wet white T.

I take the shirt from him. "Thanks. So you think we'll have to walk?"

I turn slightly while I slip the shirt on, pulling it over my wet hair. Scents of Brett surround me as I slip my arms through.

"We can hang here for a few minutes, but if a car doesn't come along we might have to hit the trail."

Without warning I feel him gently turning me toward him and helping me situate the shirt. As I tug the ends of the shirt down, his palm slides over the side of my neck before freeing my ponytail from the shirt.

His touch doesn't leave me, sliding from my neck to my shoulder then down my arm. When he reaches my hand his fingers intertwine with mine.

"I like seeing you in my shirt."

The sound of his voice and his words make me bold. "I like wearing your shirt."

I blink raindrops from my eyes, never averting my gaze from Brett's.

"Since this didn't work too well the last time, I'm going to try again." His voice is raspy, and his fingers tighten around mine. His other arm wraps around my waist, pulling me close.

"Are you going to miss me?" His question sends shivers through me.

As much as I don't want to admit it, I'm tired of fighting it. "Yes. Yes, I am."

I'm barely done speaking when his lips cover mine. Sweetness and rain momentarily caress my lips before demanding more.

If I ever thought I'd been kissed before, I was sadly mistaken.

All my warring emotions slam through me as Brett's lips take full control of mine.

Needing a grounding point, I lean against his truck not caring about the rain soaking into my jeans.

His lips don't release mine. And I don't want them to. While fireworks explode in my heart, I'm subtly aware of him unlacing his fingers from mine. Then he unwraps his arm from my waist and grabs the bed of his pickup, one hand on either side of me trapping me in his masculinity.

A low groan escapes him as he stops our kiss.

Breathless and feeling like I'm unable to move, I muster enough strength to lift my arms and place my hands on either side of his face.

His lips once again start the amazement that is his kiss.

I take my hands from his face, wrap them around his waist and pull him against me. Wet clothes, thick air, and hot kisses make my body weak and wanting more.

With just two kisses Brett Hamilton has managed to make me insatiable.

Involved

THIS IS NOT good, I think, as my lips crave more of his. I know that's a serious word to use, crave, especially after only a couple of kisses, but it's the truth.

The feel of his lips on mine has sent blood racing through my veins at top speed, trying to reach my toes to include them in the fabulous feeling. Nothing inside me wants to be left out.

His arms still have me trapped, something I'm not going to complain about. His kisses have me captivated, while my mind is a whirling mess. Brett has managed to break through all my resolve regarding falling for him.

Hot kisses leave my lips to trail along my cheek toward my ear. "I've never…" Brett starts.

"Never what?" I ask, surprised my brain can string two words together.

"Never kissed anyone wearing my shirt." He pulls back, arms still on either side of me.

"I've never kissed anyone while wearing your shirt, either."

He smiles and I realize I'll never see his lips in the same way again.

"And you better not. Ever." He leans in, his lips capturing mine once again. My hands wrap around his arms for much needed support. He steps closer, so I grab him around his waist pulling him into dangerous territory.

His lips brush across my neck. His hands push the collar of his polo making room for his kisses along the tops of my shoulders. My body pulses, awakening sensations only he can awaken. These feelings can't be possible with just anyone. A fiery zing runs from the top of my head to my rain-soaked feet.

His hands slide down my back. Instead of clenching my arms to my sides in an avoidance move, I raise them around his neck, opening my body to his. Anticipation like I've never experience before takes over.

My breath hitches.

"No," he rasps. Brett's lips leave my shoulders, sweep across my mouth as his body moves, leaving way too much distance between us.

His chest heaves, his gaze lowers, then he walks around to the back of the truck.

I stand, hands plastered against the side of the truck to keep me on my feet, while a rush of embarrassment and wonder fly through me.

And conviction.

My unsteady legs manage the few steps to where Brett stands. I reach to touch his arm, but his hand stops me. "What?" I ask.

His hand caresses mine. He shuts his eyes for a moment. "I had no idea your kisses were so amazing."

"You're not so bad yourself."

He pulls me to him, but not for more kisses. His arms wrap tightly around me and he places his forehead against mine. "If I keep learning more about you and kissing you, I'll never go to Peru."

"So kiss me."

"I'll admit I can get lost in this moment, but that's not fair to us. I know what God has for my life. I'm sorry."

"Well, I'm not sorry." I push away, wishing the rain would fall and drown out this whole scenario.

"Ann, I wish things could be different."

I turn so he doesn't see my eye-tears. I can probably pass them off as rain, but my insides are crumbling. I'm not sure what I can pass that off as.

He stands next to me, and I step away. I hear him sigh.

"We probably need to start walking." His voice is gruff. A perfect prelude to the low thunder which rumbles in the distance as if God is in agreement.

He glances at me, then motions for me to follow.

We walk side by side not touching for what seems like hours. In reality it is only thirty-five minutes before we spot a gas station. Brett uses the phone to call a locksmith who comes and picks us up, takes us to the truck then unlocks it.

"It's late," Brett says as he starts driving. "It'll be after midnight before I drop you off."

"It's not like anything is going to turn into a pumpkin, is it?"

My attempt at humor fails, and we ride the rest of the way in silence. When we pull up to the mansion, he unloads my luggage from the back of the truck.

"I'll take this in for you."

"No. I can take it. I lugged it around all weekend." As if to prove my point, I sling the shoulder strap over my shoulder, adjust my stance at its heaviness.

"If you're sure," he says.

"I'm sure. See you." I start walking toward the front door.

"Ann."

I stop, waiting for him to say something, but I don't turn around.

"I have some things I need to take care of tomorrow for the Peru trip. Some legal things. I'm not sure how long it's going to take, but I'll be in touch when I'm through."

"Okay." I would shrug my shoulders, but it's difficult with the heavy duffle bag weighing one of them down. So I start walking.

As I turn the knob on the front door I hear his truck driving away.

I go inside and head straight up the stairs. I drop the duffel bag in the bathroom before turning the shower on to extra hot.

Brett's shirt slides easily over my head. Carefully I turn it right side out. Not wanting to, I rub the wet material over my cheek, the scent of who he is gently ticking my nose.

My body almost melts again at the thought of his lips on mine.

My arms tingle at the memory of him pressing against me.

I walk to my closet and hang his shirt, still damp, in the back corner. Away from the other clothes. Out of direct sight, yet still in my possession.

An overwhelming sadness stirs my soul as I realize it's the only part of him I'll get to keep.

BRIGHT SUNSHINE mocks my fogged mind as I decide to swim some laps in the pool. Visions of Peruvian landscapes, pouring down rain, and Brett plagued any attempt I made to sleep last night.

Even the cool water can't erase the heat my body feels thinking of him. The sound of rain falling will always remind me of the sweetness of his lips on mine.

Thanks to Brett Hamilton, I don't even know who I am anymore.

Lying on the lounge chair, on the deck of the million dollar house, with the million dollar view, I think about how I would trade it all for a lifetime with Brett.

No. I shake my head like shaking it will disturb those thoughts. Those irrational notions. Those sensations that should have remained undisturbed beneath my skin.

Brett is leaving for Peru in less than a month.

I will acknowledge that I've given a part of my heart to him. He hasn't necessarily accepted it, but it's out there for him to take with him if he chooses.

Now that I've succeeded in complicating things, I need to keep my focus on the money. Spending it, inheriting it, then moving back to the comfort and security of my own home.

My home I will own without worry of a mortgage. I will give Anastasia this house in a minute. She and her mother can live here like the queens they are. Oh, and Jimmy, too. I keep forgetting he's going to be Mr. Anastasia in a few short weeks.

Too bad I won't be able to see the green and gold wedding. I'm sure it will be loud in every aspect.

"Hi, Ann."

Anastasia's voice brings life to my wedding images.

I open my eyes. She's dressed in her bathing suit and she carries a towel, book, and a drink.

"Mind if I join you?" she asks as she tosses her towel on the lounge chair before setting her book and drink on the end table between our chairs.

It's obvious she doesn't care if I mind or not.

An invisible, frigid line goes up between us despite the sparkly silver two-piece she's almost wearing.

"Shouldn't you be out spending money?" she asks.

"I can't spend money without the debit card."

"And where is the debit card?"

"I'm not sure." Which is the truth. I have no idea where Brett is or what he's doing for that matter.

"Ooh. Can't find your boyfriend today? I know where mine is. He's at work making money. Oh, but wait, he's not my boyfriend, he's my fiancé." She makes a show of flashing her ring my direction.

"Brett is not my boyfriend."

"Denial. I know you went out of town with him."

I stare straight ahead, not giving her the satisfaction of continuing the argument.

"The wedding plans are moving along amazingly well. Mama is doing a fabulous job of putting it all together very quickly. And we've received so many RSVPs already. Over half of the three hundred invites have said yes."

Three hundred? I don't even know three hundred people. "That's nice."

Despite the rays of the sun, coolness surrounds me. Whereas I had hoped my skin would feel warmth from the sun's rays, a series of chill bumps move up and down my arms and legs.

I wonder about the loud cousin Stace talked into wearing the horrible green dress. The cousin was probably enamored of Anastasia's beauty and charm. I know I was. And I went along with her whirlwind plans despite the task I had to accomplish. I had agreed to visit caterers, venues, flower people, everybody.

Now it's just her and Lovey oohing and awing over motifs, food, and flower choices.

"You know Brett is walking me down the aisle, don't you?"

I bite my lip to keep the surprise from escaping in any form. I calm my heart, hoping for a steady voice. "I didn't know. But that's nice."

And it is nice, but why didn't he tell me? Not that he has to tell me about his life, but I went away with him for the weekend. Okay, we had separate rooms and two teenagers along, but still.

Any thoughts I've had of us growing closer diminish moment by moment. The more I find out how much I don't know about this man makes me glad he chose to be the gentleman he was last night.

Although my body still remembers his touch. My lips still wish his were caressing them. But I wish I could will my body into going back to that empty feeling it had become quite comfortable with.

No such luck.

At least not today.

"I can't imagine how gorgeous he's going to look in his tux. He may be like my older brother, but let's face it, hot is hot. No denying it." Anastasia's words come out like they are cleverly devised to pierce through my skin one syllable at a time.

I glance at her. Even though she's sipping her drink, I swear there's a smirk on her face.

"I'm sure the whole wedding will be beautiful," I say, not sure of that at all. But I have no idea what else to say that will quiet her. She doesn't like me, fired me as her maid of honor, so I guess she came out here to continue the war, not offer peace.

But I'm not in the mood to fight.

I had wrestled all night with my dreams and visions of Brett, and what will never be. I have no desire to battle the day away.

"Of course the wedding will be beautiful. It has to with all of Mama's hard work. I suppose you'll be back in Atlanta by then, won't you?"

Interesting. Is her question really a question? Because to my ears it's sounding like a request.

I could toy with her. Let her think there's a possibility of me crashing her wedding. That would certainly throw her into a tizzy. As much fun as it would be watching that, again, I'm not in the mood. "I think so."

"You must have the money thing under control considering you're spending your day lying in the sun."

"It's under control."

We are a little behind, I know, but he said we should be able to make that up with a couple of nice jewelry purchases.

"I hate the thought of my inheritance being dependent on you. If it wasn't for you not inheriting either I'd pretend to be your best friend. But I know you want this money as much, if not more, than I do."

I doubt that. She'd fall out of that lounge chair if I told her I'd give it all up to be with Brett. I'm not sure which claws would come out first. Her greedy-I-want-the-money-claws, or her you-better-not-steal-Brett claws.

But giving up money to be with somebody is totally different from committing your life to telling third-world countries about Jesus.

I can tell by my thoughts I am already way too involved for my own good.

Impartation

"I REALLY appreciate the offer, but I'm going to pass." I look Brett straight in the eye so he knows I'm serious. Going to a Good Friday service is not on my agenda tonight.

"All right. But think about coming Sunday morning. Easter is always a great day in church."

No kidding. *Conviction, go away.* "I'll think about it."

"Have you eaten dinner?" he asks.

"No."

"Can you hold off for a couple of hours? Until after the service?"

"Sure."

"All right. We'll grab a bite then. Oh, and if you change your mind about coming, walk next door, and come in the front door."

"I don't think I'll be changing my mind."

"You never know."

Brett leaves, and I settle into a chair on the veranda, surprised by his offer of dinner. We haven't shared a meal all week. Lunch has been on the go between shopping trips.

No sit downs.

The beautiful view has darkened. Clouds have rolled in, and the air is still. The usual blue-sky, white-cloud look has been replaced by a hazy grayness. Surprisingly still, the air has a touch of cool to it.

Standard Good Friday weather, according to Mom.

Good Friday.

What a way to wrap up a week that has flown by with daily shopping trips, no mention of kissing, and no more interruptions from Anastasia. Brett has gone back to total accounting mode, working in cafés while I shop.

His playfulness, along with the sparkle in his green eyes, has disappeared. Why the memories and reminders of his touch can't disappear from my radar is beyond me. Every time I'm walking next to him I have to stop myself from touching his arm or grabbing his hand. I also have to rein in my staring habit.

It's obvious his agenda has taken precedence over anything else. I'm back to being just the debit card.

Maybe I'm not a very good kisser.

Although that night he told me my kisses were amazing.

Sounds of laughter drift my way. I look toward the living area. My heart sinks a little as I see Anastasia and Jimmy coming my way. They appear to be joined at the hip, her arm entwined with his, holding hands.

"Hi, Ann."

Anastasia's tone, happy as it is, puts me on guard immediately.

"Hi." I speak quietly while watching every move the two of them make. I know they have to be up to something. I haven't seen Jimmy since that crazy night he kept telling us we looked alike.

It's scary to think Jimmy has intuition.

"We passed Brett," Jimmy says. "You're not going to service tonight? Anywhere?"

Anastasia laughs. Loud. Jimmy is rubbing off on her. "She's not exactly dressed for it, is she? If Jesus dying on the cross can't convince the missionary's kid to go to church, you know there's a rebellion taking place. In here." Anastasia points to her heart.

I swallow hard. Her tone is not judgmental. It's factual. And if I'm not mistaken I see a softening in those brown eyes.

I can't let her get to me. Not like this. Not about God. "I'm not rebelling. I'm just not going. Do you guys go to the church next door with Brett?"

They look at each other like I'm crazy.

"No," Anastasia says. "We go in town to a huge church. And we always go every Easter and Christmas. We know the important dates, unlike some people."

She cuts her gaze toward me.

"Come on, Baby," Jimmy says. "We need to go. Be and be seen, you know?"

"I guess you're right," Anastasia says. "We need to be going."

They walk away, leaving me confused. Jimmy and Stace don't usually go to church. I guess Brett's actions back up his faith. So far, loud Jimmy and snap-at-me-in-a-minute Stace haven't shown me actions that mirror what I think show the Christian faith.

Even though Anastasia has been talking to me civilly lately, she still has an attitude and gets her digs in when she can.

If I'm honest with myself I'm struggling with the place God has in my heart. I do believe. But what does that mean? Even Satan and all the demons believe. But what kind of God demands a love so strong that it can pull a mom away from her child?

Out of nowhere the wind picks up. *It was your decision, not hers.*

I kind of jump out of my seat, yet stay rooted to it at the same time. My heart steels in not having fought this battle in a while. So He wants to go there, does He? *I was fifteen. Was I capable of making good decisions?*

His words swirl around me like they're air. *You thought you were.*

Really? Such a simple comeback for the complex God? *Why are You such a struggle?*

Why can't you rest in who I am? Another sensation of sweet ocean air surrounds me, and I have to push my hair away from my face.

Because maybe I can't figure out who You are! Why can't you leave me alone?

Scooting back my chair, I stand. Fully aware, I start backing toward the doors leading to the living room, the sudden stillness of the air almost scaring me.

A big swoosh of wind blows past me. *Because I love you.*

My heart flutters like warm stitches closing a gaping wound. A powerful, overwhelming love is forming in the deepest crevice of my heart, swirling into motion.

With a breath of acceptance I can be fully engulfed in this love.

Or I can square my shoulders, stand my resolve, like I've done for years, and bring down the wall blocking all His moves.

My mind sing-songs with the Psalms. Verse after verse run through my mind. Then one sounds with a resounding gong.

I sing the words softly. "Restore unto me the joy of thy salvation; and uphold me with thy free spirit."

Drawing on faith, I relax my shoulders.

And breathe.

MY STEP IS lighter as I shower and dress for dinner with Brett. I feel kind of like happy-dancing, but I keep my feet on the ground. Steady.

I don't dance well.

I wonder what kind of songs they sing at Brett's house church. Not that I would recognize anything but the old Hymns.

It *is* Good Friday. The day Jesus died for us.

For me.

I dab the corner of my eyes with my fingers, absorbing the tear that has formed, knowing I'll never get any make-up on if I keep this up.

PS swirls around my leg, meowing. I bend down and pet her. "I love you, sweetie. Yes, mommy loves you."

She closes her eyes as I pet the top of her head, that special place between her ears. She lays down, surrendering and full of expectation that I'll continue.

I do.

This whole scenario reminds me of God. We feel His touch, and we surrender with an expectation of what will be. Yet, I can already feel doubt closing in, the thought that nothing has changed. Nothing will be different.

I sit on the floor, next to PS. Like her, I close my eyes and push those thoughts away. I want to feel God. I want to feel His love.

Because frankly, I don't know what that type of love feels like.

I KNOW WHEN you accept His love stuff happens. The old becomes new. The past is forgiven by Him, if not forgotten by me. This is all knowledge that's been in my head for years.

But when Brett came walking into the living room after the church service I thought my heart was going to fly up and pop out of my eyes. I couldn't quit staring, which yes, has been an issue for awhile. But he looks different to me.

In a good way.

"Ready?" he asks.

He has no idea. "Yes."

I slide off the bar stool and walk toward him. I grab my purse off the couch then we walk to his truck. Always the gentleman he opens my door before helping me in.

We start driving. He turns to me. "You look really nice. I like the color of your dress. It gives you kind of a glowing look. Glowing in a good way."

"Thank you." I smile. I'll let him think it's the dress. Putting the love of God into words is difficult at times. And to blurt out 'I've found Jesus' would sound clichéd and fake.

And like my mom.

A part of me wishes I could call my mom in the jungle. Yet another part of me wants to tell her face to face of my impartation, you could say. Her faithfulness all these years astounds me.

But at least now I have an inkling of what propelled her.

We pull into the restaurant parking lot, but leave minutes later after finding out the wait is forty-five minutes.

"The food's good, but I'm hungry. Do you mind if we go somewhere else?" Brett asks.

I tell him I don't mind at all.

We drive about ten more minutes before he pulls into another parking lot. We are ocean side, and the place is crowded. Dusk is settling in, the grayness of the day not helping in keeping it light much longer.

Brett opens my door. His hand lingers on mine after he helps me out. We take a couple of steps then he stops and puts his arm around me. "See that island out there?"

He points to a clump of trees not too far off shore.

"Yes."

"There'll be—" he stops speaking.

"What? There'll be what?"

"I think I'll let you see for yourself. Come on, let's get some food."

I refuse to let his evasiveness annoy me.

His arm eases off my shoulders, but his hand finds mine. Can he feel my pulse pounding through my wrist as it brushes his? Can he tell how much more alive I am?

At least that's how I feel inside. Like love has burst out of my heart and is now running through my veins looking for an outlet.

We walk with the moving crowd. Some people are milling together in groups. Couples stand close to each other, laughter sounds all around us. There is the ever-present breeze, but it's gentle. Like Brett's touch.

The whole world seems like a caress right now. Like all the senses have energized with a zinging, yet tender stroke, and the whole mess swirls around me with an awareness unlike anything I've ever experienced.

This is crazy.

We stop in front of a hot dog stand.

"You are on a mission to get me to eat concession hot dogs, aren't you?" I ask.

"Look. It's an American tradition I'm going to miss when I leave. Humor me, please?"

"All right. Just this once."

Brett buys three hot dogs, then we scoot to the drink vendor and buy a couple of sodas. We take our simple dinner to the railing of the boardwalk, and stand while we eat.

"I love this food," Brett says between bites.

I must admit the hot dogs are tasty. "It's wonderful." Really, eating bugs right now would be wonderful. Okay, that's pushing it, but you get my drift.

"I like that word, wonderful."

"Me too."

"Would you like another hot dog?" he asks after I take my last bite.

"No. One was perfect."

He's finishing his second one. After he puts the last bite in his mouth he tosses our trash into the basket across the walkway. We face the ocean, still leaning against the railing, letting the breeze drift past us with an air of expectancy.

"So, what's going on?" he asks.

"What do you mean?"

"Wonderful. Perfect. New words to your vocabulary. Don't get me wrong, I like them, but that hasn't exactly been your attitude. At least not until today."

Dusk loses its grip as darkness overtakes the sky. Boardwalk lights behind us slice through the night casting shadows. Without warning, the lights disappear.

Conversations cease, a hush overtakes the crowd.

I hear a loud pop and a squealing sound before red, green and white lights burst into the sky in an amazing display of beauty and wonder. Boom after boom of color explode in the darkness.

The perfect picture of my heart.

Really?

Tears threaten behind my eyelids, slipping to the corner of my eyes. Grateful I kept a napkin, I dab the betraying tears.

Oohs and ahs sound all around us as people voice their appreciation. Obviously Brett knew this was going to take place.

"Are you okay?" he asks.

Squishing the napkins in my hand, I blink quickly, forcing the tears back. "I'm fine."

"I'm not going to push, but if you want to talk, I've been told I'm a pretty good listener."

He's a pretty good kisser as well. I nod and we watch the rest of the fireworks without words. Every nerve ending I have is ready to explode, mirroring what my newly opened eyes are seeing. My body, hot like fire, is overly sensitive to the closeness of Brett and who he is. I can imagine my skin melting if he were to touch me right now.

Seriously.

Gray puffs of smoke linger as the fireworks end and the boardwalk lights, dimmed from their earlier brightness, shoot brightly through the darkness. People immediately begin to disperse, but I don't want to move. I want to stay in this moment for a lifetime.

I look to my right. Brett has turned, facing the boardwalk instead of the water. His profile, strong and compelling, amazes me. His elbows rest on the railing. I know without a doubt women walking by can't help but stare at this gorgeously put together man.

God's creation.

Beautiful.

Wonderful.

I shut my eyes hoping to gain a balance between that person I was at noon and the person I've become since then. Talk about a roller coaster. I need to find a horizontal emotional line I can operate from. I can think from.

Because I do need to live.

"That was amazing," I say. "Thank you for bringing me here."

He turns toward me. "The city puts on the fireworks show every Friday night. It's a big draw to bring people down here to support the local businesses."

"Looks like it's working."

"It's a big tourist attraction, too."

"I'm glad it's successful. It's beautiful and probably different every week. Even if it's the same show, depending on one's state of mind, it could take on a new look."

"You're right. I've never really thought about it that way."

"Maybe we can come back and test out my theory," I say, boldly.

"Definitely." He closes the distance between us. "You know, there's something about being alone with you in the dark of the night. It has a way of removing me from all reasonable thoughts."

The love that pumped through my veins a little while ago starts pumping triple-time as his hand touches my neck. His index finger traces my jaw line from below my ear to the front of my face. It stops below my lips.

I shiver, not with cold but with expectation.

Expectation of what I now know can be with Brett. Expectation of a love, undefined by human emotions, undefined by anything my mind can fathom. I feel like I'm sitting on a love cloud as I wait for him to make his next move.

Because I can't.

Move, that is.

I'm spent with the emotions from the day. I'm spent with new sensations and thoughts that have never entered my realm of possibility.

His lips cover mine. There's nothing hungry or urgent in his kiss. It's sweet, slow and all consuming. My lips and shoulders are the only parts of my body that are physically being touched by Brett, but there isn't any part of me that isn't affected by him.

Thank goodness he breaks the kiss momentarily. I barely have time to register that I'm taking a much needed breath before his lips claim mine again.

My body and his body press together in a way that can only be described as a perfect fit. He's just the right height, width, and has an amazing ability to know how to use them both to his advantage while remaining a gentleman.

His lips kiss their way to my earlobe.

He lets out a small breath. "I have to remember we're in public."

After a swift kiss on my earlobe he leans back, his face inches from mine, but his heart ever entwined with mine.

"I can't stop thinking about you."

My eyebrows raise. A confession from the missionary? "I have to be honest," I say. "All I've thought about all week is your kiss."

Kiss, singular. Not as in only one kiss, but as in an event unto itself.

"It's been hard keeping focused on my tasks at hand. What are we doing?"

I can't decide if his question is rhetorical. I certainly don't have an answer. "We were kissing."

"Is that all it is to you? Kissing?"

I look away. Is he asking me about emotions? Feelings? No guy wants to talk about those things. But I have to remember Brett is leaving, already taking a piece of my heart with him, and if I want any heart left here in the U.S. at all, I need to play it cool. "This time next month you'll be in Peru, so yes, it's just kissing to me."

"Your kisses say something else."

I take a step back. "You think?"

He closes the gap, not letting himself get further away than I can touch.

"I know. They're saying you like me."

I do like him. But it's too risky. As much as my lighter-than-air feeling is coming aground a little, some things don't change. I know that I love Jesus and He loves me, but facts are still facts.

Brett is a missionary.

I'm not.

Inspiration

EVEN THOUGH we are still 'in public' like Brett said earlier, we are virtually alone. The vendors have closed, the people have gone back to their homes or hotels.

The occasional couple strolls by, but it's almost like we have our own private dock at the moment.

And that can be good, or not so good.

"What are you saying?" I ask, feeling my heart's edges soften somewhat toward his missionary status.

"I'm letting you know I really like you."

"I like you, too. You're really nice and you've been great to me since I've been here."

"You know what I mean. I don't go around kissing women."

"That's good to know." I stare out at the ocean. My heart would love to think that Brett and I could be together. But we wouldn't be together. We'd be separate. We'd communicate by phone, email, Skype and texting.

No touching.

Definitely no kissing.

How can love grow in a situation like that?

"Look at me." His voice is gentle.

He turns my face with his hand. I do love the way his gentle touch exudes power. But does it have the power to change the way I think?

"You are important to me," he continues. "I'm not sure a woman has ever been this important before."

"More important than Peru?"

His gaze cuts away briefly. "I've felt called to Peru for a long time. I feel that's where God wants me. And you can't compare a country to a person."

Even though my heart burst to life today, it doesn't mean I suddenly have the desire to travel to foreign countries.

I don't.

"You're going to inherit Antonio's millions," he says. "You're free to do whatever you want. There's nothing to stop you from coming with me."

An instant flashback to my teenage years floods my mind. I can hear my mom's voice as if she stood right here right now. *'You're doing great in your homeschooling. You have the opportunity to see many countries and experience what so many people only ever dream about. There's no reason why you can't continue to come with me.'*

My heart is sad and warm at the same time. I know I can feel the peace of God. But I have to remember that peace isn't an absence of conflict.

And in this case it's my heart's conflict.

"Actually there is something that's stopping me. I think it's time to live out my own dreams and quit riding coat tails on everyone else's."

IF I SEE ONE more pair of Jimmy Choo shoes I'm going to scream. I push aside the boxes in my closet looking for my flip-flops. My plain two-dollar and fifty cent flip-flops.

Of course my brain is probably not working at full capacity. My closet is filled with the scent of Brett. Yes, his shirt still hangs in the back, unwashed from the rainy night. He hasn't asked about it, and until he does it's staying right here.

At last I spot them. I shove my feet into them feeling more like myself than I have in a long time. Especially since my toes still look terrible.

I feel a sense of rejuvenation and renewal. Not just with the God feeling filling my heart, but with a clear picture of my future.

My calling.

My inspiration.

One I can nurture and grow and watch spring forth to life. And I think I know exactly what it is. I smile as ideas form in my mind.

I wiggle my toes feeling at home in my flip-flops. In my new vision. A feeling of joy I haven't experienced ever has taken over my heart.

In an underlying kind of way.

I'm still sad that a relationship with Brett won't work. Let's face it, he's gorgeous and loves God. A woman's dream man. But our dreams need to coincide and ours don't.

So.

But I can still hang out with him for the next two weeks. We still have money to spend and another lawyer's meeting to sit through. Then the very next day I'm headed to Atlanta.

I am driving the new SUV, though, and putting my car up for sale. Then I'm buying my dream Jaguar. That's for certain.

Because apparently money will be no object.

And I don't want to be here for Anastasia's wedding. Images of Brett walking her down the aisle fill my mind. She'll be so beautiful and Brett? Well, I'm sure the tuxedo will pale in comparison to his built-like-crazy body and handsome face.

And those green eyes.

I know they'll rock somebody's world.

But not mine. By the time I come back to Florida Brett will be safely in Peru, and Anastasia and Jimmy will be living in wedded bliss.

I give PS a kiss on the top of her head, resting for a moment in the sweet, content, sound of her purring before I go downstairs. Brett will be here in five minutes, and searching for my flip-flops had eaten into breakfast time.

But I do need a cup of coffee.

I barely take a sip when Brett enters the kitchen.

Moonlight, daylight, or light bulb generated light, it doesn't matter. Brett still looks amazing.

His standard jeans attire screams gorgeous.

"Ready?" he asks.

"Sure," I say. I sip a few more sips of coffee, trying not to burn my throat with the hot liquid, before dumping the rest down the drain and shoving the cup in the dishwasher.

We walk out of the front door. Brett stops next to one of the big lions and bends down, leaving something on the base of the cement statue. He stands.

"I told Ricky he could borrow my truck."

"I thought he had a key? That spare key?" Memories of his kisses fill my mind at the reminder of that night. Stuck in the rain. Awed by his kiss.

"He lost it. So I had another one made. His buddy is going to drop him by here in about an hour. He said he'd have the truck back by six."

"He's so lucky to have you." I refuse to let thoughts of Ricky and Brett surround me today. I can't help what is going to happen. Nothing I can say or do will make the hurt go away once Brett leaves.

"I'm going to give him my truck when I leave. He doesn't know it yet, so don't say anything. Don't tell Lauren either if you happen to talk to her."

Like a truck is going to make up for lack of presence. "I won't. My lips are sealed." And ever reminded of your kiss.

We reach my SUV. As customary, I hand Brett the keys. He pushes buttons and the doors unlock.

"It's the countdown to the last week of shopping," I say as he helps me into my SUV.

"One week from today and we'll never have to go into another store. At least we're almost on track with the spending. We're getting an early start so we can probably knock out tens of thousands of dollars before the stores close."

"Maybe even get ahead of the game. Cut these seven days down."

"Don't want to be around me?" He feigns hurt.

"I'm not even going to answer. We need to go to a sporting goods store. I'm taking up outdoor adventure when this is all over."

"You are?"

"Yep. I have a lot of things I want to do."

"Okay, then. We'll hit the biggest sporting goods store around."

As Brett drives, I think about my vision. I think about how it's going to change young people's lives.

I refuse to think about how much help I'll need.

God will provide.

I mentally cringe at how much I sound like my mom.

My mom.

It just now dawns on me that I'm supposed to pick her up at the airport. I pull out my phone and scroll to my calendar. My heart beats fast as I look through the days starting with May first. I let out a sigh as I see her flight comes in on Friday, May sixth at seven o'clock pm. I'll either need to leave in the middle of the night Thursday night, or head out after the reading of the will and spend the night somewhere along the way.

Knowing it's logistically possible for me to pick her up makes me feel good. If Aunt Venus picked Mom up, it would instantly put Mom on high-alert. All kinds of questions would be asked and I don't want Aunt Venus in that position.

I'll field this battle.

A slight bit of anticipation mixes with the trepidation I feel at what's going to go down when my mom finds out all that has happened since she left.

I wonder if she'll be sad at all at Antonio's passing.

I also wonder what it's like to love so hard, you spend the rest of your life running from it.

"OKAY. SO YOU weren't kidding when you said you were getting into outdoor sports," Brett says to me as we stand in line for the fifth time at the sporting goods store.

"No. I wasn't kidding. And I'm sorry we have to keep getting into line. That ten thousand dollar transaction limit is a pain."

"You're telling me. This is the last of it, though. But why do you have five soccer balls? Isn't that a little drastic?"

I shrug my shoulders. "Not really. They're all different."

"Oh," he says. "Okay."

His green eyes indicate I'm not fooling him one bit.

Several people in line behind us leave when they realize how long they were going to have to wait. The store manager became involved after I checked out for the second time, and arranged for a truck to deliver all the items I bought to the mansion next Tuesday morning.

"You're going to be one busy lady," the manager jokes as he rings up my items.

"I am and I'm looking forward to it."

"I'm sure you and your boyfriend are going to have a real nice time."

Brett and I look at each other, but neither of us says anything. Personally, I'd rather the manager think Brett is my boyfriend.

The manger's name tag says Caleb and he's not wearing a wedding ring. Since I caught him looking at me more than once, I'm content with what he's thinking.

After Brett pays, I confirm the delivery date and time. Brett and I walk out to the car, almost fifty thousand dollars lighter.

"That was awesome!" I say as he helps me into the truck.

"I can't believe you have a sudden interest in deer hunting. Something's up."

He shuts the door. At least I don't have to answer him.

"Where to?" he asks as the SUV's engine roars to life.

My stomach rumbles as if in answer to his question. "Lunch?"

"Well, since it's after four I think we better call it dinner."

"Really? I didn't realize we were in that store for so long. Time flies, huh?"

"Well, when you practically buy out the store, time flies."

I have my reasons, but none he's going to know about for a while.

Maybe never.

Because two weeks from today, I'll be back in Atlanta probably never to see Brett again.

At least not for a long time.

Brett pulls into the parking lot of a seafood buffet.

"I'm hungry. Is this place all right?" he asks.

"Sure."

"Before we go in," he says. "I wanted to ask you something."

My insides quiver ever so slightly at what his question might be. Surely it's not about me going to Peru. "Okay."

"Is there any way I can talk you into going to church with me tomorrow? It is Easter Sunday after all."

"Yeah. I'll go. That'll be great, actually. I'll be looking forward to it."

He sits there, apparently speechless.

"Surprised?" I ask.

"A little, but not totally."

"So you had a little faith in me, huh?"

"More than a little."

My phone starts buzzing in my purse. I pull it out and look at the caller ID. "Oh, it's Lauren," I say to Brett.

"Remember, nothing about the truck," he says.

I roll my eyes at him before answering my phone. "Hello?"

"Angelina. Ricky's gone."

Her voice sounds desperate which causes a slight blip in my heart pattern. "What do you mean?"

"I mean he texted me hours ago, but my phone was charging and I didn't see it until just now. It said he was at the airport and he'd be in touch with me later."

"Airport? What airport? Where was he going?"

"I don't know. I tried texting him back but he doesn't respond. I'm so worried. And the prom is Friday. Friday!"

Prom? My mind scrambles to figure out what she's more worried about. Ricky actually MIA or Ricky MIA for prom night. I turn to Brett. "Ricky's gone."

I repeat what Lauren said on the phone about Ricky being at the airport. I don't repeat her prom remarks.

"Does she know anything else?" Brett asks.

"Lauren, what other information do you have? Anything? Anything he's done recently that might have seemed strange to you?"

I hear her ragged breathing. It almost sounds like she's crying but I can't really tell. "I don't know. I can't think. I mean do you know how much money I've had to put out for this prom? Money I've worked really hard for. And now I might be sitting at home? I'm so upset."

"What's she saying?" Brett asks.

You really don't want to know, I think. I shake my head.

"Lauren. Try to calm down and think of anything that might have happened recently that will help us figure out where he might have gone and call me back. Okay?"

All I hear is sniffling and soft groaning, like a child would do. Well, she is a child, I guess. But we're dealing with a grown-up situation.

"I will," she says.

"Has she talked to Ricky's mother?" Brett asks.

I repeat the question to Lauren.

"No," she answers. "I called you first."

I shake my head no to Brett.

"We're on our way."

"Look, Lauren. We're headed over to Ricky's house now. If you hear anything from him, call us right away. Promise?"

"I will."

"Paula must be worried," Brett says as I shove my phone back into my purse.

"Could we be jumping to conclusions?" I ask. "Lauren said the text said he was at the airport. Could he be picking up a friend? Didn't you say he said he'd have your truck back by six? She hadn't even talked to Ricky's mom. It sounds weird to me."

Brett glances my way, a thoughtful expression on his face. "I guess it's a possibility. Let's just go check in with Paula. If she's home, that is."

We ride in silence. I'm contemplating Lauren's selfish attitude. Is she that concerned with the prom? Maybe I've misjudged her this whole time.

We pull in Ricky's driveway as his mother is coming out of the house. She glances at us before locking her door.

We meet her in the driveway next to her old, battered-looking car. She appears calm.

Maybe that's a good sign.

"Hi, Brett," she says. "Ricky's not here right now."

"I know. That's why we're here. This is my friend, Ann."

She holds out her hand, but not before glancing at her watch. "Hello," she says.

"Hi. It's Angelina." I shake her hand, noticing the rough feel of her fingers. This woman has not been pampered.

"Do you know where Ricky is?" Brett asks.

A puzzled look passes over Paula's face. "Well, he said he was borrowing your truck. I thought you knew."

"Yeah. I let him borrow the truck, but I didn't think about asking him what for. He's borrowed it before to do errands, so I thought that's what he was doing."

"Why the concern? Do you need your truck? Is he late?"

Once again she glances at her watch.

Now Brett and I exchange glances. I'm feeling like our visit is a bit awkward. What do we tell her? We had a hysterical call from Ricky's teenage girlfriend concerned she's going to miss the prom?

Oh, and Brett doesn't even know the prom part.

Brett takes a breath before he speaks. "Ricky's girlfriend Lauren called and said she had a text from him saying he was at the airport and he'd be in touch with her later. Do you know anything about that? Is he picking up somebody?"

"Airport? What airport?"

Brett shrugs. "We don't know. Lauren seemed a little upset. Like Ricky might have gone somewhere."

"Where would he go? Everyone he knows is here."

"I don't know," Brett says. "So he hasn't been acting weird or done anything different or out of the ordinary lately?"

Her eyes widen. "He did his laundry yesterday."

"Laundry?" Brett asks.

"Yes. I came home in between jobs and he was folding some clothes. I was stunned. This is a kid who will wear dirty clothes before he washes his own clothes. When I said something to him he told me it was time he started learning how to do some things on his own."

A chill passes over me. Foreboding sign number one.

Paula pulls out her phone. "Let me call my supervisor and tell her I'm going to be running late."

After a quick conversation she hangs up and motions for us to follow her in the house.

"If I lose my job over some nonsense this kid has pulled, I'm not going to be happy. The good Lord has blessed me with not one, but two jobs, and I can't afford to lose either one of them."

Her home is small, sparsely furnished, but spotless. The sunlight shines in from several windows making the demeanor of the house bright and cheerful.

"Let's check out his room. See where those clean, folded clothes are."

We follow her down a small hallway. She opens his bedroom door. She and Brett walk in, and I stand in the doorway. The room isn't big enough for all of us.

But like the rest of the house, it's neat and clean.

Paula somehow modestly bends down and looks under the twin bed. When she looks back at us, her expression is now worried. "His duffle bag is gone."

Slowly she rises to her feet and I see her swallowing. Her eyes are blinking fast, probably trying to hold back tears. My heart constricts at what she must be feeling.

"Okay," Brett says, breathing out slowly. "We're not going to panic. We're going to think rationally. Let's all think back to what he's been saying recently. What he's been doing."

Paula sits on the edge of the bed. She runs her hands through her short, black hair. "I don't understand. Why would he go anywhere? He has a good part-time job, a nice girl he's been going out with. He has you, me. He will have a high school diploma next month. And he lives for that soccer team he plays on."

I continue to stand in the doorway while Brett settles next to Paula. "Is there anything that's seemed to trouble him lately?"

She shakes her head. "I don't know." She sighs. "I'm rarely here when he's awake. I come in from work and he's asleep. I leave for work and he's asleep."

"Paula, you're doing the best you can to keep a roof over his head and food on the table. And he knows you're here for him."

She stands and opens his closet door. She flips past some hangers. "Some of his stuff is missing."

Her footsteps are silent as she walks to his small dresser then opens a drawer. "Yep. Gone, socks, boxers. Gone."

At that moment Brett and I lock gazes. It's then I notice an emptiness in his eyes I've never seen before.

Incredible

"HIS COMPUTER," Paula says as she stands. "I'll check his computer."

A desk is tucked into the corner of the room. A small flat screen, a keyboard and a mouse pad is all that will fit on the desk.

Paula turns the computer on. It takes a while for everything to load. But finally she pulls up the internet.

"Do you know his email password?" Brett asks.

"I do."

The sound of the clicking mouse and Paula's fingers flying across the keys fills the otherwise silent room. It's like we're all holding our breath in hopes that the email will reveal something to explain the missing duffle bag and clothes.

"I'll check the deleted email," Paula says.

My view of Paula is blocked as Brett is standing right behind her, but I hear the gasp the instant it escapes from her. "Peru?"

Peru! The word that has caused so much trouble in my life now is causing trouble in more lives.

"Peru?" I echo Paula. "What about Peru?"

Brett turns to me. "There's a flight confirmation for a one-way ticket to Peru."

"Isn't that where you are going?" Paula asks.

I don't answer as I know the question is posed to Brett.

"It is."

The tone of his voice says it all. Everything I've been trying to tell him and convey to him has become evident with those two words.

"According to the ticket the plane left Orlando at two-thirty this afternoon and has a layover in Atlanta until five twenty." Paula's voice sounds a little shaky as she speaks.

We all look at our watches. Even though I paid almost five thousand dollars for mine, it still doesn't show the time I want it to. It shows real time.

Five-thirty.

Brett pulls out his phone then starts pushing buttons.

The 'it's too late' phrase in my mind stays in my mind. I don't voice it out loud. Paula and I stare at Brett. He pulls the phone away from his ear shaking his head.

"Straight to voicemail."

This is the first time I've heard this tone in his voice. He sounds defeated. Dejected.

It breaks my heart. "Well, there's really only one solution."

Paula and Brett look at me. "What?" Brett asks.

"We go and find him."

"Of course," Brett says. "You ladies have your passports?"

"I don't have one," Paula says.

"I do." My heart starts beating like crazy as thoughts of being in Peru jumble through my mind. Peru? I never imagined going back there.

"Paula," Brett says, placing his hand on her shoulders. "You don't worry about anything. Ann and I will go. We'll go and bring him back."

"Thank you," she says, slipping from his grasp. She settles onto Ricky's bed. Silent tears run down her face.

I sit next to her. Words I don't want to say fly out of my mouth. "I promise it will be all right."

Somehow the word promise makes people feel better. I swore I wouldn't place myself in a situation where I would utter the untruthful word again.

But here I am. Giving hope when I can't guarantee the outcome.

It's called faith.

She wipes her eyes with the back of her hand. "I know. I can feel it in my heart. A peace. But I have so many questions."

I don't want to elaborate on my theory, which has to do with Ricky not wanting to be separated from Brett. I'll let Brett deal with this. Right now I just want to be supportive.

And if I'm truthful, I may have a few emotions to deal with myself.

INSTEAD OF spending Easter morning in church, we spend it driving to the Orlando airport. We were able to book the same tickets Ricky booked. Leaving Orlando at two-thirty, arriving in Atlanta for a short layover, then on to Lima, where we won't be arriving until eleven o'clock.

Brett was able to contact David Rojas Chavez and his wife, the couple Brett will be staying with for a while when he goes to Peru. Since we are coming in so late, David will meet us at the airport. A very nice gesture as it's an eight hour, not always serene, drive from Huancayo. We will stay at a hotel tonight and form a plan for the morning.

My heart saddens at the thought that Ricky will have already been in Peru over twenty-four hours at that point. There is no telling where he may be. The longer he goes without being found, the harder it will be to find him.

Quieter than usual, Brett seems to be going through the motions of what we have to do. As we settle into our seats for the trip to Lima, Brett shuts his eyes. Because of our last minute ticket purchase we weren't able to book seats next to each other, but once on the plane I convinced the guy sitting next to Brett to trade seats with me. Since Brett was all the way in the back row, it helped that my seat was close to the front.

I sigh. Brett's probably one of those people that can sleep on a plane. Not me. No matter how hard I try, my mind can never go to that place of complete rest on a plane.

Always a little nervous taking off, I clutch the armrests as the plane climbs into the air. Minutes later we are cruising. I opt out of the five-dollar headphones. The movies don't interest me.

"It's my fault, isn't it?"

Even though Brett's voice is low, it startles me. Partly because I thought he was sleeping, and partly because I don't want to answer him truthfully.

Because I do think it's his fault.

But I'm not the 'I told you so' type of gal. Instead I feel sad for him, and Ricky's mom. I feel irritated at Lauren. When she found out we were going to Peru to bring Ricky back she tried to make me promise we would be back by Friday. Brett quickly became clued in on the prom aspect, and he wasn't thrilled with her apparent selfishness.

Or maybe he was smacked with his own.

"I think Ricky's more attached than you think."

"I think I should have been paying more attention to what you've been saying."

Personally, I think so, too. But now's not the time to get into this type of discussion. "We just need to concentrate on finding him."

"You can say I told you so."

I smile. "I guess technically I could, but heart-wise I can't."

"Heart-wise?"

We're so close.

In proximity.

The air exudes his scent. The same scent that caresses me every time I step into my closet. His green eyes have darkened slightly from their usual color, which only adds a sense of vulnerability to his already gorgeous features.

The tired, anxious, worried state of my mind has me thinking of notions that can't last. Fleeting, momentary fixes, like his kiss, fill my thoughts.

A kiss that will take my mind off of this situation. When his lips leave mine though, the situation will still be the same. Ricky will still be in Peru. We still won't know where he is.

And Brett will still think it's his fault.

"Yeah. My heart doesn't want your heart to hurt."

He smiles. "That's nice of your heart."

I take my gaze off him and focus straight ahead. Maybe I'll be able to think more clearly.

"Honestly, though," he says. "I never saw this coming. I thought I knew exactly what I was doing and what was going down between Ricky and me."

"Look, there's been a lot going on. You had no idea Antonio was going to leave a will like he did. How were you supposed to know you'd be babysitting me and my debit card for a month? Then with closing your business, preparing for your move. That's a lot to deal with."

"But Ricky's a person. Man, I thought we had it all worked out. He didn't know it yet, but I was going to give him a ticket to Peru for graduation. I thought he might like to come for a visit before he started college."

I laugh. "He beat you to it."

"That he did." Then he laughs.

Our laughter, quiet as it is, seems to untie the knot hanging in the air. A whoosh of freshness sweeps over our part of the cabin. My body relaxes in the chair. I ride the air of lightness a bit too far and place my hand on Brett's.

His hand is warm. Immediately he pulls his hand from mine then gently grasps my fingers. Not being able to help myself, I turn my focus to him. To his face.

His eyes have returned to their normal warm green. His expression has relaxed and his lips are still kissable.

"We're going to find him," he says.

"I'm sure we will."

"With David's help it won't take long."

"And we can be back by Friday," I joke.

Brett's expression turns serious. "I couldn't believe how Lauren kept bringing that up. Like the prom is important."

"It is to her. Granted, it shouldn't be more important than finding Ricky, but trust me. You haven't been a seventeen year old girl before, either. Certain rationalities defy reason. And you know she has family issues, so this is probably a very big deal for her."

"I may not have ever been a seventeen year old girl, but certain rationalities defying reason have plagued me lately. Not of the prom kind, though."

I raise my eyebrows? "What exactly has been plaguing you?"

He looks at me. "Mainly thoughts of you."

Heart flutters skip across my chest at his words. But they are dangerous words. Words that have the impact to change lives. But he doesn't want his life to change, and my life can't change to a life that would be compatible to his.

Yes, very dangerous words.

"You need a redirection of thoughts."

"I think Ricky provided that. But I have to ask. Why did you so readily agree to go to church with me yesterday? I know we didn't end up there, but I actually thought you were happily on board with going."

"I was. And I'm sorry we didn't go. Easter is a very special day."

His expression falters. "You were only going because it was Easter?"

It doesn't surprise me his thoughts have drifted along those lines. The line that I was one of those people who only go to church on Easter and Christmas.

I might have turned into one of those people. Until a couple of days ago.

Settling into the uncomfortable seat, my heart comfortably settles into the new-found love I have found. Scripture in the book of Luke tells us the people were rejoicing and the Pharisees wanted Jesus to silence them. But Jesus told the Pharisees if the people didn't rejoice the stones would cry out. That's how I feel right now.

That's why I wanted to go to church Sunday.

Never mind it was Easter. The people would be worshipping.

My mom's insistence that you don't have to be in church to worship comes to mind. We can worship wherever we are with our thoughts, our hearts, our words.

Our love.

"Easter is a time of celebration," I say. "A lot of people go to church on Easter."

"You're right. They do." His voice has a sad tone to it now.

I can't let him know I've had a heart-change. He's already talking crazy about not being able to stop thinking of me. And I can't stop thinking about him.

Which scares me. Just like telling him about my love for Jesus scares me. If he knew, his mind would go places it doesn't need to go.

And I know what he doesn't. We will never be together.

Besides, we need to focus on Ricky and bringing him home. Clouding the conversation with more dead-end talks about Brett and me ever being together permanently won't do anyone any good.

THE RUSH OF the plane as we hit the runway always excites me. It means we've landed.

And being on the ground is very exciting.

De-boarding the plane takes a while. Then, even though we only have small overnight bags, the time it takes to go through customs is lengthy. We exit the secure area and start walking to meet David. I spot a man holding a sign that has HAMILTON written in bold, black letters.

"I think he's here for us," I say.

"Looks like it. Must be David."

We approach the man, juggling the items we carry as he greets us in a customary Peruvian greeting. His slight kiss on my cheek floods my mind with memories.

"Hello, Brett, Ana?" David asks.

"Yes. Hello."

This airport only brings back one memory. I remember the sadness in my mom's eyes as we boarded the plane that took us out of Peru. It's only now that I fully understand the depth of her sadness.

"Brett," David says. "To relieve your worries I want to tell you Ricky is at our house in Huancayo. He arrived this afternoon, long after I left to come to greet you. My wife, Anita, phoned me to let me know. I'm afraid the journey caused Ricky much stress and grief. Apparently his bus was held up, but no harm was done. He arrived safely to our home."

I can almost see Brett's relief as his mind processes the words of our host. I know I am relieved.

"The fact that he found you surprises me. The fact that he's stressed doesn't." Brett pulls out his phone. "I'm going to text his mother to let her know."

David lays his hand on Brett's. "Anita did that earlier. Ricky was concerned about his mom. We texted you as well."

Brett is still looking at his phone. "I see that now."

"I suggest we stay the night at a hotel not far from here. Then we can head to my home tomorrow morning to see your Ricky. I don't want Anita making the long drive here. It's too unpredictable. Are you hungry now? I know they don't serve anything substantial on the flight."

Brett looks at me. "I understand. I'm not hungry, I'm just tired. Ann?"

"No food for me. Just a bed."

"Come, then. Let's go."

It is dark as we head to the hotel, which helps the memories stay buried. There are street lights and buildings portraying a city. I know tomorrow will bring a sense of landscape and I wonder at the feelings it will evoke.

Am I ready to deal with them? What would Mom say if she knew I was here?

Are all these turns of events signs from God? I mean, just a short time ago I was unemployed, living in Atlanta dreaming about owning a pair of Jimmy Choo shoes. Now, here I am, in my old missionary stomping grounds of Peru, with a heart turned toward God, a runaway teenager, and a guy who has me thinking about love for the first time in a long time.

I certainly think about the way he kissed me.

We arrive at the hotel and are able to check in. Brett in one room, me in another and David Rojas Chavez in a third.

Brett walks me to my room.

"What a relief to know Ricky is safe," I say, standing in front of my door.

"Yeah. It's good to know. But we're going to have a come to Jesus talk tomorrow when I see him."

Leaning into my door, I try to keep as much distance from Brett as possible. Even after hours on a plane, he still looks good, and his closeness awakens my nerve endings that should be tired and unresponsive. "That phrase, come to Jesus. It always implies something so serious, yet coming to Jesus is really a joyful occasion."

"Joyful?"

"Isn't knowing Jesus joyful?"

"You're complicated, Ann." His weight shifts as he sets his duffle bag down, stirring the air.

Memories of that rainy night, standing against his truck flood my over-tired mind. Once again, his body is so close. And he thinks I'm complicated? "I disagree. I'm just a woman, in Peru, chasing an eighteen year old."

His finger traces my hairline. "I'm talking about Jesus, and you know it."

A warm sensation engulfs my face. His touch prevents me from thinking about anything but him. I grab his hand and pull it away from my face. "I don't know anything while you're doing that."

His fingers lock onto mine, not letting go. "We're here. Ricky's safe. Thank you for coming with me. Which I think you did because you've changed."

I twist my fingers out of his. "I think you're tired. See you in the morning, Mr. Hamilton."

I don't look at him as I unlock my door and step into my room. I kick the door shut with my foot wishing I wasn't so scared to share my 'heart change' with him.

But I'm not ready for the changes that might bring.

IT'S MORNING and I'm sure another sleepless night shows on my face and under my eyes. We grab a quick breakfast and coffee, and start the several hour journey to David's house.

I try to nod off during the drive, but between the switchbacks and possible armed-guard stops, I can't get comfortable or relaxed enough to shut my eyes for longer than a minute or two.

But after a couple of non-eventful, unscheduled stops, and not much interaction with Brett because of my backseat status, my weariness wins out. When I open my eyes we are stopped in front of what I assume is David and Anita's home, a modest cement dwelling, surrounded by a tall metal fence. Bars cover the windows, and I'm instantly taken back to my days in Tacna with my mom.

"I see Ricky isn't running out to greet us," Brett says, as we walk to the metal gate that encloses the house.

We enter the home. Ricky is sitting at the dining table. I can tell he's nervous, but glad to see us.

Or Brett, rather.

He probably doesn't care if I'm here or not.

Brett drops his duffle bag before embracing Ricky in a hug. As Ricky lifts his head off of Brett's shoulder, I see watery pools in those dark eyes of his. Of course, I keep that information to myself.

A woman, who I assume is David's wife, Anita, walks toward us, and greets us with the customary kiss on the cheek. I return the greeting, as does Brett, once he lets go of Ricky.

"You must be Brett Hamilton," she says. "And you?" She looks at me.

"Angelina Thomas. Thank you for opening up your home to us. I know it's rather unexpected."

"I'm Anita, David's wife. It's our pleasure," she says. "Our home is your home."

David motions for me to hand over my bag. "I'll take that for you. Brett?"

Brett gives his bag to David as well.

"You can freshen up right there." Anita motions to a small washroom.

"Thank you," I say.

"I hope you have appetites. I'm preparing a meal for us. It will be ready soon. Until then, relax and make yourself at home. I know you have a few things to discuss with this young man." She nods her head Ricky's way.

"Just a few. Have a seat," Brett says to Ricky.

Ricky slides into his seat at the table and Brett sits across from him.

"Is there anything I can help you with as far as the meal goes?" I ask Anita.

"No. Sit. I know you've had a hectic couple of days."

I sit next to Brett. Ricky gives me his 'really?' look. But hey, I've traveled a lot of miles to help find this kid, so he can get over it.

"What was this all about?" Brett asks. "What did you think to accomplish by hopping a plane to Peru?"

"Hey, man. This is where you're going to be living, right?"

"Yes."

"Well?"

"That doesn't answer my question."

Now Ricky gives Brett the look I thought reserved only for me. "I guess you're not as smart as I thought you were."

After speaking, Ricky lowers his eyes, his hands wrapped child-like around a glass of a fruity-looking water.

Brett straightens beside me. Like this realization of the things I've been trying to tell him have finally rooted into his being.

"Just because I'm here and you're there, doesn't mean things have to change."

"Are you serious?" Ricky asks.

"Logistics will change, of course." Brett's shoulders relax somewhat. "But we'll still be able to communicate. They have the internet here, you know. And phones. Many ways to stay in touch."

Brett's tone is stern, father-like. That's a tone I haven't heard before. I'm glad he's taking charge. Ricky needs an influence like Brett in his life.

"Everything is going to change when you leave."

Ricky sounds dejected. He in no way sounds like a young man who is a great soccer player, is ready to graduate high school and attend college, and has a really cute girl to take to the prom. Never mind he has a great mom who loves him.

Brett looks puzzled. "Things are going to change in your life, too. You're going to college, remember. That's a big change."

Brett's statement brings a range of emotions across Ricky's face. Moments pass and I'm starting to sense a little more tension.

"I know." Ricky's words are flat yet emotion-filled. "But I'm not going to college until August. Why can't your change wait until my change happens?"

Brett laughs. "Oh, my timeframe needs to be your timeframe?"

"Hey, if it works." Ricky takes a sip of his drink.

"I still have a few weeks left until I leave. We have plenty of time to hang out."

"If you're not out shopping with Ann. Angelina. Whatever she wants to be called. And you wanna know something else? Lauren keeps pressuring me about being in love like you guys are. I told her I don't want anything to do with love if it means you shut yourself off from everything and everyone else."

Love?

I can't believe Lauren is telling people her silly notions. I purposely keep my gaze from Brett's, although his intake of breath when Ricky made his statement didn't escape my notice. What kind of lies is Lauren filling Ricky's head with?

Lies?

Who am I kidding?

As incredible as it sounds, I am in love with Brett Hamilton.

Intentional

THE REALIZATION makes me sad beneath the joy.

I don't want Ricky to be bitter about something that will never be. Being in love doesn't change the basic facts.

"Ann and I aren't in love."

My heart dips. Even though I knew he didn't love me, something about him saying it out loud hurts.

I swallow hard, hoping Brett won't see how uncomfortable I am.

"Look," Brett says. "Life isn't easy all the time. We've talked about this before. You have to learn to adjust."

Ricky scowls. "I have an unusually high amount of adjusting to do in the next month. Everything's changing. Everything."

"As it's supposed to. These are the best times of your life."

"Yeah, well, they seem like the worst. I don't like change."

"Well, you better get to liking it. Change happens all the time."

Ricky slaps his hands on the table. "I have the answer." Ricky's voice suddenly has a happy tone to it. "I want to do missions. Right here, in Peru."

Brett shakes his head. "Go to college. Earn your degree, then we'll talk. There will be plenty of opportunities for you to do mission work right where you are until you graduate."

Ricky's happy face turns sour. He lowers his head a bit, and that hair hangs in his eyes.

Nothing more is said about missions, love, or lack of thereof.

MY STOMACH IS growling at the scents of the food being prepared. Anita tries to show me how to make the creamy yellow pepper sauce that's going over the chicken, but she's quick with her hands and her English. I'd need another lesson before I could even think about making this meal.

I smile, thinking how Brett told Ricky we were probably going to eat worms.

This meal is a far cry from worms. I manage to put a lettuce leaf on everyone's plate, which Anita tops with boiled potatoes. As we prepare each plate with the yummy lunch, I hear Brett, Ricky and David making small talk. We are about to sit down when there is a knock on the door.

David answers it. Even though my back is turned, I can tell it is someone he is familiar with. Friendly greetings and laughter float through the air as David encourages the visitor to come in and join us for the meal.

I hear introductions being made to Brett and Ricky. As I'm carrying one of the plates to the table I hear Brett's voice as the men round the corner into the dining area.

"Nice to meet you, Mr. Diaz."

I look into the eyes of Mr. Diaz, and the plate slips from my hand.

I now know how Lovey felt when she saw me.

A bit of scrambling happens as someone grabs a broom, someone else tosses me some towels, and I start cleaning up the mess I've created.

I can't quit apologizing. Anita keeps insisting that me dropping the plate isn't a big deal. Never mind we have another mouth to feed and one less plate of food.

Although I'm sure my appetite is gone. The guys think I'm clumsy. Mr. Diaz hasn't made the connection. There is no reason he should.

Maybe I should say I have a headache and ask to lie down.

Maybe you should quit running from your past.

My hand shakes slightly as I wipe the last bit of mess from the floor. I'm not sure if it's shaking because I'm now done having an excuse to avoid the men, or because I'm having to admit God's words have a truth about them.

Both options are no good.

Both options are bad for me.

Both options open my heart and soul up to a cleansing I'm not sure I'm ready for.

I slip into the washroom.

My hands brace against the bathroom sink while I try to pull myself together. I need to compose myself before sitting down at the table with a whole bunch of God.

And lost love.

When it comes to God nothing is safe. Everything is opened to a new realm of possibilities and responsibilities. People who think being a Christian is a boring life full of following rules have no clue. Being a Christian is like living life on a roller coaster, never knowing when the car is going to jump the track and steer itself onto another course.

Being a Christian is like waking up to a new adventure every day.

I say this because if God hadn't taken over my heart I'd skate by this whole Luis Diaz aspect without a thought. I might admit who my mom is. I might admit that I met Mr. Diaz long ago. But it wouldn't affect me.

Now, though, it's different. It's different because God doesn't accidentally do anything. God has a plan.

And God is very intentional.

So really, this whole Brett, Ricky, Peru, Mr. Diaz thing has gone too far for me to ignore. I'm smacked with the obvious.

God wants something from me, and that something has to do with all these people I've met and reconnected with.

Ann and I aren't in love.

Yes, I remember those words spoken just a short time ago.

I don't know what I was thinking falling in love with Brett. I suppose it was part of my plan, not God's.

See, herein is the struggle.

What God wants for us and what we want sometimes don't mesh. How do I stay strong and try to follow a path I'm not sure I even want to follow? How do I even know exactly what that path is?

A soft knock on the door is followed by Anita's voice. "Are you all right? Can I get you anything?"

Translated: How much longer are you going to be?

I smooth my hair and plaster on a smile before opening the door. "Here I am. Sorry I took so long."

Anita smiles. "It's quite okay. I, we, just wanted to make sure you were all right. Now, come. It's time to eat."

I follow her to the table. There is a place for me to sit right next to Brett.

Very close.

The table isn't made for six, so we squeeze in tight around its perimeter. Brett scoots back, stands and holds my chair for me. I notice his look of concern as we exchange glances.

Settled in, I reflect on how different it is being around him with a lot of people. I'm so used to us being alone, that the dynamics are different. Not bad, just different.

And realizing that I'm in love with Brett has changed the dynamics as much as knowing his love isn't returned.

Without warning I feel impulsive, and a streak of boldness washes over me. I decide to dive in and face whatever God has put in my path.

"Mr. Diaz," I begin. "I don't think you remember me, but my mom and I were in Tacna probably fifteen or sixteen years ago. Her name is Trixie Thomas. You and your staff were very instrumental in helping us while we were there."

Mr. Diaz sets his fork down, his gaze searching mine. "Trixie. And you are her daughter. Quiet, rebellious. I didn't remember your name being Angelina though."

"I went by Ann back then." Okay, this time last month I was going by Ann, but he doesn't need to know that.

"Ann, now that's a name hard to forget, huh?" He laughs as do the rest of the people at the table. Except me. Is he serious? Or is he mocking? He has no way of knowing my name issues, so he's probably serious.

"I prefer Angelina."

"It's a beautiful name. You are back in Peru now? To serve?"

"No. This is just a rescue mission." I look over at Ricky whose smirk doesn't fool anyone.

"I see. And Trixie, is she here?" Mr. Diaz looks hopeful and sad at the same time.

"She's not. She's in South America."

"You'll tell her I send my best?" he asks.

"I will." Years ago his best was a love for my mother that she couldn't return. Watching his heartbreak was the beginning of the end of my missionary journey. I would never burden him with that knowledge, though.

Mr. Diaz turns to Brett. "You, though. You are here to stay?"

Brett folds his napkin. "Not for a couple of weeks. I'm here on the rescue mission, too."

Ricky sighs loudly.

Brett pats Ricky's shoulder. "Ricky here has an interest in missions. I'm looking forward to working with him after he finishes college."

Even though he's biting his lower lip, Ricky can't help contain his smile.

My heart smiles, too. Ricky has something to look forward to. And the way Brett states it, I'm sure makes Ricky feel like he's grown up. Or at least almost grown up. Working with Brett must sound like a dream to Ricky.

I'm so glad God has put missions on the heart of some people. We each have our own special areas to do God's work. We can't all be missionaries.

So I wonder what God wants from me, putting me in this situation? Reconnecting with all these people and connecting with David and his wife. Pulsing the Peru feeling through my blood again.

Seeing the man whose love my mother couldn't return.

Ann and I aren't in love.

Realizing my love isn't returned.

Sadness, enthusiasm, spiritual awareness, and desire grip the air, surrounding all with the amazement of God, and who He is, and what He can work for His good.

I can't help wanting it to be for my good, too.

AFTER LUNCH, Luis Diaz leaves, but not before handing me a business card with his contact information. He gave one to Brett also, but I'm sure that was just a formality. I know what he wants me to do with my card.

I just don't know if I can do it.

I slip the card into my wallet, thankful I don't have to decide anything today.

David and Anita take us to the travel agency to book our flights back to Florida. Considering the time it takes to transfer money and drive back to the airport the soonest we could book a flight for is tomorrow night. The plane leaves at twelve-thirty a.m. and though we have a short lay-over in Atlanta, we'll be back in Orlando by twelve-thirty Wednesday afternoon.

The fact that these flights are costly is only helping my cause. Brett, I'm not too sure about. He and Ricky had a discussion about how Ricky would have to work to pay back the price of the ticket. Between paying for his passport and the one-way ticket to Peru, Ricky has almost drained his bank account.

"You're going to have to work all summer just to have a little spending money when you go to college. This was not a smart journey my friend," Brett tells him.

"Yeah, well, sometimes you have to do what you have to do."

"No, you did what you wanted to do. Big difference."

An awkward silence ensues. I'm battling my own demons regarding Brett's declaration, and I refuse to get into the middle of their battle.

It's only as we start our drive back to David's that I realize there will be two full days left to spend the money when we return to Florida.

My heart starts to race at the thought. I pull out my phone and quickly call up the spreadsheet knowing what it will say.

"We have to spend an outrageous amount of money after we return home."

I state the fact, talking to no one in particular. Both Brett and Ricky respond with "What?"

Then Brett says, "Oh."

"It's not like we can spend any money here. Customs would be a nightmare," I say.

"I agree."

"Don't forget about my quality time." Ricky's tone is factual yet fearful.

"Don't forget who's going to save your hide from your mama," Brett replies.

"Oh, yeah," Ricky says.

I continue to stare at the spreadsheet. A foreboding sensation slips through my body.

My inheritance suddenly isn't looking very promising.

Instincts

EXHAUSTED AFTER the night-flight in which no one slept, we drop Ricky off at home. Brett runs some interference for Ricky, but leaves him at the mercy of his mother who has taken the evening off work. Tired as he is, Ricky probably wishes he was scheduled to work that evening.

Brett pulls up to the mansion. "I know we have to spend more money, but I need some shut-eye. I'll be back in a couple of hours. Get some sleep."

"Don't worry," I say. "I'll probably fall asleep walking to the front door. See you later."

I'm too tired to be looking forward to seeing him again.

That's tired.

Plus my thoughts are jumbled between Peru, and God, and missions, and my mom. Seeing Mr. Diaz again opened the door to memories I wish had been left alone.

On auto-pilot, I open the front door. Grateful to see the stairs that will lead me to my bed, I put one foot on the bottom one, praying for the energy to place the other foot in front of it.

"Ann! What's going on?"

Anastasia's voice shrills through the air, piercing my foggy, void of sleep, brain. I turn toward her. "What?"

"Why did you go to Peru? Why didn't you tell anyone? You just left that note to feed your cat. We had no idea when you were coming back. And Jimmy called off the wedding. Called it off! All because you left."

Mind still in a haze, I drop my duffle bag, having trouble processing everything that came out of Anastasia's mouth. Peru, PS, Jimmy, the wedding. Calling off the wedding.

Calling off the wedding? All because of me?

"Wait," I say. "Did you say Jimmy called off the wedding? What would that have to do with me?" She can't seriously blame that on me. But as I look at her, her incensed gaze convinces me she does indeed hold me responsible.

"Do you see this?" She splays her left hand in front of my face, the fourth finger over void of any bling. "There's no ring here. He took the ring back."

Focusing my gaze on Anastasia I have to admit I've never seen her look this way. Her hair in a disheveled ponytail, black smudges under her eyes, clothes that don't match. "I'm sorry about the wedding, but I still can't make the connection between you having no ring on your finger and me going to Peru for a couple of days."

"Couple of days? Four days. You've been gone almost four full days."

I guess I'm more exhausted than I thought. "I'm here now," is all I can think to say. I also try to smile, but I'm not sure if it really happens.

"This is the worst thing," she says. "Mama and I have been on the phone, cancelling everything. Most of the deposits were non-refundable. I'm so upset."

The beautiful Anastasia seems to be crumbling before me. Calling upon any strength the Lord will give me, I breathe deep. Any animosity between us doesn't stop me from wanting to comfort her. I take a couple of steps and embrace her.

She stiffens, like she might back out of my arms, but she doesn't. Instead she rests her head on my shoulder and cries. Not sobbing hysterically crying, but a soft, tender cry which lends another depth I didn't know existed to my half-sister.

After a few moments she speaks softly.

"I think," she starts, her head still on my shoulder, her words drifting softly to my ears.

I wait. I know she'll keep speaking when she can.

"I think he was marrying me because I was going to inherit Antonio's money."

"What do you mean?" I ask.

She straightens, then wipes her eyes before placing her hand over her heart. "It appears he was marrying me for my inheritance."

I guess I'm totally sleep-deprived because this still isn't making much sense to me. "So why did he call the wedding off?"

"Seriously? You were already behind before you left. There's no way you can catch up now. No way. We aren't going to inherit anything."

I may be tired, but I guess we all have certain instincts that kick in when truly needed. "You haven't had a civil conversation with me since you kicked me out of your wedding. How do you know I'm behind regarding the spending?"

She holds her hands up, palms out. "Okay, I'll fess up. I looked at your spreadsheet a few times. When you were showering. When you weren't anywhere near that phone. I looked, okay? I had to know what was going on."

Her confession leaves me confused as to the true origin of her distraught state. What has caused the ever-beautiful, strong Anastasia to crumble? The fact she's no longer engaged or the thought that she might not inherit an apparently vast sum of money?

NIGHT HAS fallen at the mansion. Brett sits on the veranda, a laptop in front of him, the soft glow of the muted lamps casting shadows that add an almost sexy vibe to him.

As if he isn't sexy enough.

"How long have you been here and why didn't you wake me?" I ask.

Sleep and a shower have invigorated me, and I now feel an energy zinging through me that doesn't need to be zinging through me this late at night.

Because it's time to go to sleep.

But everything is off, nothing is making sense, and a part of me wants to go back to Peru where it was all simple for a day.

Really, did I just think that?

"I've been here for a couple of hours. I did go upstairs but you were sleeping so peacefully I didn't want to wake you. I know you needed to rest."

Sleeping peacefully?

Bits and pieces of the dream-dramas that kept me from sleeping soundly flit through my mind. Peru, Ricky, Anastasia, and most of all Brett. I dreamed he had walked Anastasia down the aisle and Jimmy wasn't there so Brett married her. Although uninvited I ran down the aisle yelling to stop the wedding. That I needed to be Brett's bride.

Thankful for the darkness hiding my blushing cheeks, I still turn slightly away from him, you know, in case he can see the blush.

"While I appreciate your consideration for my health, we really needed to shop this evening. We are so far behind in spending the money, and now we're really short on time."

Confident that the blush is gone, I settle into a chair across the table from him.

"We? Don't you mean you?"

Once again he's reiterating his distance from me.

Ann and I aren't in love.

How many ways can he say it?

"Have you talked with Anastasia?" I ask, desperate to change the subject from my woes to someone else's.

He looks over the top of his laptop. "Yes. I knew he would end up hurting her."

"Do you think she'll be okay? She was so distraught when I walked in the door she actually cried on my shoulder."

"Really? Tears? I guess she was at the angry stage by the time I showed up. She was yelling and saying things about Jimmy that weren't very nice."

"I can imagine. I'm sure I'd feel the same way. She said it was about the inheritance, but we, I, haven't failed yet. Doesn't it seem a little weird to you that he would call off the wedding now?"

"Jimmy has always seemed weird to me, so I guess this doesn't surprise me."

"She took good care of PS."

"What?"

"Anastasia. I had asked Lovey to feed PS and I guess she gave that duty to Anastasia, which had I known would have scared me, but it turned out okay."

"You asked Lovey to take care of your cat?"

"Yes. I know five people here. You, and you were with me. Ricky and he was missing. Lauren. I was mad at her. Which leaves Lovey and Anastasia."

"And Jimmy."

"No. I didn't count Jimmy. I don't know Jimmy."

"Agreed."

"In my opinion, Lovey was the lesser of the two evils."

"You're a trusting kind of lady."

I may not have been so trusting a couple of weeks ago. But God has a way of showing you perspectives you might not have seen before. "Right now I feel more restless than trusting."

"Restless?"

"It's all coming down in a couple of days. I mean it's like I've been in a spending kind of fog life for the past weeks, but now this is it. And then the reading of the will. After that, poof. It's gone. The whole thing. I wonder what will happen to the money if we don't inherit it?"

"Maybe it will go to a good charity."

Thoughts of all the sporting equipment I bought fill my mind.

The vision.

It can't stop here.

"I will spend that money."

"If you say so."

He doesn't mention we now have less than forty-eight hours.

IT'S NOON ON Friday. Brett and I have been on a marathon shopping spree and we've spent almost all the money.

Almost.

Every time we leave a store, I enter the total into the spread sheet, cringing as the total keeps creeping up.

And up.

I'm having a hard time swallowing, figuratively and literally. I want to tell Brett why I'm having so much trouble spending the last of this money, but he won't understand. He'll think I'm crazy.

He'll think I'm acting out of guilt. And I am. I admit it.

"This is it," I say as we stand in front of a jewelry store, feigning excitement. "We could reach the total in here."

"Let's do it," he says.

We enter the beautifully lit store. Like most of the jewelry stores we've been in there's a clean, sparkly vibe. So many different colors. I wander to the sapphire section.

"My mom's eyes are blue," I say, as I start to back away from the counter.

Brett stops me. "What's wrong, Ann."

"I can't do this." I turn to face Brett. "I called Ted's office this morning. I found out what will happen if I don't spend the money."

"What will happen?"

"If I don't spend the money, the estate goes to HOW. Hearts Of the World."

He shakes his head. "Your mother's mission organization. That's why you're hesitating."

Standing straight I look directly at him. "Yes."

"Don't play the martyr, Ann. You've been doing it for the last fifteen years. It's time to give up the role."

"I can't. It's all I know," I say, twisting away from him. The bell of the jewelry store rings as I push open the door, Brett right behind me.

My phone starts buzzing, indicating I have a call.

As soon as I see it's Lauren and I say hello, Brett's phone buzzes as well.

"Angelina. I need your help. Please?" Even through the phone lines I can tell Lauren is sniffling and sobbing as she speaks.

Ricky and Lauren were still on for prom. Lauren had sent me text after text apologizing for her seemingly selfish behavior regarding Ricky's disappearance and the prom.

Tonight.

With all that is on my mind today I had forgotten that Brett and I agreed to go to Lauren's house at six to take pictures.

"Lauren. What's wrong? Why are you crying?"

"This is the worst day of my life ever!"

I'm not the only one having a bad day.

I can barely make out the words between the hiccups and sobs, but her despair is evident. "What happened?"

"My mom is laid up in bed. She says she has a migraine, but I know she's hung over. My dad left without giving me the money to have my hair done. And, like it could be any worse, my dress is ruined."

Brett is mouthing the words 'what's going on' as he is still on the phone with Ricky.

I mouth the word 'everything' as Lauren keeps going on about how she had her dress hanging on her doorknob and her cat swatted it a few times leaving claw marks across the front, and how she had drained her checking account to buy the shoes to go with the dress and a boutonniere for Ricky so there was no way she can pay for her hair or a new dress.

Oh, and how her life was ruined.

I know exactly how she feels.

I glance at my watch. Two-twelve. "Lauren. I need you to do me a favor."

"What."

Her tone is flat.

"Dry your tears, wash your face and meet me in front of the coffee shop at the outdoor mall. I want to see you standing in front of me in thirty minutes. Do you hear me?"

"I can't—"

"You can and you will," I interrupt. "Bye."

"Hold on," Brett says into his phone. "What's going on? Ricky is saying that Lauren is freaking out because something happened to her dress and she's having hair issues. Are they still going?"

"Tell Ricky to be at Lauren's at whatever time she wanted him there. She'll be ready."

Brett shrugs his shoulders and relays the information to Ricky.

They end their conversation, and I tell Brett where we are meeting Lauren in thirty minutes.

"I don't think we have time for a Lauren-Ricky crisis. We're having our own."

"We have time. Let's go." I couldn't have planned a better scenario than this. I'm feeling a bit light-hearted now at my reprieve. Breathing is coming a little easier.

Because I know other things matter more than money. Things like being there for someone. Things like making someone feel important.

Letting someone know they are loved.

Irrevocable

AS BRETT AND I stand at the front entrance to the department store, it's not hard to spot Lauren as she walks through the parking lot. There's nothing hurried in her demeanor. Although she does glance up a couple of times, her gaze is focused downward.

She doesn't even notice the car that ignores the crosswalk pedestrian law and slams on their brakes at the last second. No, Lauren just keeps ambling across the pavement in obvious oblivion.

When she reaches us, I take my index finger and push her chin up. "Look at me," I say.

Her eyelids flit up. I'm faced with the saddest looking brown eyes I think I've ever seen. Adding to the sadness are watery pools, glistening before falling down her cheeks.

And the skin around her eyes is a little puffy.

Crying will do that to a girl.

She swipes the back of her hand across the right side of her cheek, while I handle the left side.

"Okay. This ends here. Once we walk into the store no more tears. Hear me?"

She sniffles. "I'll try."

"You'll do more than try. There's no reason why a girl should be weepy on prom day."

Her eyes widen and she holds her hands out, palms up. "Hello. I'm a girl with no dress, lousy hair, and no money. And I'm supposed to be happy because . . . ?"

"Because you're with people who care about you and are willing to help you out."

"Oh, like I'm Cinderella and you're my fairy godmother?"

"More like when you know God loves you, then you know how to love others. And right now, love looks like a dress, shoes, a make-up session and an updo."

Now I watch as Brett's eyes widen.

"Come on," I say, heading into the department store.

Brett's gaze says I really want to talk with you, but there is no time. We have less than three hours to get Lauren in shape for the prom.

I stop as we walk by the make-up counter. The girl in the white coat smiles and asks if I need any help.

"I don't, but this young lady does. Can we make an appointment for four-thirty to have her make-up done?"

"Certainly. What day."

"Today."

Her expression indicates I have a lot of gall, but her calendar says she's free at four-thirty.

"We'll see you then," I say.

"I don't have any money," Lauren says as we exit the department store into the big mall.

"Did I ask you if you had any money?"

Brett is walking next to me. "We need to talk."

"Later. We'll have all evening to talk."

"If we wait until tonight we'll be having a very different conversation."

"I'm aware of what I'm doing and what is going on." I look at Lauren. "Here we are. Let's buy a dress."

Lauren hesitates outside the dress shop.

"Come on," I say.

"I can't. That place is so expensive. I'll never be able to pay you back."

"Did I ask you to pay me back? No more thoughts of anything but you looking beautiful for tonight."

I grab her hand and we walk in. Colors, textures, glitz, and glamour line the racks and walls of the dress shop.

"Start looking for a dress. I'll be right back."

"I don't know where to begin."

"You better figure it out. We're on a time crunch here."

Leaving Lauren in the dress shop I spy a salon. I start walking knowing Brett will follow me.

"This is crazy, Ann," he says as we weave our way through the people.

"Helping someone in a time of need isn't crazy."

"Where did that comment about God's love come from a few minutes ago? Do you really believe that?"

We're standing outside the salon, people walk by oblivious to our situation. I take a deep breath. "Yes. I really believe that."

He smiles. "I knew you had changed."

"Only God can change a heart, and it seems like He changed mine."

I walk into the salon.

"How can I help you?"

A girl about Lauren's age stands behind the counter, her carefully made up face barely hinting at a smile. Her severely pulled back red hair makes her appear older than she is.

"I'm in a bind," I start. "I have a girl in that dress shop," I point to the shop, "whose prom is tonight. Due to unforeseen circumstances, let's say, she needs an updo now. As soon as she picks out her dress. Can you help me?"

"Now? Like I don't know. Everyone is like booked."

She glances behind her and I follow her lead. Two of the eight chairs are in use. I see a couple of ladies standing at the back talking.

I point to them. "They have appointments?"

"Yes. But their clients are like running late."

I click my fingernails on the glass counter. "Would the assurance of like a hundred dollar tip like encourage either one of those ladies to like do an updo for my friend?"

Pulled-back hair girl doesn't even blink at the mimicking of her speech pattern.

"Like, I'll go see."

"You do that."

She walks to the back leaving a hefty scent in her wake reminding me of Ricky's cologne overload. Nothing remotely close to Brett's gentle on the nose scent.

"A hundred dollar tip? Are you serious?" he asks.

"Sometimes you have to make things happen. Money talks."

"Now you're going to spend the last bit of money on someone else and doubly void the will."

The made-up pulled backed hair girl returns. One of the ladies that had been standing in the back is following her.

She holds out her hand. "Hi. I'm Kathy. I'd be happy to help you out with an emergency updo."

Kathy's smile immediately puts me at ease.

"Great. I'm going to grab Lauren, and we'll be right back. Give us ten to fifteen minutes?"

"Sure. I'll be waiting."

"Thanks."

I leave pulled-back hair girl and Kathy standing behind the counter and walk to the dress shop. Brett is right there beside me all the way.

"Did you hear what I said?" he asks.

"I heard."

"Why are you doing this? Inherit the money then donate it to HOW if that will ease your guilt."

I stop outside the dress shop. "Anastasia won't donate her half. If I inherit this money I would literally be stealing the money from my mom."

I see the wild look in his eyes, the are-you-crazy look on his face. "You would not. You can't keep living in the past. I know you don't want to be a missionary. As much as I want you to, I know it has to be your decision. But you can't keep living for your mother's approval, either."

"Approval? You think that's what this is all about?"

"I think you've been fighting her for a long time, and now you have an opportunity to gain her approval by donating a boatload of money to her mission organization."

His words cut deep, but not deep enough. "I'm not seeking her approval. I just want her to love me."

My admission causes me to blink rapidly, the squelching of tears causing my throat to hurt.

Brett embraces me. His strong arms engulf me as I lose the battle with my tears.

"I'm sorry," he says. "But no amount of money is going to buy what you're looking for."

I look at him, not caring about the tears falling down my cheeks. "I'll have to tell her that I knew. What will she think when she knows I spent all this money on unnecessary things?"

His thumbs brush my tears off my cheeks. "I know you have a plan, Ann. I don't know what it is, but I know you have one. Go with your instinct. Your gut. I can't promise you'll find what you're looking for regarding your mother, but I can promise God is already blessing what's in your heart."

He speaks the truth. I know he does. "I know it's crazy for me to think I can buy love. But it doesn't matter what I do, it isn't enough to keep her here."

"That doesn't mean she doesn't love you. It simply means she doesn't know how to show it."

She does love you.

Chills cover my arms while warmth flows through my body. I close my eyes. My mouth starts moving, the one hundred forty-seventh Psalm washing over me like a cleansing rain. *'He healeth the broken in heart, and bindeth up their wounds.'*

Thank you, Jesus.

I rest momentarily in the words given to me.

A shopping bag, carried by a young girl, bangs me in the leg.

"I'm sorry," she says, not making any eye contact.

"It's okay." I step away from Brett. From the safety of his arms. I'm on my own now.

Truly.

The healing has begun, but I have another situation to rectify. "What about Lauren?" I ask. "I have to pay for her dress, her hair. I promised."

Brett's green eyes sparkle. "I've got you covered. You can pay me back when you're a millionaire. Go in and buy yourself a really pretty, really expensive dress."

"And it will be finished."

"It will."

"And irrevocable." My breath hitches as I speak the words.

I enter the store with a smile on my face and peace in my heart.

Intrusion

I SIT IN TED'S office, along with Lovey and Brett and Anastasia.

I'm wearing the funeral dress I arrived with. Kind of a reminder of who I truly am.

I'm wearing the flip-flops as well.

After this visit I'm going back to the mansion, grabbing PS and starting home. I need to be at the Atlanta airport tomorrow night to pick up my mom.

Then that will lead into a very long overdue conversation.

One my already messed up heart is gravitating toward, while my mind is asking if we really have to go there.

Yes. We have to go there.

But that's tomorrow.

Today is today.

Ted walks in, causing me to sit a little straighter. Like it proves I'm really paying attention.

For a lawyer he sure is smiley. And he's humming. A catchy tune, no less. He opens a folder before focusing his gaze on me, then Anastasia. He turns toward me once more, his smile becoming bigger, before turning again toward Anastasia.

Brett's fingers tap the arm of the chair in what appears to be a furious beat. I only have a view of his profile, but his expression seems flat. Quite the contrast to Ted's.

"Hello, Brett, Angelina, Anastasia, and Lovey. Good morning to all of you."

I guess it's his big frame keeping him in his luxurious lawyer chair, because everything else about him seems to be floating.

I guess handing over a lot of money can give one a good feeling.

He taps the papers he's holding on the desk before clearing his throat.

A soft knock intervenes into his agenda. The wooden door opens slowly, slightly.

Ted has a puzzled expression on his face.

"Hello?" he asks. "Can I help you?"

"Yes. I believe so if you are Ted Reynolds."

If the blood could drain from my body it would be doing so now. That voice is the voice of my mom.

Trixie Thomas.

"I'm Ted Reynolds. But I'm afraid I'm in a meeting right now. I'm sorry Gretchen wasn't out there to greet you. Please step into the waiting area, and I'll be out shortly."

My mom chooses this moment to fully step into the room. She looks tiny, tanned, and tired. Her khaki skirt hangs loosely on her frame, while a brown pullover shows off her curves. Her scuffed beige utility sandals, as I call them, grace her feet. Her toes are ever unpolished, while her heels always look like they could use a good lotion.

A loud gasp resounds through the room.

Lovey.

I probably should stand to greet my mom who is taking in the scene in front of Ted's desk.

Her hand flies to her mouth as her gaze stops on Anastasia and Lovey.

I watch in slow motion as my mom crumbles to the ground.

At least I come by it honestly, I think, as Brett, Ted and I race to my mom, who has fainted.

MY MOM COMES to, mumbling about jet lag and lack of food. I see panic in her eyes, but keep that information to myself. If she wants to keep quiet about what really caused her to faint, that's her prerogative.

It's all very awkward.

She sits up, and insists she can stand.

Brett and I help her and lead her to the small love seat in the corner of the office.

"Here, drink this."

I turn to find Gretchen holding out a cup of water.

"Thank you," my mom says. She takes small sips of the water, while time seems to hang in the office.

Gretchen leaves, but Brett and I are still standing in front of my mom, like we are guarding her. Like if we part, the wide open space in front of her will be invaded.

As I glance over my shoulder, I realize the danger of that happening. Lovey is standing, arms at her side, at the ready. Anastasia is next to her, arm around her mom's shoulder. Maybe that's the only thing keeping Lovey standing still.

I think it's only a matter of time before we have some mama-drama happening.

Mama-drama and daughter drama if she stays here. I can't believe this is happening. My palms are sweaty. My heart races, and I can't seem to catch my breath.

I wonder how much she knows. How she found this office.

Found me in this office.

The silence needs to be broken, and she is my mom.

"Mom, are you okay?" I ask.

She takes another sip of the water. "As okay as I can be finding you cavorting with the enemy."

"Cavorting? Not hardly," I bend down and whisper. "They can't stand me. And what are you doing here? You aren't supposed to be home until late tomorrow night."

"I came home early to surprise you. Venus told me the whole story. Antonio's dead."

She has a sad look on her face. Or maybe she's just tired and I'm misreading her.

"Yes. He died in March."

"That's too bad."

She stands, and Brett and I back up. My mom looks around me before gently pushing me aside. She walks toward Lovey. "Did you marry him? Are you his widow?"

Lovey laughs a low, dramatic laugh. "No. Antonio was a single man when he died."

My mom stops in front of Lovey and Anastasia. "You must be Anastasia. You're beautiful. Just like my Ann."

"Thank you." Anastasia slowly removes her arm from her mother's shoulder, as if the lions are a little tamer now.

"Many years have passed, Trixie." Lovey's voice is stoic.

I'm holding my breath, no one is smiling, and the showdown, which has waited thirty years to take place, is about to start.

"They have. And with passing years comes maturity. Wisdom."

"Are you saying you don't want to claw my eyes out?" Lovey's expression remains flat. Serious.

Challenging.

Mom rubs her arms. "Ah. Those were my parting words to you, weren't they?"

"They were. And rightly deserved, I might add."

I release my breath, as an apparent truce of some sorts starts to take place.

"Not really. Looking back I realize I should have directed them toward Antonio, not you."

"I should have respected your vows," Lovey says.

"I should have respected yours."

As I suck in my breath I hear quiet gasps from around the room.

"Were *you* married to him, Mama?" Anastasia asks.

"Not legally. We said some vows one summer night out by the pool. Silly and childish."

"Not at the time," my mom says. "That summer they were real and had meaning."

Lovey tilts her head. "So he told you about us?"

"Only after the girls were born. It was his way of explaining why you were pregnant with his child."

"It was all very dramatic," Lovey says.

"It's amazing what one man's selfishness can accomplish. Our daughters grew up without their father. Without knowing each other."

"One man, Trixie? Weren't you acting selfishly when you swept Angelina away? He was a broken man after you left. That's why he never wanted Anastasia to know he was her father. He was afraid I'd eventually leave, too."

"I did what I needed to do to protect my daughter."

"I think you were protecting yourself."

My mom crosses her arms, a battle stance of sorts, I guess. "Think what you'd like to. I know my truth."

"He was about to make it all right, you know."

"Make it right?"

"Yes. He'd found Angelina and was on his way to Atlanta to meet her. Then he was going to tell Anastasia the truth. He was hoping his daughters would get to know him and each other. But he had a heart attack on that plane."

I look at Anastasia, who despite blinking furiously, has tears spilling from her eyes, which causes me to tear up.

Pressing my thumb against the corner of my eye, I try to stop my tears. As if stopping theses outward signs of emotion can stop the intrusion of the truth.

"Like I said earlier, with passing years comes maturity and wisdom," my mom says, her voice void of any emotion.

Lovey drapes her arm around Anastasia, pulling her close. "There, now, don't cry."

I look at my mom still standing alone, making no effort to move toward me. To comfort me in this crazy situation. If she knew the rest of the situation I can't imagine what she would say.

"Why don't we sit?" Ted says. "Mrs. Thomas, you are welcome to stay."

No! She can't stay!

Brett motions my mom to sit in the chair he was sitting in. Which would put her between us.

She shrugs before accepting his offer.

We all settle in our fancy chairs as Ted speaks.

"What a great occasion it is to bring you all together for the final reading of the will."

A different tension fills the room. Not the possible mama-drama tension from a few minutes ago. No, this is more like electric currents running through the air. Like a small intake of breath would implode the room.

I refuse to look at my mom. My legs and hands are shaking.

"Since all conditions have been met and carried out, the monies will be transferred via wire transfer. Angelina and Anastasia, I'll have papers for you to fill out and sign before you leave. Now, for the last part of the will. It's actually a letter written by Antonio."

I look at Anastasia. She stands and starts moving her chair closer to mine. I meet her half-way and we sit.

"All settled?" Ted asks.

"Yes," we say together, as Anastasia grabs my hand.

Dear Angelina and Anastasia.

If Ted is reading you this letter, it means I have passed away never telling you I was your father. For that I am sorry. There are so many things in my life I would have changed if I could, but knowing I have two beautiful grown women for daughters wouldn't be one of them. Angelina, I'm saddened we didn't get to know each other. Anastasia, I'm sorry I didn't know you like a daughter.

The stipulations of the will probably seem strange to everyone. But I'm a simple man, and I have a simple explanation. Angelina, I know you grew up in virtual poverty. Traveling the world, material items were few and far between. I'm figuring by now you are probably so tired of spending money, it's the last thing you want to do for a while. And I knew if there was something at stake, you would do well. So I put Anastasia's inheritance in your hands, knowing, if nothing else, you wouldn't fail her. And since Ted is reading this letter, you have done well. I'm a man of few words, so I apologize for the brevity of this letter. I also apologize for never truly being a father to both of you. Enjoy your inheritance, spend it wisely, leave some for your children, and most importantly, don't be like me. Go after what you want and love well.

With all my love, Antonio.

Anastasia and I are still holding hands. I know she's crying.

I'm sure she knows I'm crying.

I don't look at my mom. I'm too scared. Scared that I will see absolutely no emotion from her at all.

Sometime I'll have to tell her about the will and all its stipulations. And I'll have to tell her what would have happened had I not passed the test.

But that will have to wait.

Right now, I'm in mourning.

I WILL SAY it was a little awkward when we arrived at the mansion. Mom quickly said she needed to freshen up, so I showed her to a room upstairs. That was over twenty minutes ago. I can't help but think she's trying to pull herself together.

Even on the hottest, most tired days in the jungle, I had never seen my mom faint. I've seen her go days without real food. I've seen her still going and going after days without sleep.

She's always seemed so strong.

"There you are."

Yes, she must have refreshed. Her voice is strong and confident like usual.

I'm sitting on the veranda where all things seem to go down here at the mansion.

It's no longer *the* veranda. It's my veranda and my mansion.

Anastasia has inherited a house across the bay that no one even knew Antonio owned. She's apologized profusely about her behavior during her very short engagement.

We're friends again.

And Antonio's letter bonded us in a way we never expected.

"Hi, Mom."

She pauses, looking around, before she fully steps on the veranda. "So, this is yours, now?"

"It is," I say as she walks over to the table.

She pulls out a chair, settling into it like it's the last thing she wants to really do. "How ironic."

"I prefer to think of it as coming full circle. This is where we started out, isn't it?"

"The furnishings have changed and there's been quite a bit of updating, but yes, this is where we started out."

The more luxurious the surroundings are, the more my mom looks out of place. From her worn clothes to her short fingernails, she defies all this mansion stands for. "I understand why we didn't stay."

She brushes her bangs out of her eyes. "You can't possibly know the shame I felt. The humiliation and embarrassment of knowing your father not only fathered another child, but was still carrying on the relationship after he swore to me it was over."

Feeling on edge, I breathe deeply as if it will take away the tension. The tension caused by knowing I am going to fail my mom, just like Antonio did. "I agree it was a complicated hot mess. There's no way anyone can say what they would do in that position."

"You're right. So what about you? What are you going to do in your position?"

"What position?"

"With this, of course." She sweeps her hand across the veranda. "This house. The money. The stuff you had to buy to inherit all this."

God, could you have given me a more perfect segue? "There's more."

Mom shakes her head. "More?"

Part of me wants to hide like a coward while delivering the news. But another part, a stronger, new part, knows I need to face her, literally. "You know from being in the meeting this morning that I had to spend a million dollars rather quickly to inherit Antonio's estate. For me and Anastasia. What you don't know is that if I had failed, Antonio's estate would have been given to a charity. And the organization was—"

"HOW. I know."

Relief mixes with anxiety so I'm not sure of the best way to react. "You knew?"

She nods her head. "I've had a copy of that will since you were an infant."

Scooting my chair back, I stand. "What? And you never told me?"

Her rough hand pats the table. "Ann, sit down. Who knew Antonio had a bad heart and would die at such a young age? I thought I had years to broach the subject. And who knew he would add the stipulation regarding that handsome accountant having to monitor your every purchase. Antonio was much too romantic for his own good."

I sit, but only on the edge of my seat. I stare at her, trying to reconcile what she has just told me. "You have no idea how I've struggled with this."

"You spent the money."

I nod my head, my lip the recipient of my teeth causing pain to make sure this is all real and not some crazy dream I'm going to wake from. "I did."

"I suppose now you won't want to work. You'll employ some help here and let them cook for you and wait on you. Oh, and I forgot, you can tan by the pool all day long. I see you've already been partaking of that activity."

"I thought you would be upset. Because I spent the money, your mission doesn't receive the money."

"I'm not worried about HOW. They will come along fine without more of Antonio's money."

"More?"

"He's been donating for years. And if you want to donate money, they'll be fine with it. I'm worried about you. What all this will do to you."

I want to talk to her about my change, about Jesus, but it doesn't seem like the right time. To blurt out 'I've found Jesus and I'm going to be fine and make smart decisions' will sound like I'm trying to make excuses for keeping the money and the house. "I'm still your daughter. Nothing is going to change."

She stands. "That's what I was afraid of."

Talk about ironic? Who knew her biggest fear and mine were the same.

Her sandals make no sound as she walks away. My gaze follows her until she disappears up the stairs.

I continue to sit on the veranda, the coming nightfall a source of comfort for the place my mind is right now. My mom and I have a lot of healing to do.

The ding-dong of the security system invades my thoughts. Not being able to help myself I smile, knowing Brett will be walking in here any second.

But after a few seconds I still don't see Brett. I don't see anybody. But I do hear a car's engine roar to life.

I run to the front door in time to see my mom's rental car pulling out of the circular drive onto the street.

She's gone again.

Without me.

Ingrained

I'M STILL STANDING at the front door when I see Brett's truck pull up.

"Was that your mother I passed on the street?" he asks as he walks toward me.

"It was. She just left."

"Just left as in just now left? Or just left as in she just left and you didn't know?"

"She didn't even say goodbye."

"Maybe she just went for a drive."

That's what I was afraid of.

"I don't think so," I say, recalling her words mere minutes before she left. We still have so much to talk about. So much to resolve. I guess she's a runner. Running from her problems rather than staying and facing them.

"Are you okay?" he asks, genuine concern in his expression.

"Yes. I'll be okay. I'm used to it, remember?"

"Nobody should be used to that," he says walking toward the living room.

I follow. The veranda doors are open wide, the breeze blowing the ocean-scented air into the room. "I want to thank you for everything," I say.

He leans against one of the doorframes to the veranda. His hair blows softly while my heart does crazy things. "I didn't do anything, really."

"You saved me from myself." I sit on the arm of the couch. My couch.

"Saved you from Stace's wrath." He smiles.

I love seeing him smile. "Guess what? My mom knew. She's known about the will for years."

Concern etches his face. I know he feels for me. "Do you think she'll come around?"

"Maybe. If she quits running long enough to have a conversation. I believe you. I believe she doesn't know how to show love."

Speaking of love, he looks so good standing in the doorway.

Ann and I aren't in love.

Every time I try to think of him with my heart, the words he spoke in Peru replay in my mind. They haunt me with the finality of what we'll never be.

He pushes off the doorframe, his walk toward me slow and deliberate. At least that's how I see it. He may just be emotionally spent as well.

"I hope this isn't a case of like-mother-like-daughter. Do you know how to show love, Ann?"

He stops in front of me, his whispered words carried on the wind.

I stand. "I think I do," I say, knowing my words are risky.

"I'd stay if you'd ask me to."

With those words, he places his hands on my shoulders. His touch is gentle, but what he is saying weighs down my heart.

Visions of living a life I didn't want to live, surface. There is no way I'd ask him to give up his dream. It's what his father and mother did. It's what I did for my mom for so long. I know the damage that will cause. "I don't want you to stay," I say.

His gaze never leaves mine, but his eyes sadden. "Then I guess this is goodbye."

He lowers his head, then brushes my lips with his. My eyes close while my heart officially breaks at the touch of his lips on mine. I swear they would cry if they could.

His kiss is brief, a total contrast to the long-term destruction he's caused my heart.

I feel him walk away and purposefully don't open my eyes. My tongue lightly traces where his lips touched mine as if the gesture will seal the tingling sensation there forever.

Foolish.

It's only when I hear the door close that I realize I've been holding my breath.

I open my eyes and breathe.

I stare down at my funeral dress thinking how appropriate it was for me to wear this today.

Antonio, my mom, then Brett.

Inheriting millions can't replace what I've lost.

Soft sounds of celebratory music float into the room from downstairs. Lovey and Anastasia are having a packing party. They can't wait to move into their own mansion.

The absurdity of it all hits me. I need to leave.

I make my way up the stairs. Passing by all the shopping bags still sitting on the floor, I call for PS.

When I don't hear a response, I head into the closet. There she is, curled up in her favorite corner.

I turn around, spying the backpack I arrived here with. I'm already wearing the dress and the flip-flops. It doesn't take me long to locate the other items I brought with me and shove them in the backpack. I fling it on the bed and grab PS's carrier, then scoop her up and place her in it.

She meows softly, and I apologize to her.

My keys and my purse are in the living room.

Taking one last glance into the closet, past tens of thousands of dollars worth of clothes I always thought I wanted, I spy it.

His shirt.

Still hanging in the corner.

Slowly I walk to it. I slip it off the hanger then press the dark material to my cheek, his scent a gentle reminder as to why my heart is aching so.

He'd forgotten about his shirt, just like he'll forget about me.

I fold this bit of Brett carefully, as if it has feelings.

The shirt may not have feelings, but it evokes feelings in me that I'll always remember. Feelings that are ingrained in my spirit, my heart.

I walk to the bed, unzip my backpack, then place the shirt on top of my things. I look around the room at all I'm leaving behind.

Without regret, I zip the backpack closed, knowing I'm leaving with what is important.

A little piece of Brett and a whole lot of Jesus.

Insight

I OPEN THE door to my condo, relieved to be home. I drove without stopping for the night. I'm exhausted, mentally and physically.

My bed has never looked so inviting.

I let PS out of her cage. She immediately runs and jumps on the bed.

Walking like a dazed robot, I strip off the funeral dress and shower. After putting on a comfy pair of pajamas, I slide underneath my covers, my pillow feeling strangely foreign after sleeping on the pillow at the mansion for so long.

The mansion.

My mansion.

Thoughts of what I'm going to do with it flutter briefly in my mind. I thought for certain I'd be able to fall right to sleep, but my mind doesn't seem to want to shut off.

The mansion. Anastasia. Brett.

Brett.

Forcing my exhausted body out of the bed, I walk to the backpack I left sitting inside the front door.

I set it on the couch then unzip it.

There is it. His shirt.

Feeling a little weird, but not caring, I take the shirt with me and walk back to the bed.

I place the shirt on the pillow next to me. Just so it's close. The Brett scent comfortably settles in around me. Longing and sadness fill my heart. Why couldn't he be a normal guy and keep his normal CPA job?

Why did he have to have a heart for foreign soil?

Why did I have to fall in love with him?

PS comes and curls up next to me, like she senses my broken heart. I run my hand over her soft fur, her purring a sign of her contentment.

I don't think I'll be purring for quite a while.

I WAKE UP late early Saturday afternoon and start rushing around. It's only after two cups of coffee, showering and dressing I realize I was only rushing because of the late hour.

I have no plans. Nowhere to go. Nothing to do, per say.

The urge to see Aunt Venus is strong, but I know Mom will be there.

And I'm not ready for that conversation yet.

I'm surprised and anxious when I hear a knocking on my door. Has my mom come to not show her love again? Taking advantage of the peephole, I look out.

I brace the doorframe. Even through the distorted peephole view, Anastasia is still beautiful.

And Lovey is still stoic.

Taking a deep breath, with shaky hands and a somewhat relieved heart that it isn't my mom, I unhook the safety chain and open the door.

"Hi." Anastasia's tone is hesitant.

"Hi. Come on in."

I step aside and Anastasia and Lovey walk in.

"I hope you don't mind this impromptu visit."

"No, I don't mind, but I am surprised to see both of you here."

They laugh, but Lovey's laugh is louder.

"I know you mean, me," she says.

I guess I could lie and deny it, but it's the truth. Lovey's presence here does surprise me. I wonder at her agenda.

Anastasia's too, for that matter.

"Well," Anastasia starts, "Now that I have lots of cash, we decided to fly up here and see you since you left without saying goodbye. We have a couple of rooms at the Ritz on Peachtree Street. We'd love to take you out to dinner."

"As much as I'd like to believe you came all the way here to take me out to dinner, I think there's a little more to this visit."

An awkward silence hangs in the air.

"Why don't you guys have a seat," I say, pointing to the couch. "Can I get you something to drink?"

"No, we actually had a little drink in the limo on the way here."

I sit in my desk chair as they sit on the small couch. "You took a limo here?"

"We did. Why not?" Anastasia asks.

"No reason," I answer, wondering how long Anastasia's money is going to last. "I would have come to the Ritz if you had called me."

"Oh, it was much more fun to surprise you."

I wonder at her good mood. I guess her broken engagement pales in comparison to inheriting a vast sum of money.

"I have to admit I'm surprised." And a bit disappointed, but I won't tell them that.

I won't tell them a part of me was hoping it was Brett at the door. Not that I would have known what to do with him. Nothing has changed between us.

We haven't talked since I left.

Lovey looks uncomfortable sitting on my couch. Her straight-back, kind of regal body language contrasts with my cushy couch. I bet my new furniture, that hasn't arrived yet, is more to Lovey's taste.

As if watching her trying to get comfortable isn't uncomfortable enough, I spy PS out of the corner of my eye, and before I can say anything, she jumps on Lovey's lap.

"Oh! Scoot! Now!"

Anastasia reaches over, sweeping PS up into her arms, saving Lovey from her cat dilemma. "Mama. It's just a cat. She won't hurt you."

PS seems quite taken with the attention Anastasia is bestowing on her, while Lovey is meticulously trying to pick the cat hairs off of her gray slacks.

Anastasia kisses the top of PS's head. Then she sets her on the floor before looking at me.

"We wanted to say thank you, Sis. Thank you for working hard to spend the money. We want to do something with the money, some of the money, to help people. We're just not sure what right now, but we'll think of something."

Now I'm really surprised. I guess money can change people, and it doesn't always have to be for the worse. "I'm glad we're friends again. Sisters again."

Anastasia stands. "That's the best part, isn't it? Can I have a hug?"

We hug. A real, sisterly hug. It feels good.

"You are coming back to Florida, aren't you?" she asks as we end our hug.

"Eventually. I'm not sure when, though. I have a lot of things to figure out."

How to mend my broken heart being one of them.

And putting my plan into play another one.

Visions of all the items I purchased come into my mind. The sporting equipment, the electronics. Adrenaline rushes through me and I grab Anastasia's hands. "You said you wanted to help people, well I need your help."

"My help?" Anastasia asks.

"Yes. I bought a lot of items from the sporting goods store. Items that can be donated or sold. I'm not sure of the best way to go, but I was thinking we could rent a warehouse. Maybe have a store where people can purchase items really inexpensively and the proceeds can go to an organization. Like the one Brett went through to be a big brother to Ricky."

Anastasia pulls her hands from mine then clasps her's together. She has a wildly excited look about her. "We? I love the sound of that. And what if we add another aspect. We could have a little spa. We can do pedicures, manicures. Maybe hire somebody to do facials?"

"Can I be the first customer?" I ask, looking down at my feet, still in need of a pedicure.

"You'll be the before and after ad," Anastasia says.

A knock on my door silences our laughter.

"Excuse me," I say, walking to the door.

Once again I look out the peephole. This time I have no illusions of it being Brett.

And I'm not disappointed.

A distorted image of my mom comes into view.

Great.

Another showdown.

"Hi," I say to my mom. "Come on in."

She smiles timidly, then steps in. "I was driving by and saw what looked like that gigantic SUV of yours. So I pulled in and looked in the passenger seat. I saw PS's bed on the floorboard, so I knew you were home."

"I'm glad you did," I say.

I see her eyes widen and I know she's spotted Lovey and Anastasia.

"Oh, I had no idea you had company. I'll come back another time."

She places her hand on the door.

"Trixie. Wait. Don't leave."

Lovey's voice rings through my condo. If it is sending chills up my spine, I can't imagine what it's doing to my mom.

My mom's hand stays on the doorknob. Nobody moves. Time seems to have stopped. My heart hammers at wondering what Lovey wants to say to my mom.

Will my mom turn the knob and leave, running once again?

I watch as she slowly turns the knob and takes a step towards the door.

Taking a couple of quick steps, I place my hand on her shoulder. "Mom. Please don't go. Please don't run from this."

Her hand drops from the doorknob. She shrugs my hand off her shoulder and turns. "What is it you want from me, Lovey?"

Lovey fingers a necklace she is wearing. A beautiful, delicate-looking topaz ring hangs from it. "This is the ring Antonio gave me the night by the pool when we said our vows. He told me the brilliant stone matched my eyes. Have you ever heard such nonsense?"

My mom walks to Lovey and I scoot close to Anastasia. She grabs my hand and we watch together as my mom briefly and quickly hugs Lovey. Then my mom steps back, clasping her hands together. "Actually yes. I have heard such nonsense. From his lips as well. Only my ring was blue, the color of the beautiful skies and my equally beautiful eyes. Or so I was told by Antonio."

She opens her purse and pulls out a small box. Lifting the lid, she reveals a sparkling blue-stoned ring sitting regally on white velvet.

Lovey unhooks her necklace. They exchange rings and smile.

"Before you came in the girls were talking about opening a store where people could buy discounted items and the profits be given to organizations that are giving back to the community," Lovey says.

"Very nice. Is this store going to sell jewelry?" My mom asks.

"I think it might. Especially if we have some exquisite pieces to donate."

"Aquamarines and topazes are very nice stones. Might bring a nice price, even discounted. What do you think?" My mom gazes at Lovey.

"I think great minds think alike. Here, Anastasia," Lovey hands Anastasia her ring.

My mom in turn hands me her ring. "Your first items to sell. How does it feel?"

AFTER A LITTLE more planning, Lovey and Anastasia leave. The door clicks shut as if announcing it's now time for my mom and me to chat.

She sits on the couch and pats the spot next to her. "Sit with me."

I do.

"There's so much to explain, I really don't know where to start."

"How about the beginning? Thirty years ago?"

She takes my hand in hers, a totally foreign thing for her to do. My skin prickles as I'm not used to touches from my mom. Gestures like this are reserved for the needy and wanting.

Which is me right now. I smile at the irony of it.

"I've always loved Jesus. Ever since I can remember. When I left with the group that summer I was eighteen, I expected the trip to be like the others. I had no idea how my life would change."

"So that's when you met Antonio?" I don't think I'll ever refer to him as my father, or dad. It somehow doesn't seem right. Even after the letter.

"It is."

Her smile and dreamy eyes remind me of how I must look when I think of Brett.

"He was a little older than me, extremely handsome, and I thought he was the most kind and caring person I'd ever met."

"So he was helping with the mission?"

"No." She laughs. "I thought he was at first. But basically we met in a parking lot."

I sit back. "A parking lot?"

"Yes. We had parked the bus in a big parking lot. The people we had connected with in Florida were there to pick us up in cars to take us to our destination. Antonio was one of the drivers. What I didn't realize then was that he was a fill-in. Someone had cancelled out at the last minute, and since they were friends with Antonio they asked him to come and take a few of us to the mission site. So he did."

"But he wasn't part of the group."

"No. I sat in the front with him while he drove us to where we were staying. There were three others in the back seat carrying on their own conversation, so Antonio and I had our own. It was about a thirty-minute drive."

"What happened after that? Did he join the team?"

She laughs. "No. But he did know where I was staying. I'd come back to the hotel to find flowers in the room. Or chocolates. One time there was a bottle of champagne. I thought my roomie was going to lose it.

"I ended up going out with him just to tell him he had to quit doing those things. But Antonio was a very persuasive man. One non-date turned into lots of real dates, and when that bus pulled out of the parking lot I was waving goodbye to my friends while I stood next to Antonio. I still remember the feel of his arm on my shoulder. So possessive. Which at the time I thought was romantic. If only I'd known that it was really a weight."

I'd never seen this side of Mom before. This vulnerability. This rawness of feelings. I don't even know what to say.

"I quickly found a job, rented an apartment, which I broke the lease on two months later when I found out I was pregnant."

She pulls her hand away from mine and stands. She crosses the room to walk to the windows. Pulling the blinds up she looks to the street. Like it will help her tell the next part of the story.

"We both loved you from the start, Ann. We did. There was never any talk about anything but getting married and being parents to you. Which we did right away. Marry, that is. A quiet, small ceremony in that gazebo in the cul-de-sac in front of his house. But it was beautiful. And I never stopped loving Jesus. I just thought for a while He didn't love me anymore."

I stand and walk over to her. "Why would you think that?"

She shrugs. "Guilt. Shame. Antonio wasn't a big church goer, so I got out of the Word. I made Antonio my world. Big mistake. Especially when my world was being worldly with Lovey."

"When did you find out?"

"Not until I was in the hospital giving birth to you. The day of my biggest joy and my biggest sorrow. When that nurse came in and told Antonio Lovey was about to give birth and he was needed, the look in his eyes gave him away."

She laughs. "He had previously told me the gardener had gotten her pregnant. I was gullible and naïve, believing him. Then when we were checking into the hospital so was she. Something in my gut stirred then, but I was so excited and scared about your birth I brushed it off."

"What was it about his eyes?" I ask.

"I can't explain it, really. I just knew. And he knew that I knew."

"Awkward."

"Very. He left and the nurse bustled about me like she hadn't said words that shattered my world. I think holding you was the only thing that kept me sane at that moment."

A warmness seeps through me. "I'm glad I could help."

She braces her hand on the window frame. "He promised me, while he was holding you, that it was over with Lovey. And again I believed him."

I honestly have never seen my mom cry. Her quivery voice gives me the hint that might change. Soon. I don't know what to say. This is her story.

She lets go of the window frame and turns. She leans against the frame and crosses her arms. "But when I realized he had lied to me, I knew I had to leave. I couldn't put you through the kind of trauma a life with Antonio would have been."

"Look at the drama he's caused during his death. It would have been twice as bad in life, I'm sure."

"Here we are," she says. "Thirty years later, and here we are. You the recipient of Antonio's millions."

"Half recipient. Don't forget Anastasia."

"How could I? She looks just like her mother."

"They're both beautiful."

"Like you. I think that Brett Hamilton finds you beautiful as well."

"Mom, please." PS rubs against my leg and I pick her up, her purring a comfort to me.

"What's his story?"

I laugh. "Ironically, he's a CPA turned missionary. He's leaving in a couple of days for Peru."

"Peru?" she asks.

"Yes." Still holding PS, I walk to where my purse hangs by the door. My hand shakes slightly as I pull out the business card. I have no idea how this will be received.

"It's a long story, one I'll tell you later, but I ran into an old friend. He asked me to give you his best. And this card."

Even though Mr. Diaz didn't specifically state I was to give my mom his card, it certainly was implied. So I stand in front of my mom and hand her the card.

She blinks rapidly as she stares at the card. "Where did you—"

"It doesn't matter," I say. "He wanted you to have it."

"Very ironic," she says, her eyes now taking on a teary sparkle I haven't seen in a while. "Back to you and that CPA. You love him, don't you?"

I nuzzle PS. "I'm not sure."

"I suspect you do. I also suspect you are throwing away true love because you resent what I did."

My body chills, even with PS's warmth. "Mom. It's not that. I don't want to be a missionary."

"Quit thinking about what you don't want and focus on what you do want."

More chills. Silence. My small condo seems to be shrinking by the second.

"What do you want?" she asks.

She leans forward, and for the first time I realize I'm scared that she might actually show affection. I'm so glad I'm holding PS. "Always what I can't have."

She gives me a puzzled look. Total Trixie-style. "What you can't have?" she asks.

"Yes. I wanted a mom who would be home with me. I wanted a father that I'll now never know."

"I'm sorry. I may not have made the best decisions, Ann. I apologize."

She brushes the card across her fingers.

"My name is Angelina. You even changed my name."

My words seem to take a toll on her. She steps away from me to sit on the couch. Her shoulders slump, a look I'm only used to seeing in the midst of true crisis. Famines and poverty-type crises. Not a mom, daughter crises.

"For my sanity I had to. I couldn't bear it if you knew him. Knew that life. I couldn't lose you, too."

Me knees want to pool as I'm struck with God-given insight into her world. I breathe deep to stand straight as her life hits me, and I say what needs to be said. "I'm not Antonio, mom. I do love you. I will always love you."

I set PS on the floor. I don't think a group hug is what mom needs right now. Sitting next to her on the couch, I embrace her. She stiffens and hesitates, but only for a moment.

Her arms wrap around me with everything she's been holding in over the years.

"Like Antonio said, don't be like him. Don't be like me," she says, her voice soft, yet loud in my ear. "Love well, Ann. Go after what you want."

Ann.

Who I am and always will be.

"I will, Mom. I promise."

She starts singing softly. "Lord our Lord, how excellent is thy name..."

The Psalm touches me as does her voice. "Lord our Lord ..." I start and she joins me in song.

And in heart.

In Love

THE ONLY THING I am sure about is that I need to talk to Brett before he leaves.

Since I am a woman of means, now, I book a ticket, the price not even a consideration.

The reconciliation with my mom set my heart free in a way I couldn't imagine. Not Jesus-free. Only He can do that, but in other ways. Ways that shed light on how skewed my vision was for some things.

I arrive at the Atlanta airport International terminal in plenty of time. I had dropped PS off at Aunt Venus's, with a promise from her to take great care of her until I return.

I also dropped off my brand-new Jaguar XK.

I check in, and start walking toward security, my backpack slung over my shoulder. The security line isn't long, and I make my way through the scanners.

Only when I'm cleared and I start walking does my heart start beating rapidly. No escalators, no train in this new terminal. Just the concourse.

The concourse where Brett will be waiting for his connecting flight.

That flight from Atlanta to Peru.

I see the gate number ahead, and I slow my walk. I try to slow my heart rate, but it doesn't happen.

Delaying, I know, I stop and buy a bottle of water. I quickly quench my thirst then twist the white cap back on, and drop the bottle in my purse.

It's not hard to spot him as I near the gate. His profile I would know anywhere. The seats on both sides of him are taken, so I'm not sure how to approach him.

That dilemma is solved when he looks up and sees me. The surprise on his face makes me smile.

And when I smile, he smiles. Then he gathers his bag and newspaper, and ditches the paper in the trashcan as he walks to me.

"Hi."

I want to run into his arms, but I keep a safe distance from him. "Hello."

"This is a surprise."

His eyes are sparkling that green color, while his nearness gives me a joy I haven't felt since he walked out of the mansion that night.

"I came to give you something."

He sets his bag down. "What?"

I unzip my backpack and pull out his shirt. "Here. You forgot this."

He laughs. "Really? You came to the Atlanta airport and have obviously bought a ticket to somewhere or you wouldn't be in this part of the airport, all to give me my polo shirt?"

"That's only part of the reason," I say, noticing he's not taking the shirt. I lower my arm, the shirt still in my grasp.

"What's the other part?"

I hesitate, only because I know I might get hurt. Because I probably won't hear the words I want to hear from him. But I don't care. I have to tell him how I feel. "I was advised to love well and to go after what I want."

"You were. And you said love?"

Ann and I aren't in love.

This subject is so unfamiliar to me. These feelings, these risks. But I am determined not to let him leave without knowing the truth. "I know you don't love me. Yet. But I had to let you know that I love you."

His eyes warm as he places his hands on my shoulders. "And what makes you think I don't love you?"

I can't believe I literally have to spell this out. "Because you said so in Peru. 'Ann and I aren't in love.' Those were the exact words you told Ricky."

He shakes his head. "I remember. There was no way I could tell him I was in love with you. I was afraid of his reaction."

I squeeze the shirt tighter. "So you didn't mean them? Those words?"

He leans over and kisses me lightly on my lips.

The polo almost slips out of my hands, but I hold on. Just like I'm holding on to the feel of his kiss.

He squeezes my shoulders softly as he ends the kiss. "No. I didn't. I wanted to tell you differently, later, but when you refused my offer to stay, I couldn't tell you."

"Can you tell me now?" I ask, trembling.

Once again his lips cover mine. But this kiss is more demanding, rocking my world. Now the polo does slip from my hand as I wrap my arms around his waist, not wanting the kiss to end.

He takes his lips from mine, but they don't go far. "I love you."

My heart races at his words. We stay in each other's arms, our heads close together, the polo at our feet, conveniently covering my still unpolished toes.

"So, what's the plan, Angelina?"

I look at him, into his gorgeous green eyes. "Angelina?"

"Personally I like Ann better. But I love you, and if you want to be called Angelina, it's okay with me."

His hands are warm as I grasp them. "I'm tired of trying to be someone I'm not. You knew it all along. I'm an Ann, not an Angelina."

He squeezes my hands. "And you're mine."

"Yes, I am. And I have a ticket to Peru."

"Is this what you really want to do? Go to Peru?"

"I want to make a difference. I'm making plans to set up a store just north of Hampton Cove to sell items to people in need at a discount. Anastasia and Lovey have agreed to run it, while I keep the books. Anastasia is even going to give extremely discounted manicures and pedicures. A service I probably should have taken advantage of, but I had more important things on my mind."

"Yes you did," he says, bringing me close to him. "Do you want to get married in the States or in Peru?"

"Married? Are you serious?"

"Well, I can't officially ask you until I can buy a ring."

Being in his arms is the most natural feeling ever. It's where I'm supposed to be. "So you're unofficially asking?"

"I am."

Not running from love definitely has its benefits. "Then I unofficially say yes. But I have a favor to ask."

His fingers trace my back. "Anything."

"I want to get married in the gazebo in the cul-de-sac."

He looks puzzled. "The gazebo?"

"Yes. It's where my mom married Antonio. And I know it didn't work out for them, but we're not them. I've always thought it was beautiful. It seems like the perfect place."

"If it's that important to you, then yes."

"Thank you," I whisper before brushing a kiss across his lips.

"We will now begin boarding flight seventy-three, non-stop service to Peru," the airport employee announces over the loud-speaker.

"Are you ready, Ann?" Brett asks, tightening his grip on me like I might decide to bolt at the announcement just made.

I think back almost a month when I sat in the airport with my mom. It's amazing how God can change a life in such a short time.

"I've never been more ready," I say.

He reaches down and picks up his shirt. "We can't forget this."

"No, we can't," I say, shoving the shirt into my backpack.

I zip my backpack standing in the warmth of Brett's arms.

"Let's go," he says planting one more lingering, amazing kiss on my lips.

His kiss reminds me how rich in love I am.

The End!

Coming Next

Rich in Hope

Book Two of the *Richness in Faith* Trilogy

Isaiah 61:3

To console those who mourn in Zion, To give them beauty for ashes, The oil of joy for mourning, The garment of praise for the spirit of heaviness; That they may be called trees of righteousness, The planting of the Lord that He may be glorified.

—NKJV

Beautiful

I MADE A LOT of money when I was beautiful.

But I'm not beautiful anymore.

So now I'm broke.

The cab door squeaks as I open it before the cab driver, Malcolm, his identification read, can come around. Patience is not a virtue that I possess at the moment.

Pointing toward the trunk, I indicate to Malcolm that I don't need his help exiting the cab, but I do need his help with my bags.

With a scowl, even though he's wearing a festive Santa hat, he complies.

My gaze travels to the unfamiliar million-dollar plus house I'll be inhabiting for the next few weeks. The sage green stucco one story sits in the center of the cul-de-sac, a silhouette against the dawn.

Quiet.

Alone.

Like me.

At least for a couple of days.

The trunk slams. Trying to breathe normally, I clench the cab fare in my hand, refusing Malcolm's offer to help take the luggage to the front door. As the early morning breeze kicks up, my blonde hair swirls around me.

I wish the long, luxurious locks would wind around my face and head, like a tall turban, and cover the hideous markings of a supposedly simple surgery gone very wrong.

The sunrise splashes orange and yellows across the gray sky as it begins to rise. The December air is much warmer here in Florida, sharply contrasting the flat-out cold temperatures I left behind in New York City. The city that never sleeps.

The city that doesn't forgive is more like it.

As I hand Malcolm his fare, one of the twenty-dollar bills becomes caught in the wind. It doesn't travel far, and Malcolm and I try to stomp on it at the same time. My boot wins.

In the rush to save the bill, I'm distracted. The auto-response of looking directly at him as I hand him the bill that tried to escape causes the reaction I've become familiar with, yet can't become used to.

His widening eyes, which quickly turn to pity, seep into my being.

My hand shakes as I give him the rest of the money then stand, my lack of control unfamiliar and irritating. A storm of uncertainty rages inside me as I grab my luggage with both hands and start pulling. The weight of the luggage forces a slow pace, while the sound of the luggage wheels thumping over the brick driveway drown out the cab's exit from the cul-de-sac.

But the sound doesn't drown out the mantra playing through my head.

It's not looking good, Jenny. I'm afraid there'll be scarring. Jenny, the cheek is very hard to reconstruct. Months to recover.

And then from my parents the ever faithful, *you'll always be beautiful to us, Jenny.* The same words they spoke to the overweight, lonely girl I was in school. I'm now almost thirty and am in danger of reliving my childhood. Not the overweight part, but the lonely part.

In fact, I think it's already started.

Tears I thought no longer existed, prick the corners of my eyes, blurring my walk to the front door. Sheer habit forces me to blink them away, refusing to focus on the hopelessness of my situation.

I pull the house key my best friend Katherine gave me out of my jean pocket as I reach the front door. The front door which when I enter through it, will let me escape the festivities of Christmas. Will let me hide and be hidden from the world.

Having this avenue of escape has been one of the things that has kept me from totally losing it, totally curling into a heap on the floor, totally deciding my life is over.

But in reality, life as I know it *is* over. The hope I had for the future I always envisioned is gone.

All because I was a little too vain.

What I wouldn't give to see that tiny pimple on my cheek again.

It only takes seconds to unlock the door and let myself in.

The house is quiet, like it's asleep, and I'm sure the sound of me tugging my luggage inside would wake it if it were alive. My expensive luggage now sits on the expensive marble floor. Finding the house key a place in my purse, I realize I'm over-dressed, too warm, and exhausted. Flying at night has never been something I've enjoyed, but it is much less populated. And since staying away from people for a few weeks is my goal, it's what I had to do.

As the door clicks shut, I breathe a thankful sigh.

Alone at last.

And I'm thankful there are no Christmas decorations. I'm not in a pretty bow, mistletoe kind of mood.

Only now can I truly relax.

This beautiful house will help. An elegant wrought-iron chandelier hangs overhead. The living room is straight in front of me, so I look down the hall to my right, deciding that's where the bedrooms must be. I grab my suitcases and head to the second door on the left. I stand outside the room Katherine told me I could use until she arrives in a couple of days.

Cautiously I step inside, my gaze sweeping the room.

Relief escapes in the form of a sigh as I see the walls and dresser tops void of mirrors. Perfect.

Katherine's memory of this room was spot-on.

Smiling, I think back almost ten years ago when Katherine and I met. We were both after the same modeling job. Turns out they hired us both and we became best friends.

With a sense of comfort, because thinking of best friends and being surrounded in luxury can do that to a girl, I bring in my suitcases from the hall, one that holds my clothes, and the other one that holds the items that will launch my new career.

Or destroy it.

Catching my breath from the unfamiliar strain of actual manual labor and potential second-career failure, I notice the white furniture and king-size bed. The burgundy and tiny white polka-dotted bedspread is cute and feminine. Long, wide windows grace both outside walls of the corner room, which will let in plenty of light during the day. Wanting nothing more than to put on my pajamas and curl up into the comfy-looking bed, I reason I need to unpack.

After all, there's no one here to do it for me.

I try lifting one of my suitcases onto the bed, but the overloaded bag is extremely heavy. So, I climb up, boots meeting gorgeous bedspread, and use every ounce of strength I have to pull the flowery luggage onto the bed.

I'm now at the point of almost sweating, but I press on, shoving the over-sized, useless decorative pillows against the headboard. I yank my other suitcase onto the bed, the reality of my new, hopefully temporary, life sinking in as I sink into a sitting position against the useless decorative pillows.

No bell-hops, no doormen.

No housekeepers or cooks.

Just the three of us, me myself and I.

Welcome to Jenny's DIY.

Well, it can't be that bad. Leaning forward, as I put my finger on the zipper to open my luggage, I become aware of a scent in the room. A subtle scent that reminds me of outdoors. Woodsy outdoors, not beach-like or tropical.

Probably one of those air fresheners plugged into a wall somewhere. After all, the bathroom is right off of the bedroom.

I unzip the suitcase that holds my clothes, then eye the dresser. I also see the doors to the closet. Looking back at my suitcase I realize this is going to be a project.

Might as well start.

As I slide off the bed I notice a photograph on the nightstand. Picking up the photo, I smile as I take in the image. A lion has both of its paws wrapped around a man. I can only see the man's profile, but the dynamics of the photo threaten to burst through the glass.

This lion loves this man.

And this man must be Stephen Day, Katherine's brother. According to Katherine he's a renegade, rogue, wildlife photographer who can't stay in one place for any length of time. And right now he's half-way across the world in some remote country she couldn't pronounce, taking pictures of four-legged creatures she'd never heard of.

Which is why we're borrowing his house.

The photo seems much too bold to be in this room, on this tame, plain white nightstand with its frilly, lacey-looking lamp.

I return the photo to the nightstand before grabbing a stack of clothes out of my suitcase. Walking to the dresser, I set my clothes on the top of it as I open the drawer.

A foreboding feeling comes over me at the sight of clothing in the drawer. Making sure my stack is straight and not ready to tumble, I walk out of the room and look around.

Second room on the left, Katherine said. So, yes, I'm in the right room. I step back into the room. Burgundy bed spread with white polka-dots, exactly like she described. No mirrors just like she remembered.

I have to be in the right room.

I pull out the top clothing item in the drawer.

Black boxer-briefs.

As I hold them, a freshly laundered scent mingles with that woodsy scent. My cheek may be scarred, but my brain isn't.

Somebody is staying in this room.

"Never seen briefs before?"

The black briefs slip from my hands at the sound of the oh-so masculine voice. I watch as the briefs miss the drawer and land silently on top of my brown boots.

My mind flies back to childhood and the story of the three bears. I can't help but laugh as the words 'Who's been sleeping in my bed' try to block out the 'never seen briefs before' question.

I look up, turning slightly. Immediately my laughter dies. I swallow the huge lump in my throat, now feeling like Malcolm the cabbie with my eyes widening. Only mine widen in surprise.

And as a woman who appreciates beauty, what a nice surprise.

A put-together-in-all-the-right-places man leans against the doorway, making the doorway appear much smaller than it had when I walked through it moments ago. His rich brown hair, hint of sideburns, and gorgeously angled face are model-worthy. And it doesn't stop there.

Lips that any girl would love to kiss, part slightly to reveal white, straight teeth.

Muscular arms, flat abs, no shirt, black running shorts, just-the-right-amount-of sexy legs, and brand-new looking running shoes root me to the unfamiliar point of being unable to say a word.

Not even hello.

Oh, and did I mention the sheen of sweat that only enhances all the attributes I've run through my head?

At least I hope I haven't voiced any of my thoughts.

He's staring straight at me. He doesn't look away. His dark-eyed gaze evokes no pity.

Actually, it hardens the longer I stand here. Like I'm invading his space.

Looking down at the drawer, then across the room, I realize I am invading his space.

My suitcases are strewn across his bed. My hands are literally in the cookie-jar of his stuff.

Personal stuff, too.

He pushes off the door frame in a smooth move. "The beautiful Jenny Harris has come to visit."

He knows my name?

He starts a slow, lazy walk toward me. "Even my underwear," he says as he bends down to pick up his black briefs, "are so enamored by her beauty, they literally fall at her feet."

His sweaty, heady scent slices through my 'I'm not beautiful anymore' mantra that constantly buzzes through my mind.

I swear I can feel the heat off his body.

Except that it's probably only my face flushing at everything about him.

But he's so close.

I can reach out and touch him if I wanted to. And I want to, just to make sure he's real.

Because I think the photograph has come to life.

Discussion Questions

1. Because Ann's mother chose to do missionary work, Ann felt like her mother gave more of herself to strangers than she did to Ann. Have you had a similar experience? If so, how did it make you feel?

2. Ann had never met her father or her half-sister. Is there a family member in your life now that you met later in life? Are you close?

3. If you had to spend a lot of money on yourself, what would you buy? Do you think spending money would become tiring or burdensome? Why or why not?

4. Ann learned a lot about Brett by the way he interacted with Ricky. Have you been a mentor to someone? Has someone mentored you? How important do you think these types of relationships are?

5. Ann learned that her mother was running from her own insecurities. How do you handle yourself when you feel insecure about something?

6. John 3:16 is the theme of *Rich In Love*. What Bible verse has impacted you lately?

7. Ann finds herself falling for Brett, even though he's going after everything she's trying to stay away from. Have you ever felt like God was challenging you by placing things, people, or situations that you are trying to avoid, directly in your path? How did you handle them?

8. Ann has a cat, Princess Sari. PS for short. Do you have a pet? Does your pet bring you comfort?

9. If you could be a missionary in any country in the world, where would you go and why?

10. What was your favorite scene? Why?

Dear Reader,

There's such joy in being given the opportunity to share God's love through storytelling. There is no love greater than the love He has for us. Thank you to my editor, Deborah Smith, for believing in the story. I must also thank her for giving me my very first deadline which revealed what an amazing cook my husband is.

I'd like to give a huge shout out to Ash and Audra McEuen and their family. They're on an amazing journey with God in Peru, showing people the love of Jesus Christ. Thank you for reading and offering insights to the Peruvian life. We all continue to be in prayer for you and missionaries around the world who are bringing life to Matthew 28:19-20.

A big thanks to Audra Harders, Dianna Shuford, and Jill Vaughan for reading the beginning of this novel way back when and adding insight. Ane Mulligan, Ciara Knight, and Angela Breidenbach, your encouragement along the way means so much to me.

Our awesome group blog, F.A.I.T.H. is made up of women who God has laid it upon their hearts to write His stories. Angie, Christy, Mindy, Jenn, and Missy, we live, love and laugh well together. A great combination.

Linda Musgrave, hugs and thanks to you for your love of reading and your willingness to read my book through. Your heart is huge!

Meg Moseley and Maureen Hardegree—never will I write a book that I don't think about you and our critique sessions and all I learned from them. You are dear friends who are in my heart forever.

In Bermuda lives an awesome writer named Cathy West. I met her online, and had the privilege of meeting her in person this past year. Thanks for being my critique partner and guiding my stories in the right direction, instead of on the wandering path they tend to go. We'll go to church one night together. Promise!

To my critique partner, Missy Tippens, whom God put in my life long before critiques were even talked about, I'm so thankful the Lord crossed our paths more than once. You continue to bless me, reel me in, and show me love through this crazy journey.

Brenna, Chris, Alex, Sarah, Melanie, Jason, Ally B, Tyler, Lisa and Brian. Wow! I am tremendously proud of all of my children, their spouses and my grandchildren. I love you all more than it will ever be possible to say or show you. Know that I write with you in mind.

Lenny—Love!!!! You are my love. You are my life. I'm thrilled that I now know what an amazing cook you are.

Jesus Christ, who sacrificed once for all, author of our salvation, I love you.

I appreciate everyone who reads the books authors toil and sweat over. We do have a story to tell, and I thank you for choosing my story to read.

—*Lindi Peterson*

About the Author

Lindi Peterson definitely believes happy endings are just the beginning. She lives out her real life romance with her husband in a small Georgia town. When she's not writing, she loves to read, bowl and spend time with her family.

Visit her at lindipeterson.com and thefaithgirls.com

DELETED

Made in the USA
Lexington, KY
10 February 2015